The Barnum Museum

Stories

·

STEVEN MILLHAUSER

POSEIDON PRESS

New York   London   Toronto   Sydney   Tokyo   Singapore

Poseidon Press
Simon & Schuster Building
Rockefeller Center
1230 Avenue of the Americas
New York, New York 10020

*POSEIDON PRESS is a registered trademark
of Simon & Schuster Inc.*

*POSEIDON PRESS colophon is a trademark
of Simon & Schuster Inc.*

*Designed by Karolina Harris
Manufactured in the United States of America*

1 3 5 7 9 10 8 6 4 2

*Library of Congress Cataloging in Publication Data
Millhauser, Steven.
The Barnum Museum: stories/Steven Millhauser.
p. cm.
Contents: A game of clue—Behind the blue curtain—The
Barnum Museum—The sepia postcard—The eighth voyage
of Sinbad—Klassik komix #1—Rain—Alice, falling—The
invention of Robert Herendeen—Eisenheim the illusionist.
I. Title.
PS3563.I422B37 1990*

813'.54—dc20   *90-32697*

*CIP
ISBN 0-671-68640-2*

Permissions appear on page 239.

To Charlotte Millhauser
and the memory of Milton Millhauser

Contents

■

A Game of Clue

The board. The board shows the ground plan of an English mansion. The nine rooms are displayed along the sides of the board and are connected by a floor consisting of a series of identical yellow squares the size of postage stamps. In the middle of the board, on a stairway marked with a white X, rests a black envelope. Each room bears its name in the center, in black capital letters: the STUDY, the HALL, the LOUNGE, the DINING ROOM, the KITCHEN, the BALLROOM, the CONSERVATORY, the BILLIARD ROOM, and the LIBRARY. Each room contains furniture, drawn in black outline and pictured from above, as if we are viewing the room from the center of its ceiling. One corner of the board is partly concealed by the edge of a saucer, on which lies a smoking cigarette.

The table. The board lies not quite in the center of a green folding table, which shines with a dull gleam in the glow of two lights: the overhead porch light, encased in four squares of frosted glass, and the small red-shaded lamp attached to one of the porch walls. Additional light comes through the four small panes of the kitchen-door window, part of which is covered by translucent yellow curtains. If we view the table from directly above, as if our vantage point were that of the moth beating its wings against the glass of the overhead light, we see that the green border of the table is crowded with objects: a coffee-stained saucer on which lies a smoking cigarette; four pads of Detective Notes; a green quarter-full bottle of wine, bearing on its label a purple sketch of a grape arbor with three purple birds flying overhead; two yellow hexagonal pencils, one round black pencil (supported by a hand), and one round shiny-green pencil; an opaque glass bowl, white on the inside and orange on the outside, containing a few broken three-ring pretzels lying among crumbs and pretzel salt; a nearly empty stem-glass of red wine, which bears on its cup, in white letters, the legend BROTHERHOOD: AMERICA'S OLDEST WINERY; two tulip-shaped glasses of red wine; a slender wineglass one-third full of 7-Up; a half-empty cup of coffee; a transparent green glass bowl of potato chips; and a small china plate showing, beneath a scattering of brown crumbs, a blue stone bridge overlooking a blue stream with three blue ducks, one of which is raising its head toward the outstretched blue arm of a girl in a blue bonnet. In the course of the game, while the tokens move on the board, these objects also move; some of them move small distances, whereas others, like the bowl of potato chips, the bowl of pretzels, and the bottle of wine, exchange places or move to different, unpredictable places on the table. In addition there are, at the moment of observation, three hands on the table: one hand taps restlessly between the saucer with the cigarette and the nearly empty glass of wine; the side of another hand, lightly tanned, lies quietly on the table while the pad of the forefinger moves slowly, slowly back and forth against the glistening tapered thumbnail; and a third hand, holding the round black pencil, writes a question mark beside the words *Professor Plum* on the Detective Notes and at once erases it.

▪

Jacob. Jacob Ross, twenty-five, sits tapping the fingers of his right hand on the tabletop as he stares unseeing at the fan of five cards in his left hand: the LIBRARY, the KITCHEN, the BILLIARD ROOM, Professor Plum, Mrs. White. He is so angry that he feels it as a pounding in both temples and a beating in his throat. He is so angry that he would like to weep, to cry out, to kill, to sweep his long hand across the board and fling from the table the tokens, the weapons, the die, the black envelope, but when, by old habit, he imagines how he appears to whoever may be watching him, he sees only a look of tense concentration, an exaggerated and brooding attention to the cards in his hand. But he is angry. He is enraged. At Marian: for speaking to him in a certain tone of voice, in their father's study four hours ago, immediately after dinner. At Susan: for their epic argument in the car that afternoon, lasting from 3:37 (by his watch) on the Mass Pike to 5:54 (by his watch) under the railway trestle by the Post Road, exactly two minutes and thirty-six seconds before he drew up in front of his parents' house. At David: for saying nothing, for concealing his hurt, for flooding him with forgiveness. At himself: for spending eight hours a day (2:00–6:00 and 8:00–12:00) six days a week at his desk for the past four months unable to write a single new word of what was to have been Part One (*The Book of Childhood*) of the greatest American poem of the second half of the twentieth century, after a period of five months during which he had accumulated 180 pages of manuscript in a minuscule handwriting in a single spiral-bound notebook (Narrow Ruled). He is enraged at his failure, at his evasions, at his later and later awakenings, at the slow erosion of his belief in his destiny, at the inexplicable wreckage of his dream, at his inevitable future as an embittered professor of English at a major university, at the unknown obstacle, at his daily defeated will. Jacob taps his fingers against the tabletop, not metrically but in a nervous and disordered rhythm that exasperates him as if the hand belonged not to him but to some clumsy stranger inhabiting him and smothering his brain. "Colonel Mustard," he says sharply, not looking up. "In the library. With the revolver."

Pray forgive me. Colonel Mustard enters the LIBRARY and sees, standing with her back to him to the left of the fireplace, Miss Scarlet, in a tight crimson dress, reaching for a book in the bookcase. At the sound of the opening door she turns suddenly; the book drops to the floor. "Oh, I didn't—" she says, crouching swiftly to pick up the book and with her other hand sweeping a lock of pale hair from her eye. "Pray forgive me for disturbing you," the Colonel remarks, closing the door quietly behind him. Her crouching knees, one higher than the other, press through the clinging crimson, which seems stretched to the breaking point. It is an effect not lost on the Colonel, who feels, in his right palm, a sudden sensation of taut silk and tense thigh. Proper now, aren't we. Ripe for it.

The library. Viewed from above, the LIBRARY is a symmetrical figure that may be thought of as a modified rectangle: from each of the four corners a small square is missing. The resulting figure has twelve sides. As in all the rooms, the furniture is pictured from above and drawn in black outline. Thus the lamp on the central table reveals only the hexagonal top of its shade, whereas the standing lamp beside the fireplace reveals the top and side of its shade, the slanting line of its stand, and the slender oval of a base we assume to be circular.

Marian. Marian Ross, twenty-four, rolls the red die, which tumbles past the DINING ROOM into the LOUNGE and comes to rest beside the lamp. Four. Marian is no longer angry at Jacob, who was not one, not two, not three, not four, but four and a half hours late on David's fifteenth birthday; who'd been expected for lunch but who arrived, without a phone call, four minutes before dinner; who stepped from an unknown car in the unannounced company of some girlfriend or other; and who said something impatient and unsatisfactory about a broken alarm clock, while Miss Slenderella stood with a little frown and suddenly introduced herself with an outthrust hand and a tinkle of silver bracelet: hello, I'm Susan Newton. Marian moves her piece, Miss Scarlet—she always chooses Miss Scarlet —from the LIBRARY in the direction of the distant BALLROOM. Two or three moves from now she will enter the BALLROOM, which she holds in her hand, and will suggest that the murder was committed there by Mr. Green, whom she also holds in her hand, with the Revolver, which she does not. After dinner, in her father's study, she asked Jacob why he hadn't called. His evasive reply angered her. "You should have called. It's David's birthday." "Should have, should have. Christ, Marian." She called him selfish, and he walked out of the room. Now she wonders: was she too harsh? Marian loves Jacob and knows he is unhappy. He has passed his orals brilliantly at Harvard but has refused to begin his dissertation. He argues that scholarship and poetry both require a lifetime of devotion and that he has only one life. His decision to write for a year has brought him no peace. Was it necessary for her to use the word "selfish"? Couldn't she have found a word with less sting, like "inconsiderate"? He had looked at her with hurt surprise. Is it possible, Marian asks herself, that her outburst was directed not at Jacob but at Susan Newton?—for having the bad taste to come with Jacob on an intimate family occasion, for being Jacob's girlfriend, for being beautiful and desirable, for having an easy life. Marian's own life is unsatisfactory. The men she meets are superficial or humorless, her assistant editorship in the science division of a textbook publisher interests her less and less, she is dissatisfied with her appearance (hips too broad, hair impossible), she has a sense of waste and drift. At twenty-four she is already afraid of ending up alone. Or worse: of making a safe marriage out of fear of ending up alone. Where did she go awry? Robert's words, when she broke with him: "You talk too much about your family. What about me?" Jabbing his forefinger into his chest. "What about me?" She can still hear the sound of his finger thumping against the breastbone. Marian looks at her cards: the BALLROOM, Mr. Green, the Revolver, the Wrench. The thought comes to her: am I selfish?

Tokens and weapons. Of the six original tokens, made of wood and shaped like pawns, five remain: the red token (Miss Scarlet), the yellow token (Colonel Mustard), the green token (Mr. Green), the white token (Mrs. White), and the blue token (Mrs. Peacock). The purple token (Professor Plum) has been lost for years and has been replaced by the top half of a black wooden chess knight. There are six weapons: the Rope, the Knife, the Candlestick, the Revolver, the Wrench, and the Lead Pipe. The Rope is a small piece of white rope, formed into two coils, one on top of the other, and knotted at the ends; the five remaining weapons are made of metal. The Lead Pipe is soft and can be bent back and forth. Unlike the tokens, which are essential to the conduct of the game, the weapons are merely decorative; their movement from room to room serves no purpose, except perhaps an atmospheric one, and in no way affects the strategy of the game

The porch. One wall of the porch is shared with the kitchen, one wall is shared with the garage, and two walls contain screened windows: four in the longer wall that faces the garage, and three in the shorter wall that faces the kitchen. All seven windows are partially covered by the narrow wooden slats of roll-up blinds (dark green), held in place by ropes that pass around pulleys at the corners of the upper windowframe and around hooks under the windowsills. The rolled-up portion of the long blind lies in a slightly slanting line across the four windows. Marian sits with her back to the long blind. To her left is Jacob, with his back to the wall of three windows. Behind him, in the wall angle formed by the windows and the garage, is an aluminum chaise longue with a flower-pattern cushion on which lie a small black AM-FM radio with extended antenna, a section of the *New York Times* folded in half twice so as to display the crossword puzzle, and an open Clue box with partitions for the cards, the tokens, the weapons, the die, the black envelope, the Detective Notes, and the instructions. The Clue box lies aslant on its upside-down green boxcover, whose split corners have been fastened with package tape. On the wall above the chaise longue hang the red-shaded lamp and a Navajo sand painting from Albuquerque, New Mexico, showing three identical stick-figure Indian girls with outstretched arms. Susan sits to Jacob's left, with her back to the garage. She faces Marian and the slightly slanting line of the rolled-up portion of the blind. Beneath the rolled-up blind, through the four screens, she sees mostly darkness. In one corner she can also see a porch light and part of a front porch post across a street. To Susan's left, facing Jacob, sits David, with his back to the kitchen door. The four-paned window of the kitchen door is partially covered on the inside by translucent yellow curtains. Two wooden steps, painted gray, lead up to the door. There are two more doors on the porch: the wooden maroon door, which opens to the garage, and to which is fastened a used Connecticut license plate with two white letters and four white numerals on a blue ground; and the aluminum porch door, which opens to the back yard and is located beside the four windows near the kitchen wall. The top panel of the aluminum door is glass, and is mostly covered with a dark red strip of cloth with black and gray geometric designs, hung there for the sake of privacy by Martha Ross, who received it from a friend traveling in India. The narrow lower panel is a screen; it is changed to glass in the fall. Whenever Marian, Jacob, or Susan rises from the table in order to go to the kitchen, or to the small bathroom past the kitchen near the entrance to the cellar, David moves his chair forward under the table. He wishes to leave plenty of room for the person coming around the table toward the two steps leading to the kitchen door, even though there is room enough. When David looks to the left he can see, reflected in the narrow band of glass beneath the dark red strip of cloth, the back of his chair and a piece of his light-blue shirt. When he looks to the right he can see, over Susan Newton's shining hair, a green, red, and black lobster buoy from Maine, hanging by a rope from a hook in the wall.

David. David Ross, fifteen, puts down the black pencil and stares at his four cards: the STUDY, the CONSERVATORY, Miss Scarlet, and the Rope. As early as the fifth grade, when Jacob, home from Columbia, had sat down and taught him to play, David had begun to notice flaws in the game. Of the total of twenty-one cards (six suspect cards, six weapon cards, nine room cards), three were placed in the black envelope in the center of the board and eighteen were dealt to the players. When three people played, each person received six cards; but when four people played, two received five cards and two only four cards—a distinct disadvantage for the four-card players, each of whom had one less clue to the murder than the five-card players did. The unfairness had disturbed him; and although it was partly rectified by the fact that the deal passed from player to player, David had always secretly discounted games with four players. All that afternoon he had waited eagerly for Jacob, assuring his mother that things would be all right, calming Marian, who had arrived from Manhattan on the 10:48, and imagining elaborate, desperate explanations for Jacob's lateness (the train from Boston had been delayed an hour; Jacob had gone out to change a five-dollar bill in order to call and had missed the train; he hadn't called because he was afraid of missing the next train, which was due any minute but had also been delayed). When Jacob finally pulled into the driveway four minutes before dinner with an unknown girl in an unknown car, David's relief at seeing Jacob, his sense that things would be all right now, was mixed with a sharp disappointment: there will be four players, the games won't count.

Doors and passages. On the board there are seventeen doors, all exactly the same: yellow, with four gray panels. Like the furniture, they are pictured from above, in sharp perspective: they are inverted trapezoids, the top of each door being nearly twice the length of the bottom. The four corner rooms have a single door each; the DINING ROOM, the BILLIARD ROOM, and the LIBRARY, two doors each; the HALL, three doors; the BALLROOM, four. In addition to their single doors, each of the corner rooms has a SECRET PASSAGE, indicated by a black square containing a yellow arrow. When a token is in any of the four rooms containing a SECRET PASSAGE, it may, on its turn, advance immediately to the room diagonally opposite. The doors and passages are the secret life of the game, for they permit the tokens to enter and leave the nine rooms, and it is solely in the rooms, and not in the yellow squares or central rectangle, that play takes place, by means of continual guesses at the three cards concealed in the black envelope.

The pleasures of secret passages. Professor Plum walks in the SECRET PASSAGE between the LOUNGE and the CONSERVATORY. He enjoys traversing the house this way: the passage corresponds to something secretive, dark, and wayward in his temperament. The erratic earthen path, the dank stone walls, the dim yellow glow of irregularly placed kerosene lanterns, the spaces of near-dark, all these soothe and excite him, and bring back those boyhood rambles along the bank of the brook in the wood behind his father's house. He thinks of Pope's tunnel at Twickenham, of the emergence of eighteenth-century English gardens from the rigidity of French and Italian forms, of the grove of hickory trees in the wood, of asymmetrical architecture and the cult of genius. Professor Plum does not suffer from delusions of boldness. Part of the pleasure of the serpentine dark lies in knowing that he is walking between two well-known points, the LOUNGE and the CONSERVATORY, and it is precisely this knowledge that permits him to experience a pleasurable shiver at the appearance of a lizard in the path, the fall of a mysterious pebble, the ambiguous shadows that might conceal the murderer, the sudden extinction of a lantern on the wall.

A **woman of mystery.** Miss Scarlet enters the BALLROOM and sees with relief that she is alone. The silent piano, the empty window seat, the polished parquet floor, the high ceiling, the gloom of early evening coming through the high windows and making a twilight in the dying room, all these comfort her in a melancholy way, as if she might lose herself in the mauve shadows. And yet, as she crosses the floor to the window seat, she imagines herself observed, in her evening dress of close-fitting red silk (tight across the hips, flared below the knees, dropping to midcalf), takes note of the firm delicate neck, the soft waves and curls of her short blond hair, the slight but firm-set shoulders, the long svelte stride, the motion of hips under the small, elegant waist: a woman desirable and untouchable, a woman of mystery. She detests the Colonel. She detests him even as she imagines his eyes following her slow, swinging walk across the echoing room; detests his faintly flushed cheeks, his bristly brown-and-gray mustache, the small purplish vein at the side of his nose, the short neat hairs on the backs of his fingers, above all, those melancholy and relentless eyes. They are organs of touch, those eyes—she can feel his indecent gaze brushing the back of her neck, rubbing lightly against her calves, drawing itself like a silk scarf between the insides of her thighs, brushing and lightly rubbing. His eyes appear to include her in a conspiracy: let us, my dear, by all means continue this little farce of civility, but let us not pretend that you do not wish to be released from your restlessness by the touch of my thumbs against your stiffening nipples. The Colonel is patient; he appears to be waiting confidently for a sign from her. She asks herself suddenly: have I given him a sign? His eyes hold abysmal promises: come, I will teach you the disillusionment of the body, come, I will teach you the death of roses, the emptiness of orgasms in sun-flooded loveless rooms.

A warm night in August. It is nearly midnight on a warm August night in southern Connecticut. 11:56, to be exact. Through the screened windows of the Ross back porch comes a sharp smell of fresh-cut grass and the dank, salt-mud, low-tide smell from the Sound three blocks away. A stirring of warm air moves through the porch and touches the lightly sweating foreheads of the four Clue players. Six sounds can be distinguished: the shrill of crickets, the gravelly crunch of footsteps passing along the street at the side of the house, the rising and falling hiss of a neighbor's lawn sprinkler, the faint music of a jukebox from a seaside bar ten blocks away where the summer people from New York and New Jersey have their cottages, the soft rush of trucks on the distant thruway, the hum of the air conditioner in the bedroom window of the neighboring house near the back porch. These sounds mingle with the snap of a pretzel, the scritch-scratch of a pencil, the click of an ice cube, the soft clatter of a tumbling die. The glow of porchlight spills beyond the screens and touches faintly the catalpa in the side yard. A solitary passerby, walking on the gravel at the side of the road, sees, through branches of Scotch pine and the exposed portion of the screens, the four players in their island of light, distinguishes a woman's bending shoulder, a white upper arm, a tumble of dark thick hair, and feels a yearning so deep that he wants to cry out in anguish, though in fact he continues steadily, even cheerfully, on his way.

A pause on the way to the kitchen. Mrs. Peacock, proceeding toward the KITCHEN from the LOUNGE, pauses not far from a door to the DINING ROOM. Through the half-open door she can see part of the mahogany table, the branch of a silver candle-stick, the gleam of the cut-glass bowl on the sideboard. Mrs. Peacock appears to be waiting for something, there by the partly open door. Does she expect to see a line of red blood trickling through the door, does she expect to hear the sound of a candlestick thunking against a skull? Her lavender dress is a trifle mussed from the day's exertions, really it is far too warm in these airless corridors, she must look a fright. In the KITCHEN she will drink a glass of cool water. Mrs. Peacock prides herself on looking neat. She has always been attractive in a girlish sort of way, though too short: she has always had to look up into faces, as if offering herself for inspection: please notice my nice smile. Not like Edith White: all eyes turned when she entered a room. Mrs. Peacock thought *he* had noticed, but evidently she had been mistaken. Why is she lingering in the airless corridor? What is she waiting for? Through the half-open door of the DINING ROOM she can hear the silence, falling drop by drop.

Susan. Susan Newton glances up from her cards—the HALL, the LOUNGE, Colonel Mustard, the Lead Pipe, the Knife—and sees again the fatal profile: the line of David's nose and upper lip exactly reproduces the line of Jacob's, except for some faint difference difficult to account for. Is there more calm in David's profile, less sense of inner force pushing outward into form? Susan is continually startled and disturbed by the physical likenesses among the Ross children: Marian has Jacob's eyebrows and cheekbones, though her face and features are wider —she is less elegant, less beautiful than Jacob. Susan is struck by how all the Ross faces register emotions sharply, as if her own emotions were unable to find expression in her face, as if her face were an instrument less developed than theirs. The harmony of the faces at the card table excites her but shuts her out: she is so clearly alien. Although David's kindness has touched her, she senses Marian's dislike. Marian is a powerful woman with lines of tension between her eyebrows and a surprisingly rich, throaty laugh. It's as if she is continually releasing herself from some constriction through the act of laughter. Jacob has been cold to Susan all evening. She is angry at him for making her come unannounced on David's birthday, for making them late, for making her an accomplice. He has been sharp with her lately, unkind, impulsive, autocratic. She understands that his anger at himself, his furious disappointment, is making him desperate: perhaps he wishes to confirm his sense of failure by failing with her. The understanding does not help, for she can feel Jacob removing himself from her in a series of small, precise withdrawals. He will leave her soon, her *homme fatal*, she can feel it in her bones, and in her unhappiness she turns again to look at David, startled to see, in the long, slightly upturned upper lip, the thick, nervous eyelashes, the devastating hook of hair over the crisp collar, a purer, gentler Jacob. "Mrs. White," Susan says. "In the kitchen. With the rope."

Mr. Green hesitates. Mr. Green, formerly the Reverend Green, stands frozen in the shadows of the northwest corner of the BALLROOM, watching Miss Scarlet advance toward the window seat. He wishes to step noiselessly from the room and vanish along a corridor, but he fears that his slightest motion will startle her into attention. Mr. Green does not dislike Miss Scarlet, but she makes him uneasy; young women in general make him uneasy. He does not know where to look when he speaks to them, and in particular he does not know where to look when he speaks to Miss Scarlet. To look away is rude; to stare into her restless, twilight-colored eyes is unthinkable; to fasten his attention on her full small mouth is to have the sensation of being about to be swallowed; to lower his eyes, even for an instant, to her distinctly separate breasts is an indecency. Mr. Green is a bachelor of thirty-eight who lives with his mother and still sleeps in his boyhood room. The same bookcase that once held Howard Pyle's *Book of Pirates, The Merry Adventures of Robin Hood, Kidnapped,* and *The Three Musketeers* now holds Skeat's *English Dialects from the Eighth Century to the Present Day,* the thirteen volumes of *A New English Dictionary on Historical Principles, Celtic Scotland* by W. F. Skene (3 volumes), the county volumes of the English Place-Name Society, all the volumes published by the English Early Text Society, including 194 volumes (up to 1933) of the Old Series and 126 volumes (discontinued in 1921) of the Extra Series, as well as philological quarterlies, dialect dictionaries, Anglo-Saxon and Middle English grammars and morphologies, and miscellaneous publications of the Camden Society, the Pipe Roll Society, the Canterbury and York Society, the Scottish Text Society, the Caxton Society, and the Rolls Series. A tendency toward the eccentric, held in check and made respectable by faith, has been released and accentuated by the loss of faith. Mr. Green has a passion for English place-names (he is the author of "A Contribution to the Study of Cheshire Place-Names of Scandinavian Origin," published in *Transactions of the Historical Society of Lancashire and Cheshire*), obsolete card games (ombre, primero, noddy, ruff and honour), gem lore, Pictish history, ogham inscriptions, a theory of Wyatt's versification according to which a strong pause is the equivalent of a stressed syllable and a line contains an irregular number of unstressed syllables, pre-Celtic Britain, and the history of armor. Mr. Green walks twenty miles a day and is subject to attacks of melancholy. He is comfortable only in the presence of children and elderly women; he fears the Colonel, likes Mrs. White, and is especially fond of Mrs. Peacock, who reminds him of a favorite aunt. In a properly regulated society, he has been known to say wryly, all girls on their twelfth birthday would be removed to Scottish castles, from which they would be released on their sixtieth birthday after forty-eight years of instruction in harmony, prosody, and needlepoint. In the shadows of the northwest corner of the BALLROOM, Mr. Green is riven with distress. If she should discover him, standing in the shadows, his silence will be impossible to explain. It might even appear that he has been spying on her, as she walks in her nervous stride across the long floor of the BALLROOM, swinging her hips, swinging her hips, touching herself on the sleeve, running a hand along the side of her hair, touching herself on the hip. Mr. Green has come from the LIBRARY, bearing with him a book on Norman castles that now lies on a chair with claw-and-ball feet beside his left leg. He cannot pick up the book without fear of being heard by Miss Scarlet, who is approaching the window seat. She will sit down and see him standing in silence across the room. He must not appear to be aware of her when she sees him, but when he looks away he feels that she is turning to look at him, now, this very moment, and he looks back abruptly to make certain that he has not yet been seen. It occurs to him that he cannot possibly pretend to have been unaware of her long walk across the echoing floor. His position is worsening by the moment.

A secret. David's love for his brother runs so deep that he feels it as an oppression in his chest. David feels there is something wrong with him: he imagines other people too intensely. He has forgiven Jacob for his lateness, which he attributes to some difficulty or sorrow in Jacob's life, but he has no clear sense of Jacob's trouble and is hurt at being excluded from it. David feels older than Jacob, as if he were the one who could give comfort. He can sense Marian's anger at Jacob, her dislike of Susan, and Marian's own trouble, which he detects in her eyes, in her self-disparaging remarks, and in an occasional tone of voice. He feels sympathy for Susan, whose uneasiness is plain to him; he is disturbed by Jacob's coldness to her and desires to be kind to her, in part to make up for his own initial disappointment at her presence. He sees that she is pretty, possibly beautiful, though he observes this neutrally, since it is not a kind of prettiness or beauty that attracts him: there is something cool and sculptural about it, a beauty of the moon. He admires most of all the color of her hair, a light brownish red shot through with threads of blond. The thought of her hair disturbs him, for he has a shameful secret: he imagines the pubic hair of all women, even of his sister, a habit that began at the age of twelve when he saw his first nude photograph in one of his father's photography annuals. David thinks continually about the bodies of women; although he is without sexual experience, he has a strong sense of sexual corruption. He feels that if Susan knew what he was thinking she would be shocked and would despise him; and as he studies his cards—he knows that either Mrs. White or Mrs. Peacock is the murderer—he feels a burst of gentleness toward Susan, as if she must be protected from himself.

Cards. There are twenty-one cards: six suspect cards, six weapon cards, and nine room cards. Each suspect card shows a large, colored token in the foreground and, behind it, the head and shoulders of the suspect, in two colors or three. Each weapon card pictures a weapon in a single color: yellow or blue. Although the rooms on the board are gray, and the furniture in black outline, each room card shows a pale orange room with furniture in two, three, four, or five colors (red, yellow, blue, and two distinct shades of green). Three cards—the CONSERVATORY, the HALL, and the Wrench—have been lost over the years and have been replaced by traditional playing cards labeled appropriately. Thus David's CONSERVATORY card is a seven of clubs with the word *Conservatory* printed in blue ballpoint across the top; Susan's HALL is a two of spades with the word *Hall* printed across the middle; and Marian's Wrench is a five of diamonds with the word *Wrench* printed above the central diamond.

Nymph reclining. As Colonel Mustard silently enters the BALL-ROOM by the door nearest the BILLIARD ROOM, he is aware of two things: Miss Scarlet sitting at the window seat with her back to him in one of her ludicrous attitudes (head lifted, hands loosely locked against raised knees, a show of white stocking, glossy heels on floor: Miss Scarlet exists as a series of tableaux vivants, animated from time to time by little bursts of hysteria) and Mr. Green standing in a corner intently studying his pocket watch. The Colonel's decision follows swiftly: get rid of Green, rearrange the picture on the couch (Nymph Reclining: a study in rose and marble, disposed upon a background of red plush velvet, the whole set off by tumbled white silk underthings, glossy ink-black pubic curls, and a brilliant silver chain dangling from one languorous wrist). "I say, Green," remarks the Colonel, "have you the . . ."—time, he would have said, but Mr. Green turns abruptly, cracking his elbow against the wall and gasping with pain, while from the window seat comes another gasp and a rustle of rearrangement: Nymph Upright, Tense, and Cold. Legs sharp as scissors, the long femurs shut tight like the silver sides of a nutcracker: crack crack, a scattering of broken shells. It occurs to the Colonel that there may be a certain satisfaction in disencumbering Miss Scarlet of her propriety.

Samuel's dream. In an upstairs bedroom Samuel Ross, age fifty-seven, wakes from a troubling dream. He has not been sleeping well lately. Martha lies in her separate bed beside him, facing him, asleep. In the dream he was back in his childhood apartment on Joralemon Street in Brooklyn Heights. His father, Solomon Ross, né Rostholder, wearing a brown vest with a pocket watch, was seated at the kitchen table, bent over his account books. Suddenly his father's face had a stricken look, the pen dropped from his fingers, he stood up holding his chest; and a stream of bright blood burst from his mouth onto his vest. Samuel shakes his head once and sits up in bed. His father died at the age of sixty-four, when Samuel was twenty-one. In six years David will be twenty-one and Samuel will be sixty-three. Samuel thinks: I have seven years left. From the porch he hears the sound of voices, laughter. He thinks: it is David's birthday. He thinks: my children are home, the family is together. I am happy now. He thinks: forgive me, Father.

Borders. The nine rooms are surrounded by a green border, which itself is surrounded by a narrow black border that forms the outermost edge of the playing board. Unlike the smooth green border, the black border is grainy in texture; it forms part of the black paper used for the back of the Clue board and has been carefully folded over each of the four sides. The colorful playing surface is a square sheet of smooth paper pasted over a slightly larger square of cardboard. Under the green border you can see the slight elevation caused by the black paper, which extends nearly half an inch beneath the smooth surface.

Of course! Mrs. White—the widow White—stands in the KITCHEN staring at an object in her hand. It is smooth and heavyish, with a gleam or shine; through it she can see her hand. She runs her long thumb along the side, over and over, watching the play of the tendon. Of course: it is a glass. It is a glass of water. I am standing in the kitchen with a glass of water in my hand. A glass. Of water. In my. She is standing, in the kitchen, with a glass of, and it is all strange, so utterly strange. Is it perhaps a dream? Fifteen years of making the best of it (how well she has adjusted!), fifteen years of long dreary afternoons (how well she looks!), and then last night, was it only last night, the earth-shattering proposal, flames of happiness, and next morning the cold corpse at the foot of the stairs. Mrs. White stares at the mysterious glass in her hand: how did it get there? She hears a noise and turns to see Mrs. Peacock—dear, dear Evelyn—enter the room.

From the window seat Miss Scarlet. From the window seat Miss Scarlet watches Mr. Green retreat awkwardly from the BALLROOM, shutting the door behind him a little too loudly and enclosing her with the Colonel, who strides to Mr. Green's corner, picks something up, and begins to walk toward her across the long, polished floor. She feels that she is watching her doom approach, as if the intensity of her detestation no longer mattered. Men are of two kinds: the coarse, sensual, and indifferent tribe, who wish to enact their curious little rituals upon her arranged, convenient flesh, and the gentle tribe, with their pale hands, wry phrases, and alarmed eyes. If she were an empress, she would choose for her lover a beautiful fourteen-year-old boy with small round buttocks and strong white teeth: she would instruct him slowly in the art of love, she would be mistress and mother to him, goddess and tender sister. Miss Scarlet feels there is something shameful in this fantasy, which she has revealed to no one. As the Colonel approaches she feels his gaze lapping at her, rising insolently along her legs, sliding along her hips like thumbs. Miss Scarlet feels arranged by his gaze, emptied of interest, rendered desirable and trite: he confers upon her a sensation of absence. He unsees her: makes her invisible. "A pleasant evening," the Colonel remarks, flawlessly banal, placing something, a book perhaps, on the window ledge and glancing incuriously at the romantic twilight dying over the black yews. "Is it," he continues, turning upon her silken throat his melancholy gaze, "not?"

Ballrooms. For Jacob, the BALLROOM is the *salle de bal* in the château de Fontainebleau, dimly remembered from a day trip during his summer in Paris, when he turned seventeen: the glossy floor stretching away, the sunken octagons in the ceiling, the chandeliers plunging from the great arcades, the tightly clutched copy of the *Oeuvres Complètes* of Rimbaud purchased at a bookstall on the Seine and carefully cut with his Swiss Army knife, the tormenting breasts of a tour guide called Monique. He can still see her coppery braided hair and the white, loose blouse, suddenly heavy with breasts from a twist of the shoulders. His seventeenth birthday: two years older than David. Jacob is glad to be rid of adolescence; he worries about David, but doesn't know how to protect him. For Marian, the BALLROOM is a nearly forgotten black-and-white movie in which a bride, abandoned by her groom, dances a waltz alone, round and round, *one* two three *one* two three, as the members of the hired orchestra exchange nervous glances and continue playing. For David, the BALLROOM is the high school gym, festooned with pink and green crepe paper for the spring dance. He tries to see another, more plausible ballroom, but the images are vague—a British officer with neat mustache and slicked-back hair gazing across a room at a girl with masses of blond ringlets overflowing with ribbons—and keep turning into the high school gym. For Susan, the BALLROOM remains unimagined: a gray rectangle on a board.

Other rooms. The board does not mention the other rooms of the mansion, rooms that are nevertheless implied by the board and have their own life apart from the game: the three wine cellars with their tiers of bottles in slanting rows, the two beer cellars, the servants' bedrooms in the cramped upper story, the gun room, the scullery, the butler's pantry, the serving lobby, the breakfast room, the day nursery, the summer smoking room, the winter smoking room, the glass pantry, the governess's rooms, the night nursery, the larders, the maids' sitting room, the maids' lavatory, the housekeeper's room, the servants' dining room, the five bathrooms, the six bedrooms in the family wing, the eight guest bedrooms, the dressing rooms, the anterooms, the refrigerated cold store, the garage with its motorcar (a Daimler). And let us not forget the entrance court, the rose garden, the park, the pleached avenues, the summer pavilion, the ruined rotunda in the lake, the hunting lodge, the carp pool glistening in the sun . . .

Martha. Martha Altgeld Ross lies dreaming of summer at Blue Point. She is cutting beans into a pot on the unrailed back porch. Jacob is swinging on the wooden swing that hangs from the twisted apple tree. Under him his shadow is swinging through the tree-shadow onto the sunny unmown grass. Sun streams onto her hands, onto the apple leaves, onto the beanstalks on their rickety poles, onto Jacob's plump strong legs stretching, stretching into the blue air. Suddenly she puts down the knife, runs down the unpainted steps into the yard, seizes the ropes of the swing. Jacob is startled and looks up at her with his dark, earnest eyes. She snatches him from the swing and kisses his stomach, his neck, his long-lashed eyelids. O my handsome boy, my son. She feels crazed with love. Martha is sitting on the swing, with Jacob on her lap. Higher and higher they go, she is laughing, she is happy, sun and shade ripple over her outstretched legs. Jacob is laughing. O how do you like to go up in a swing, up in the sky so blue? O I do think it the pleasantest thing. Sunlight glints on the pot of beans on the porch. O my handsome baby boy. Tears burn in her eyes, she is heavy with love. She is calm now.

Ritual. Although it is past midnight and he is already tired, David plans to stay up the entire night, if necessary, in order to be alone with Marian and Jacob, and then with Jacob. When Marian visits, she and David always stay up and talk after their parents go to bed; when Jacob visits, he and David stay up till three or four in the morning, or even till dawn. The long night with Jacob is a well-established ritual, which David looks forward to intensely, for aside from the sheer excitement of late, forbidden hours it is a way of asserting intimacy. Surely Jacob will not fail him on his birthday. David is aware that his formulation of the thought contains a doubt: he isn't entirely certain of Jacob, who arrived four and a half hours late, with an unannounced girlfriend, and who now sits remote and unhappy at the other end of the table. Jacob's unsatisfactory reason for his lateness—he hadn't fallen asleep till five in the morning and had slept until noon—is, from another point of view, reassuring: if Jacob has slept late, then he will stay up late, quite apart from the question of obedience to their late-night ritual. Of course, this line of reasoning is far from decisive: the badness of last night's sleep might easily lead to early tiredness. It's true that even if Jacob goes to bed early, they will be sleeping in the same room, since Susan has been given Jacob's attic room and the folding cot has been set up for Jacob in David's room. But isn't it possible, isn't it even likely, that Jacob will sneak upstairs with Susan, in defiance of his mother's chaste arrangements? The possibility of no talk, no late-night summer walk, no assertion of the ritual, is so disturbing to David that he pushes the thought away with another: after all, even though Jacob was four and a half hours late, even though he is sitting remote and unhappy at the other end of the table, they are playing Clue, as they always do.

Not uninteresting. The Colonel, who is continually threatened by an appalling boredom, does not take pleasure in easy conquests. He is therefore surprised, indeed disturbed, by the ease with which matters seem to be taking their course: the rigid arm unwithdrawn from the negligently brushing hand, the thigh tensed but motionless under the testing palm, the silken knees irresistant to his slight pressure of parting. The Colonel is not a profound student of human nature, but he is quick to understand that the exaggerated ease of surrender is intended to convey contempt: you may stick my body, which I value less than an old, discarded hat, with your swollen red member, it is nothing to me, who live elsewhere. In this sense Miss Scarlet intends her swift surrender to be the precise opposite: a resistance deeper than flesh, a spiritual negation. The thought pleases the Colonel; Miss Scarlet continually proposes erotic riddles that require complex solutions. It is important, he reflects, to linger now, seated beside her on the window seat, his torso twisted toward her as she leans back fully dressed but already a little disheveled against the far pillow, with her stockinged feet on the seat-cushion, her knees raised and parted a hand's width, her crimson hem draped over the tops of her knees—affording the Colonel a piquant view of her elegant silk stockings, her long thighs in the mauve shadows, her fashionable pink crepe de chine knickers with plissé frills (the Colonel is extremely knowledgeable about ladies' undergarments), the clearly outlined pink fold between the slightly parted thighs, the transverse crease that divides one raised thigh from the firm but flattened base of the coyly proffered buttock. It is yet another of Miss Scarlet's poses—all in all, the Colonel reflects, a not uninteresting one.

A trifle anxious. At a bend of the path there is a stretch of darkness, and Professor Plum experiences a delicious confusion. Although he has passed this way before, he cannot remember whether the black passage proceeds straight for the next few steps, or continues to turn in the same direction, or turns the

other way. Each time he descends from the civilized world of
well-appointed rooms and high windows to the dank dark of
the SECRET PASSAGES he has the pleasurable sensation of losing
his way, of immersing himself in an alluring and alien realm of
flickering lantern-lit walls, unlit stretches of darkness, black fissures and crevices, sudden cavelike openings. The paths are
growing increasingly familiar, but at the same time they are
accumulating strangeness, for the growth of familiarity releases
him to search for new details, not seen before. The two passages, moreover, really constitute four different paths, depend-
ing on his point of descent, since it is impossible, in the
semidark, to commit to memory the precise pattern of turns or
the exact number and order of crevices, fissures, and curious
outcroppings; and as if to conspire with the dark, and increase
his sense of uncertainty, he cannot always recall whether he is
on the way to the KITCHEN, the STUDY, the LOUNGE, or the
CONSERVATORY. The four descents to the two passages are strikingly different: the rickety wooden stairway leading down from
the KITCHEN, the rusting iron handrail rattling in the wall over
the stone steps behind the secret door in the LOUNGE, the grass-
grown earthen steps descending from the CONSERVATORY, the
circular stairway behind the sliding panel in the STUDY. Professor Plum reaches out a hand and touches the damp wall; it
appears to be crusted with loose, brittle growths, several of
which drop lightly to the path. The sense of strangeness is, to
be sure, carefully contained within an encompassing sense of
the familiar; the passages, however dark, surprising, and uncertain, always lead to one of the four rooms. It cannot be other-
wise. Professor Plum advances slowly, with his hand on the
wall. It is like the experience of reading a detective novel: a
rigorous design bristling with dangerous surprises and leading
to an inescapable end. But is this an original thought? Has he
perhaps read it somewhere? Lantern-light is already visible on
the path; the Professor, who has begun to be a trifle anxious,
feels a little burst of relief, of disappointment.

Physical. It is an old board, which goes back to Jacob's child-hood. The line down the center, representing the place where the board folds in half, has become more visible over the years; the paper has gradually worn away over the fold, exposing the gray cardboard beneath, so that a thin gray line now runs through the center of the HALL, across a row of yellow squares, through the central rectangle, across two rows of yellow squares, and through the center of the BALLROOM. The O in the word LOUNGE is shaded with a pencil. Part of the shading has been erased, but the erasure has removed an arc of the O and the gray color beneath the shading, and has left a white smudge. A small brown stain beside the R in BILLIARD ROOM, on one side of the fold, corresponds to a pale stain, identical in shape, on a wall of the DINING ROOM, on the other side of the fold. A faint pencil line is visible in the LIBRARY. A darker, wavy line shows in two yellow squares beside one of the doors of the BALLROOM.

Rooms. The Ross house has eight rooms: a kitchen, living room, dining room, and study (formerly a playroom) down-stairs, three bedrooms upstairs, and an unheated bedroom (for-merly a study) in the attic. There is also a small screened porch in back, in the space between the kitchen and the attached ga-rage. When David was born, he slept in a cradle in his parents' bedroom for three weeks, before being moved to a crib in Mar-ian's room. Marian, aged nine, moved into Jacob's room and stayed with him for nearly a year. When Marian was ten, she moved back to her room and David's crib was moved into Jacob's larger room for a trial period; to everyone's surprise, Jacob liked having David in his room and spent many hours sitting on the floor with him, reading books patiently over and over and showing him how to fit the bright red apple and the bright yellow banana into his fruit puzzle. When Jacob entered high school, his father converted the playroom to a study and Jacob moved up to the room in the attic, where he used an electric heater in the winter. Jacob liked being alone at the top of the house, in a room with a slanting ceiling, a room whose walls were entirely lined with bookshelves. David missed Jacob but liked having complete control of the room; he felt he was taking care of it for his brother, who still kept some of his clothes in the closet. When Jacob left home for Columbia, David, aged eight, felt that his brother had moved to a still higher room. Every day for nearly a month he climbed the stairs to Jacob's room in order to straighten the books and make certain everything was all right; one day he stopped going up there, and did not return until Jacob came home for Thanksgiving. He began staying in the living room when Marian practiced her Czerny exercises and Chopin études, and he had long talks with her before going to bed. When Marian left home for Barnard, David did not feel that the house had grown larger: he felt that two rooms had been lost, since there was now no reason to enter Marian's room or Jacob's attic room. One night when his parents were asleep he went into Marian's room and crept into her bed; he thought he could smell her perfume on the pillows. When he woke up in the middle of the night he did not know where he was; he thought that he must be in Grandma's apartment in Washington Heights, and only when he remembered Grandma lying proud and white in the coffin did he realize his mistake.

Still life. Miss Scarlet is struck again by the Colonel's ability to turn her into an arrangement: to be inspected by that banal gaze is instantly to become a tableau, a wax figure, a mediocre artist's gilt-framed still life (the staring fishhead, the glossy green grapes each with its careful highlight). She feels, in that pause of inspection, that she has achieved the condition of utter banality. It is a condition more extreme than death, for to die is to continue to exist in the body; but she has ceased to exist in the body, she is impalpable, the cells of her flesh have dissolved in the solvent of a trite imagination. Despite her revulsion for the vulgar Colonel, Miss Scarlet is grateful to him for permitting her to savor this annihilation.

Research. David has not yet told Jacob of his morning's research. In anticipation of Jacob's visit, David spent the morning at the library, searching for facts about the history of the game. After two hours of failure, he was in the Fine Arts section sullenly and half curiously turning the pages of an illustrated book about British board games when he made his triumphant discovery. Clue was not an American game at all. It was a British game exported to the USA in 1949 and sold in the States by Parker Brothers, who had introduced small changes in design. The British game was called Cluedo, a bewildering name that David decided was intended to allude to another British board game, Ludo. The book showed a color photograph of the board, which was strikingly like the Clue board with one notable difference: the rooms were without furniture. Other differences between the two versions emerged: the mansion of Cluedo was owned by Dr. Black, not the embarrassing Mr. Boddy of Clue; the colored border running around the ground plan of the mansion was light red, not green; the backs of the cards bore no illustration. The suspects were the same, except that Mr. Green was the Reverend Green: Jacob would enjoy that, he would spin some wild theory to account for the change from Reverend to Mister when the game crossed the Atlantic. The British murder weapons were the same, but three of them had different names: the Wrench was called the Spanner, the Knife was called the Dagger, and the Lead Pipe was called Lead Piping. David is so eager to reveal the results of his research to Jacob, who will know how to appreciate each detail, that the thought of an obstacle is intolerable to him, and he suddenly imagines Marian seizing Susan by the hair and plunging the Knife into her throat. He is shocked at the thought, and glances guiltily at Susan, startled to see her staring directly at him.

Feminine stratagems. The Colonel reflects that Miss Scarlet is the kind of woman who, by primness of temperament and propriety of upbringing, cannot confess to herself a crude desire for sexual adventure, and in particular a desire for sexual adventure with a coarse womanizer like Colonel Mustard. It is therefore necessary for her to disguise from herself the fact of her craving, while at the same time arranging for its satisfaction. This problem she has solved instinctively and brilliantly by the tactic of striking scornful attitudes whenever she finds herself in the Colonel's presence. Her attitudes serve the double purpose of affirming her sense of decorum and drawing continual sexual attention to herself. She has in effect pursued him relentlessly through deliberate demonstrations of indifference. Miss Scarlet, the Colonel surmises, can permit herself to be seduced only if she persuades herself that she feels contempt for her seducer, thereby removing responsibility from herself while inviting his attentions through disdainful poses tinged with erotic display. The little game, rich in nuances, holds specific but limited charms for the Colonel. It is always of course a pleasure to observe the unfolding of feminine stratagems however transparent, but the Colonel cannot find indefinitely stimulating the two-dimensional role created for him by the charming Miss Scarlet. From the very beginning she has produced in him an odd and distinctly unpleasant sense of constriction. In her continual flight from herself, her relentless assumption of attitudes, her striving to become nothing but an object, she diminishes him: he becomes a cartoon villain in her gallery of pornography (The Disdainful Maiden and The Aging Lecher). Her provocative little pose, on the velvet window seat, in the mauve light, appears to be an invitation to pleasure, but in fact it is an invitation to death: its intention is to confirm the Colonel's mediocrity, to divest him of imagination and thereby turn him to stone. It is to evade this divestiture that the Colonel prolongs his refusal.

▪

Words. The nine names of the rooms, in black capital letters, constitute eleven words: the seven single-name rooms and the two double-name rooms, BILLIARD ROOM and DINING ROOM. Five additional words appear in the center of the board: beneath the word CLUE, in large white capital letters with black shadows, appears the word THE, in small black capital letters, and beneath the word THE appear the words GREAT DETECTIVE GAME. When we observe the board so that the word CLUE is right-side up, then we see, in the lower left-hand corner of the playing board, in the green border that runs around all nine rooms, the words © 1949 JOHN WADDINGTON, LTD. In the same green border, in the lower right, we see four lines of print: PARKER BROTHERS, INC./SALEM, MASSACHUSETTS/NEW YORK SAN FRANCISCO CHICAGO/MADE IN U.S.A. Still other words appear on the board. The four rooms with secret passages all contain words: in a corner of the STUDY are the words SECRET PASSAGE/TO/KITCHEN/(ONE MOVE), in a corner of the LOUNGE are the words SECRET PASSAGE/TO/CONSERVATORY/(ONE MOVE), in a corner of the KITCHEN are the words SECRET PASSAGE/TO/STUDY/(ONE MOVE), and in a corner of the CONSERVATORY are the words SECRET PASSAGE/TO/LOUNGE/(ONE MOVE). Finally, six of the yellow squares adjacent to the green border contain the word START, with the name of a different suspect under each one: MISS SCARLET, COL. MUSTARD, MRS. WHITE, MR. GREEN, MRS. PEACOCK, PROF. PLUM. If we consider the date 1949 to be a single word, the abbreviations U.S.A., LTD, and INC. to be single words, and combinations such as NEW YORK, PARKER BROTHERS, and MR. GREEN each to be two words, and if we ignore the symbol ©, then on the Clue board we find seventy-five words.

Jacob did it. Susan lowers her eyes, ashamed to have been caught staring at David. Now he too will dislike her: the outsider, crasher of birthday parties, Jacob's shikse, insolent starer. She cannot look at Jacob, who has insisted that she come with him and now is drinking too much wine and shutting her out. She cannot look at Marian, who resents her presence and wants her dead. She cannot look at David, who has caught her staring at him, spying on him. She can look only at her hateful horrible cards: the HALL, the LOUNGE, Colonel Mustard, the Lead Pipe, the Knife. Oh, Jacob did it. On the porch. With his cold, cold eye.

Mr. Green's dilemma. Mr. Green stands in the corridor near another door of the BALLROOM, not far from the DINING ROOM, paralyzed with uncertainty and chagrin. He has left the BALL-ROOM in a manner so awkward, sudden, and inexplicable that he feels it only proper to return and proffer an apology. At the same time, the thought of entering the BALLROOM again after his disgraceful exit is so painful that as he imagines it he draws an audible sharp breath. Besides, how can he possibly explain to Miss Scarlet, whose gasp was caused not simply by the Colonel's sudden words in the silence but by the shocking revelation of Mr. Green's presence, that he had been standing in a corner during her entrance into the room and had remained there without a word during her long walk across the echoing floor? The thought of entering the room again is itself unspeakably painful to Mr. Green, but in addition to entering the room he will be obliged to walk across the long, loud floor, carefully observed not only by Miss Scarlet, whose initial surprise at finding him in the corner will have had time to darken to indignation, but also by the Colonel, in whose presence, under the best of circumstances, Mr. Green feels uncomfortable and anxious, and who now, as witness to Mr. Green's inglorious retreat and as a probable confidant and champion of the injured Miss Scarlet, will await Mr. Green in the manner of a stern father barely willing to listen to an excuse already dismissed as contemptible. Mr. Green will not know where to look; he will not know what to say; the entire purpose of his return, which should be to clarify a possible misunderstanding and render him less foolish or odious in their eyes, will be undermined by his undoubted inability to utter a single word and the general impossibility, even if he were not at a loss for words, of explaining his shameful behavior. Despite these extremely compelling reasons for evasion there remain, nevertheless, equally decisive arguments for confrontation. It is too much to hope, for example, that he can avoid either or both of them during the remainder of his visit. It might therefore prove even more painful in the long run if he does not, immediately, face up to the inevitable. Besides, he has left behind his book, a clumsily written but learned study which he took with him from the LIBRARY with the express intent of finishing it before dinner. Mr. Green takes a deep breath, raises his right foot, and does not move.

Sprechen Sie Englisch? "How's Dad been?" Jacob asks out of the blue, looking up abruptly from his cards. David is startled and exhilarated: things are going to be all right after all, the family is sticking together, everything's bound to be all right. "Oh, he's been all right," David answers. He knows that Mrs. Peacock did it, with either the Revolver or the Candlestick; his father is slumped in an armchair, a revolver at his feet, a red hole in his temple. "Actually there was one, I don't know, episode." Marian turns her head sharply. "What episode, Davey?" "Episode," Jacob says, frowning thoughtfully and pulling at his chin. "Episode, episode." His face assumes a hopeful expression. *"Sprechen Sie Englisch?"* "Well," David says, "you know how he likes to park as close to his classroom as possible? So he doesn't have to carry his briefcase too far? Well, last month someone took his space, so Dad had to walk across the whole parking lot with a load of books. He told Mom he was so short of breath he had to sit down. Now he's bought an extra copy of every book for the course and he keeps one copy in his office and one at home." "You never told me that,"

Marian says. "Davey, you promised to tell me, no matter what." "Mom made me promise not to tell. You know how Dad is." "And he won't see Hershatter?" Jacob asks. "No way. He tells Mom, but she's not allowed to tell me. But she does, sometimes. He gets furious if she tells him to see Hershatter." "Am I living in a bad novel?" Jacob says, flinging up an arm. "What is this crap? Can't Mom get him to see Hershatter?" "You try getting him to see Hershatter. Mom says he gets too angry. She doesn't want to upset him." "She doesn't want to upset him? He can't walk across a parking lot and nobody's allowed to know?" "He's been better lately," David says, "really." Jacob stares at David; for a moment his arm is suspended in the air. He lowers his elbow to the table and leans his forehead into the heel of his hand. His long fingers are thrust into his hair and his eyes are heavy-lidded. "Dad is sick," he says slowly. "He needs to see a doctor. If he keeps on like this, he's going to die." "Jake," Marian says, placing a hand on his forearm. "It's David's birthday."

Professor Plum makes a discovery. As he advances once again along the SECRET PASSAGE toward the KITCHEN, or is it the CONSERVATORY, Professor Plum notices, around a darkening bend in the path, a narrow fissure in the rough stone wall. He has noticed it before. In the half-darkness lit only by the distant flame of a kerosene lantern, he stops for a moment to give it his close attention. The fissure rises from the floor to the height of his forehead; it is wide enough to admit a man sideways. The Professor is in no great hurry to arrive at the CONSERVATORY, or is it the KITCHEN—indeed, his supreme pleasure is to traverse the passages—and on a sudden impulse he steps sideways from the path into the fissure, bending his head awkwardly and protecting his spectacles with a hand. Behind the entrance the fissure widens and admits the Professor to another dim-lit passage. It is much like the one he has left but covered with a strip of carpet and lined with shelves containing a variety of amusing objects: small colorful glass jars, faded magic-lantern slides, pipe racks filled with pipes of many shapes, lacquered wooden boxes. The Professor advances by slow steps, looking back at the receding fissure, which closes into darkness. He plans to follow the new passage only a short distance, before turning back and continuing on his way.

Cards (2). The backs of the cards show a magnifying glass in whose lens is pictured, in blue-black and white, the posts of a gate, a curving walk, and a gabled mansion with four chimneys. Each chimney is crowned by three chimney pots. A large blue-black tree with bushy blue-black foliage, situated between the gate and the mansion, spreads a curving branch above part of the roof. Each gatepost is surmounted by a finial composed of a cone with concave sides topped by a sphere. Each sphere, in the foreground, is large enough to contain the door of the mansion, in the background. On the handle of the magnifying glass are long parallel blue-black lines, suggestive of palpable ridges like those on the circumference of a coin.

Love and death. Jacob crushes down a reply and, with Marian's hand still on his arm, remembers suddenly the new baby home from the hospital: he and Marian standing on both sides of the cradle looking down at David. He thought: he looks like me, in the album. The unexpected resemblance gave him the sense that he was the father, that he was peculiarly responsible for this child: his child. He sees his father's grave face, hears the solemn words: Jacob, Marian, I want you to love your brother always, do you understand, you're all he'll have when your mother and I are no longer here. Jacob tried to understand, but the words frightened him; he wondered why they were no longer going to be there.

A deeper significance. Miss Scarlet, fixed by the Colonel's mediocre imagination in an attitude of banal surrender, senses that matters are not proceeding quite as they should be. The smooth revolting precision of the Colonel's advance upon her has suffered interruption, indeed breakdown. At first Miss Scarlet imagines some merely masculine trouble, but gradually she divines a deeper significance. The Colonel, in order to enjoy himself, requires a small pleasure she has failed to provide. Her stylized offer of herself, which perfectly expresses his vulgar and trivializing fantasy of conquest, nevertheless irks him because it deprives him of a pleasure still more banal: the overcoming of an obstacle. Miss Scarlet does not cease to marvel at the fascinating depths of the Colonel's inexhaustible banality. It is in order to provoke in her a show of titillating resistance that the Colonel lingers on the threshold of seduction, and it is in order to prolong his hesitation, and postpone the degradation of his touch, that Miss Scarlet remains motionless on the window seat in an attitude of erotic invitation.

The two Mr. Greens. Slowly, very slowly, Mr. Green advances toward the BALLROOM door. He has not made up his mind to enter, but he has made up his mind to advance slowly in the direction of the door, in the hope that forward motion, with its apparent decisiveness, will demonstrate to his doubting mind that decision is possible. But with every step forward there rises, in Mr. Green's mind, a new reason for retreat. It is as if the fact of forward physical motion has released his mind from the need to find reasons to advance, thereby permitting it to exercise its full powers in producing evidence for retreat. Mr. Green is therefore moving in two direction: forward, physically; backward, mentally. A diagram would show twin figures back to back, each with its foot raised, each with its head turned over its shoulder.

▪

Is that all? David, frightened by Jacob's words, glances over his cards at the board and sees a square of cardboard with yellow and gray plane figures on it. The flatness of the board startles him: it is a depthless world, devoid of shadow. There are no rooms, no doors, no secret passages, only the glare of the overhead light on the black lines, the yellow spaces. For a moment he wants to shout: is that all? is that all?

A new life. Marian removes her hand from Jacob's arm but continues to think about her father. He is sicker than she knew; the signs are there, she has been deceiving herself. The thought of her father's death is so disturbing that she feels a ripple of panic pass across her stomach; she looks up guiltily, as if she has been detected in a crime. Her father's absence from her life, a life that hasn't even begun yet, is not possible. She will speak to her mother in the morning. She will call more often. She will begin her life. She will change her life. She will meet someone. She will do something. Marian thinks: stop. You are growing morbid. Stop. You are being selfish. It is David's birthday, a day of celebration.

Go back. Professor Plum has not advanced far along the carpeted passage when he comes to an open place from which three other passages stretch away. In the open place sit several old armchairs and couches. The Professor is a cautious man. He is perfectly aware that he must not lose his way, must under no circumstances permit himself to yield to the temptation of unknown passageways; but it is precisely this awareness that frees him from the constraints of caution, and permits him to continue his exploration of the unknown, for he knows that he is not the sort of man who takes foolish and unnecessary risks. Even as he admonishes himself to return to the SECRET PASSAGE before he loses his way, he is deciding among the new, alluring passages. One is hung with paintings; one is lined with writing desks, highboys, and wing chairs; one contains two rows of closed red doors. The Professor hesitates a moment before choosing the passage of red doors. After walking a short way he tries a door and is admitted to a flight of carpeted steps going down. Go back, the Professor reminds himself, as he descends the stairs.

A lack of imagination. The Colonel, paralyzed in a pose of suspended seduction, is beginning to grow a little bored. He has no intention of sparing Miss Scarlet, but her inept imitation of whorish abandon cannot sustain his indefinite interest. He would like to get on with it and repair to the BILLIARD ROOM for a whiskey and soda before dinner, but every possible advance is fated to confirm Miss Scarlet's crude imagining of him. To act is to become her fantasy, to assent to his inexistence. The Colonel feels himself dissolving into an imaginary Colonel with a trim mustache, pulled-back shoulders, and reddish cheekbones. Utterly unimagined, devoid of detail, he is beginning to fade away.

David looks up. David wonders whether he is the only one to notice that Susan is playing badly. Her Suggestions reveal that she has no grasp of strategy; he knows that she doesn't have the STUDY, Professor Plum, or the Revolver, yet on her last turn she named all three, as if guessing at random instead of using her own cards to make controlled guesses. The poor quality of her play disturbs him, and he tries not to look up when it is her turn, for fear that his irritation will show on his face. True, she has never played before this evening—David has never known anyone who hasn't played Clue, and he imagines it as a misfortune, a childhood deprivation, as if he had been told that she had never eaten a piece of chocolate or visited an amusement park—but the rules are easy and the principles of inference elementary. It isn't likely that Susan, a Radcliffe graduate who majored in mathematics, cannot follow the game, and David senses a deeper reason: something is wrong between her and Jacob, she is worried and distracted, she is filled with an unhappiness that doesn't show on her cool, lovely face. And when he looks up suddenly from his cards, in order to see whether she is concentrating on the game, he is unsettled to see, three feet away, staring over Marian's shoulder at the porch windows, the large, beautiful, sorrowing eyes of Susan Newton.

The doorknob. Mr. Green's hand is resting on the knob of the BALLROOM door. He hears nothing within. It is possible that Miss Scarlet and the Colonel have left, and that Mr. Green can enter with impunity and retrieve his book; but there are other explanations of the silence. The room is large and the door is thick; it is quite possible that a conversation at the far end cannot be heard by someone standing outside the door, his head bent almost to the wood, listening intently. It is possible that Miss Scarlet and the Colonel are within, but silent. It is possible that Miss Scarlet has left the room by another door, leaving the Colonel alone, or that Miss Scarlet is alone, having been abandoned by the Colonel. It is possible that they are within but have been joined by a third person, say Professor Plum, who had not expected to find them there and whose unanticipated appearance has rendered everyone silent. It is possible that Miss Scarlet, Colonel Mustard, Professor Plum, Mrs. White, and Mrs. Peacock are all inside, facing this very door, awaiting the return of Mr. Green, whose comic disappearance has been discussed at length. Indeed, as Mr. Green stands with his head bent close to the wood, he is surprised at how the possibilities proliferate: it is possible that neither Miss Scarlet nor the Colonel is inside but that someone else, whose appearance caused them to leave, has remained; it is possible that Miss Scarlet has been murdered and is lying with her throat cut on the window seat;

it is possible that Mr. Green is inside and that he is imagining himself outside, with his hand on the doorknob and his head bent close to the wood of the door. Even as the possibilities multiply, Mr. Green realizes that he does not know whether he desires Miss Scarlet and the Colonel to be present or absent, since he is not certain whether he wishes to confront them and apologize, or to evade them and retrieve his book in peace; and as he watches his hand begin to turn the doorknob he does not know whether to be astonished at his audacity or ashamed of his timidity.

The bodies of women. David is disturbed by how much time he spends thinking about the bodies of women. He is released from this necessity only rarely, under the influence of a stronger passion, and Susan's presence on his birthday is disturbing in part because she interferes with his release into family feeling. Although she is dressed modestly, in a vanilla silk blouse and tan corduroy skirt, David is aware of her breasts pushing lightly against the thin cloth, especially when she leans forward to roll the die; and when she crosses and uncrosses her legs, or shifts her position slightly on the padded wooden chair, he is disturbed by the soft sounds of cloth, the creak of the chair, and the hushed slippery sound of sliding and rubbing skin. Susan had arrived in nylon stockings, but when she came down from her room he saw that she had taken them off. Stockings themselves, their scratchiness and glisten, have always disturbed him, but the fact of their removal disturbs him even more, as if she had suddenly drawn attention to the act of lifting each leg in turn to roll down the tight, clinging stockings, as if, carelessly lifting each leg in turn, she were taunting him with the suddenly exposed flesh of her upper thighs, as if, lifting each leg in turn, higher and higher, she were attempting to slip her legs into his mind and leave them there, lifting turn by turn, forever, while she vanished into Cambridge, Massachusetts. One afternoon, in the year before Marian left for college, David had entered her room to look for a piece of paper. He was startled to see Marian standing in a half-slip, facing him. At the sight of the heavy white breasts with their red wounds he felt a rush of fear and sorrow, even as he felt something relax at the back of his mind, as if he had suddenly remembered a word that had eluded him. Marian instantly crossed her arms over her chest, gripping her shoulders with her hands. What David remembers is the white-knuckled fingers, the crushed, painful look of the breasts, the proud and sorrowful turning away of Marian's face, and the fact that although she turned her face to one side, she did not turn her body away.

The Colonel makes up his mind. At the sound of the turning doorknob the Colonel turns his head sharply toward the distant door and is aware, even as he turns, of the silk-and-flesh slapping together of Miss Scarlet's knees and the sudden stiffening of her limbs as she prepares to fling herself upright. The Colonel, although he once beat a man senseless with his fists, is essentially a discreet man, who prefers not to be caught in compromising situations. Nevertheless, during the moment when he hears the turning doorknob and the clapping together of Miss Scarlet's knees, he realizes two things: he is not going to permit Miss Scarlet to escape her banal destiny, even if the door should open to admit a regiment; and the banging together of her knees, the tensing of her body, the look of sharp alarm constitute Miss Scarlet's sole failure to assume a pose, and render her suddenly desirable. As she struggles to rise, the Colonel admires for a moment the tendons of her neck tensed like ropes, the harsh twist of her torso, the lines of strain between her elegant eyebrows, before throwing himself on her expertly.

Late. It is growing late. Susan yawns through tightly shut teeth, slitting her eyes and giving a faint shudder. She wonders whether Jacob will tuck her in and talk to her, she wonders whether he will make love to her in the narrow bed in his attic room before leaving for the cot in David's room. Marian's large eyes are half closed; she leans her temple on the heel of a hand, so that the skin above her eyebrow is taut, giving her a look of alertness that clashes with her drooping, sleepy air. Jacob has been steadily drinking glasses of wine and cups of coffee; the whites of his eyes are cracked with red, his irises glitter. Now he leans forward on both elbows and runs three fingers of each hand slowly along his temples, over and over; his thick, springy hair has a slightly mussed look. David's eyes are tired, and burn with Jacob's cigarette smoke; his heart is beating quickly, as if he has been running. Upstairs, Samuel Ross lies asleep on his back, breathing through his mouth, rasping lightly. Martha Ross, turning heavily in her sleep, half wakes and hears voices from downstairs. She must tell Sam that the children are still up, the children, yes, but again she is asleep. Across from the Ross house a light goes out in an upstairs window of the Warren house. Sandra Warren, closing her eyes in the dark, can hear through the open window the sound of the exhaust fan in the Rosses' attic and a faint sound of voices from the Ross back porch as she thinks of Bob Schechter coming out of the water with his hair flattened down and his streaming body shining in the sun. A foghorn sounds. The tide is going out; on a blanket on the dark beach, two lovers lie facing each other, stroking each other's cheeks. Far out on the water a blinking lighthouse shows where the dark water meets the dark sky, before plunging both into blackness. On the other side of the beach a dull red glows in the sky, from the shopping center a mile away. Again the foghorn sounds; on the Ross porch, David listens to it and thinks of train whistles, night journeys, distant cities, all the unseen places longing to be seen.

The rigors of civilized life. Better and better: at the bottom of the stairs Professor Plum comes to another passage, from which he notices stone stairways going up and down. At this point it is still not too late to turn back. The Professor has only to return to the carpeted steps, climb to the top, turn left along the passageway of doors, and proceed to the open space, which stands at the end of the carpeted passage that leads to the fissure; as he rehearses this information, he continues along the new passage, which is intersected by other passages. The Professor is enchanted—by a stroke of luck, he has discovered a honeycomb of secret passages under the mansion. No doubt the original owner, bored by the rigors of civilized life, constructed this shadowy escape from the sunlit realm; or perhaps a number of owners, each discovering the fissure in the SECRET PASSAGE, constructed independent systems of passageways that they cunningly joined to existing systems. As he explores the proliferating realm of crisscrossing passages, connected by numerous stairways to passages above and below, the Professor does not forget that he is on his way to the KITCHEN, or is it the CONSERVATORY. At any moment he plans to turn back.

An unscreamed scream. As Miss Scarlet struggles with the Colonel, she opens her mouth to scream but does not scream. To scream is to secure rescue, to assure the flinging open of the door, the clatter of feet across the hard floor; but rescue means discovery, and Miss Scarlet does not wish to be discovered sprawled beneath the odious Colonel with her crimson dress above her hips and her pink crepe de chine knickers at her knees. She cannot but hope that the door will remain closed; even to struggle is to risk discovery. The unscreamed scream struggles inside her, ripples across her abdomen, makes her fingertips itch. Miss Scarlet realizes that her sudden, involuntary resistance has aroused the Colonel, whose dull brain no doubt teems with juicy images of struggling maidens; she further realizes that the necessary cessation of struggle will satisfy his trite image of conquest. As the seconds pass, and no other sound is heard at the far end of the BALLROOM, Miss Scarlet marvels at the way in which the world has conspired with the Colonel, for whom even the act of vision is hackneyed and hand-me-down, to absorb her into the realm of the imaginary.

Hair. The game is winding down now, and Marian wonders whether David has had a good birthday. He appears to be engrossed in the game; he studies his cards intensely, continually makes marks on his pad, shakes the die over and over in his fist, flings it vigorously onto the board. He is taking on some of Jacob's characteristics, as he sometimes does: when he flings the die onto the board he gives his wrist a twist that is Jacob's, and he talks to the die in Jacob's voice: come on baby, three baby, three big ones for Brother Dave. Jacob has thrown himself into the game; his excitement, which has infected David, makes Marian uneasy. There is sweat-shine on Jacob's cheekbones and on one side of his nose; his thick hair, ruffled by his thrusting fingers, has sprung out of place. David's hair has always been different: straight and pale brown, it falls slantwise across his forehead almost to his eyes. From time to time he sweeps it up with a hand, leaving a few long hairs fallen. Marian looks across at Susan, startled by the beauty of her hair. Marian has always been troubled by the thick abundance of her own hair, which breaks the teeth of combs. She remembers David's childhood hair, silky and brown, the fineness of it, and the sweetness of his scalp's smell. Susan looks tired. She is far from home, in a strange house. She too is part of David's birthday. "Susan," she says, reaching for the bowl of potato chips and realizing that it's the first time she has said the name aloud. "Can you use some more of these?"

In the darkening corridor. In the darkening corridor Mr. Green stands with his hand on the turned doorknob. It seems to him that he hears dim sounds from deep within the dangerous BALLROOM, but the sounds are so faint that they may be nothing more than sounds of the house itself. The house is full of sounds: loose window sashes knock in their frames, water pipes mutter, floorboards creak, the very walls seem to breathe and sigh. The memory of his discovery in the shadowy corner, and of his awkward, guilty retreat, is so vivid to Mr. Green that he cannot continue his arrested motion. With alarm he realizes that his current posture is no less dubious—anyone happening along the corridor might well mistake him for an eavesdropper, for his hand is on the knob, his forehead is bent forward almost to the wood of the door. Indeed, it would not be difficult to imagine that he harbored a weapon in his waistcoat. Mr. Green looks stealthily over his shoulder: no one. He is alone. He thinks of the quiet arbor in the garden behind his mother's house, of the well-worn leather of the armchair in his room. His mother had been right: he would not enjoy the weekend.

The Black Hag. The Colonel, at the instant he enters Miss Scarlet, begins to lose interest in her. Miss Scarlet has exhausted her purpose as prey; her remaining usefulness is severely limited. The Colonel prides himself on not being a sentimentalist. His interest, he reflects, will steadily diminish as his thrusts increase in intensity until, at the famous moment, Miss Scarlet will become superfluous: and the Black Hag, bending over him with cold fingers and heavy-lidded eyes, will claim him once again.

The die. The die is a translucent red cube with slightly rounded corners. The spots are sunken, opaque, and white. It is difficult to tell whether the spots are small holes in the surface that have been painted white, or whether they are small white plugs that have been set in holes in the surface. Through any of the six translucent sides, other spots are visible as little reddish lumps shaped like the heads of bullets.

Poor thing. Miss Scarlet slips nimbly from her body and takes up a position not far from the window seat, where she observes with interest the scene before her: the Colonel's pale, well-muscled, heaving buttocks peeping out from beneath his agitated shirttails (the Colonel is naked only from the waist down), the young woman's raised knee pressed back against her ribs by the Colonel's splayed hand, a tangle of pink and white at the ankle of the other foot. The young woman's visible arm is stretched out, the hand limp at the wrist; her face is turned to one side and her eyes are closed. She looks for all the world as if she has been slain—only, from time to time, a barely perceptible tremor passes over her body. Poor thing, Miss Scarlet thinks.

Stunning. Susan is not deceived, by Marian's gesture, into sudden intimations of intimacy. She is grateful anyway. She sets down the bowl beside her glass of wine, bites into a saddle-shaped chip, and looks directly at Jacob's sister, whose face is already turned toward David. At that moment, in that light, at that precise angle, Marian's unlovely face is stunning: her high cheekbone shines, the tide of her hair rolls along her face and dashes down on her shoulder, the sharp proud line of her forehead and nose slashes across the dark green blinds like a blade of light. Susan's hair has been admired since early childhood, but she feels that its straightness shows lack of character. She has always been attracted to forceful, intelligent, unbeautiful women stronger and bolder than she. In high school her best friend had wild hair and braces, wore torn jeans and floppy lumberman's shirts, practiced the violin three hours a day, and once punched a boy in the mouth when he refused to stop torturing a cat. Susan is willing to be proud of her hair because

Jacob adores it, but if she were Jacob she would be more critical. Jacob is stern when it comes to her taste in literature (Faulkner is a gasbag) and music (rock music is what Yeats meant by "mere anarchy is loosed upon the world"), but he is reverent toward her body, which makes him seem careless. If she were a man, she would want to plunge both hands into Marian's torrent of hair. If she were a man, she would reject herself and choose Marian.

Mrs. Peacock and Mr. Green. Mrs. Peacock cannot endure the presence of Mrs. White for another second: the slumped shoulders, the dark eyes glistening with desolation, the hands moving helplessly, the air of dazed bewilderment, all these inspire in Mrs. Peacock a sense of suffocation. She must escape from this room that is filling up with grief, a grief that rushes outward in all directions, pushing down everything in its path, pressing against the walls, hurting her skin. "Yes yes, dear," Mrs. Peacock says, "it will be all right," and escapes from the desperate gaze, the inconsolable bulk of flesh. She makes her way down the corridor toward the DINING ROOM, passing on her way the corridor to the BALLROOM, where she is surprised to see Mr. Green standing with his hand on the doorknob, his head half bowed. At the sound of her footstep Mr. Green whirls to look at her, gives a gasp, then fumbles at the door and thrusts it open, disappearing within. A queer one, Mr. Green. One might almost think he was afraid of her.

Endgame. David knows that the murder was committed by Mrs. Peacock, with the Candlestick, in one of three rooms: the BILLIARD ROOM, the DINING ROOM, or the BALLROOM. The game is winding down now; it is simply a matter of moving his piece across the board from room to room, eliminating the incorrect ones. Although Susan's guesses have grown more skilful, she does not appear to know either the murderer or the room, but David is less certain of Marian and Jacob. Jacob almost never loses at Clue; his logic is flawless, his instincts sure. Marian, in her quiet way, is a dangerous player who can never be ruled out. David knows, from his system of checkmarks and *X*'s, that Jacob has identified Mrs. Peacock and the Candlestick; he is almost certain that Marian knows both, though he can't be sure about the weapon; all three of them are moving from room to room, searching for the final clue. This part of the game always draws attention to another disturbing flaw in the game's design: although play is supposed to be based on logical inference, it admits a high proportion of sheer chance, since each time a player's token is accused of the murder it must be moved to the room in question. One is continually being whisked away, to the wrong part of the board. Jacob is known to absorb this whimsical element of the game directly into his strategy, and to make a useless Suggestion deliberately, for the sake of removing a token as far as possible from its apparent destination. He has already pulled David across the board to the STUDY, which he knows David holds in his hand, thereby delaying David's progress and wasting a move of his own; the result is to give Marian an advantage in the race to new rooms. The game cannot last much longer. David is pleased to see Jacob bending intensely over his Detective Notes, trying to wrest an additional secret from his complex system of marks; Jacob seems in a better mood, he has been drawn into the game. David wonders what will happen next. Will there be another game? It's almost one in the morning. Will Susan retire and leave the three of them together, to talk in the living room? Marian seems tired; perhaps she too will go upstairs. Will Jacob want to stay up till dawn? Will they walk to 7-Eleven and buy Cokes at four in the morning? Will they go down to the beach and walk out to the end of the jetty and sit looking across the black Sound toward Long Island? The foghorns are silent now; maybe the sky has cleared. Will Jacob want to talk? Will he talk about Dad? About Susan?

His writing? David hopes he can somehow let Susan know that it's all right for her to be here on his birthday. He shakes the die in his loose fist, enjoying the tension of the game, holding back, savoring the moment when he will suddenly open his hand and watch the red die tumble across the bright, loud board.

Just going. As Mr. Green hurtles into the BALLROOM he sees, on a corner of the distant window seat, Miss Scarlet sitting with her hands in her lap. Ten feet away the Colonel stands with his back to Miss Scarlet and his hands clasped behind his back. Miss Scarlet looks up, the Colonel turns his head: they are waiting for an explanation. Mr. Green cannot speak. His cheeks are aflame, his heart is pounding, he feels light-headed with embarrassment. The Colonel goes to the window, picks up a dark object, turns sharply on his heel, and begins striding toward Mr. Green. The Colonel is going to strike him. The Colonel is going to murder him. Mr. Green cannot move. "I say, Green," the Colonel says, striding directly up to him. "Forgot your book." The Colonel thrusts out the book. Mr. Green feels a bursting sensation in his heart; tears of gratitude prickle his eyes. "I am so terribly sorry," Mr. Green says. "I mean happy, of course. I do hope I haven't—" "I was just going," the Colonel remarks.

The black envelope. The black envelope is a little larger than the cards it contains and is open at one of the narrow ends. In the open end is a shallow semicircular notch intended to ease removal of the three hidden cards. On one side of the black envelope appear the words CLUE CARDS, printed in dim silver. On the other side the structure of the envelope is visible: a single sheet of black paper has been folded in such a way that narrow strips overlap the side and bottom; the overlaps are glued in place. Years of use have caused the black envelope to tear at the corners of the open end; minuscule black hairs of paper twist from the splits.

In which the Colonel is thirsty, and goes to the kitchen for a glass of water; and what he finds there. The Colonel feels a slight dryness in his throat after his late exertions and, as he passes the KITCHEN, decides to drink a glass of water before proceeding to the BILLIARD ROOM. When he enters the KITCHEN he sees, in the middle of the room, buxom Mrs. White, standing sideways and holding in one hand a tilted but unspilled glass of water. She is staring straight before her, with her lips slightly parted; her cheeks are wet with tears. Her slumped shoulders, her gleaming cheeks, her loosening braids of hair, her air of desperate disarray, all these form a pleasing foil to her ample well-corseted bosom and handsome high posterior. "Pray forgive me for disturbing you," remarks the Colonel, and closes the door gently behind him as Mrs. White turns her dazed wet face in his direction. The Colonel makes a quick calculation. There will still be time for a game before dinner.

A sound of shattered glass. The Professor has counted seven tiers of crisscrossing passages, but he is no longer certain of the number because many of the passages dip and climb, attaching themselves to higher and lower tiers without the evidence of steps. The multiplying passages cannot be endless, the Professor reminds himself: that is a delusion born of anxiety. Evidently the builder, or series of builders, desired an impression of extravagance, of freedom, as if a single SECRET PASSAGE moving from one known locus to the next were a form of intolerable constriction, for attempts have been made to disguise or blur the intermingling of passages and create confusion in the unwary wanderer. Passages scrupulously resembling other passages have been introduced, so that the illusion of having returned to familiar ground is continually created, only to be disrupted by a deliberate change in the pattern; passages containing shelves, furniture, and paintings lead suddenly to primitive passages where large rocks lie on the earthen paths and water trickles along the stony walls. It occurs to the Professor that perhaps he has been ceaselessly retracing a small number of cunning passages. Or it may be that he has been following a slowly widening and deepening series of passages, a series that he has far from exhausted, a series that has barely begun. His legs are growing tired, and despite the cool air he is perspiring. He stops for a moment to wipe his eyeglasses, which slip from his fingers to the hard path. He hears a sound of shattered glass. He crouches and pats the ground; grains of moist dirt cling to his fingertips. When he picks up his eyeglasses, he brings them close to his eyes and sees that the lenses are unbroken. He stands up quickly. I am imagining things, he says aloud. You are talking to yourself, he says aloud. His voice is very clear. He puts on his eyeglasses and begins walking briskly. This is not happening, he says aloud. Ahead of him, the path divides in two.

Is it possible? In the mauve dusk Miss Scarlet sits in the corner of the window seat smoothing her crimson dress, black in the twilight, over her knees. The Colonel has escaped through the door. Already the late episode is fading, becoming implausible. Is it likely that she? Is it possible that they? The Colonel, after all, has never seen her. He experiences women solely as a series of banal erotic images; he transforms real flesh into figments of his imagination. The Colonel is a magician: in that dark, unseeing gaze, women vanish. Miss Scarlet cannot have been present at the unlikely scene at the window seat, because the Colonel's lovemaking is strictly solitary. The thought is somehow bracing. In the violet gloom Miss Scarlet pinches herself on the forearm and gives a little gasp of pain.

She looks up suddenly. "Mr. Green?" she asks, straining her eyes. But Mr. Green is no longer there.

Jacob raises his glass. Jacob rolls a three: two short of the DINING ROOM. The game is almost over. He raises his wineglass and says, "Happy birthday, Davey." David looks down, flushing with pleasure. Marian places a hand on his hand. "Hey. Happy birthday." David looks up to see her smiling at him; her tired, sorrowful eyes brim with tenderness. Susan pushes back her chair and stands up. She steps around the table, bends over suddenly, and kisses David on the cheekbone. "Happy birthday, David," she says. He can smell the clean scent of her blouse, mixed with a tang of something else: skin? hair? The kiss was a little high, just under his eye. He hears her sit down. David looks quickly at Susan, at Jacob, at Marian. His sister's hand is warm on his hand, his cheekbone still feels the pressure of Susan's lips, his brother's greeting sings in his ears. He would like to tell them that they can count on him, that he will take care of them, that everything will be all right: Jacob will be famous, Marian will be happy, Susan will marry Jacob, Dad will never die. He knows that the words are extravagant and says them only to himself. "Thank you," David says. For a moment, it's as if everything is going to be all right.

In the attic. It is late, on a summer night. In the Ross attic, light from a streetlamp passes through a window-screen, makes its way past the spinning, misty blades of an exhaust fan, and falls dimly on a narrow stretch of floor flanked by old bookcases filled with childhood toys. One shelf holds an uneven pile of abandoned board games (Sorry, Parcheesi, Pollyanna, Camelot), a puzzle showing on the cover a three-masted ship with billowing sails plunging in black-green waves, a pile of Schaum music books with colored covers and miscellaneous sheet music such as "The Flight of the Bumblebee," "My Old Kentucky Home," "*O Mein Papa,*" "In the Hall of the Mountain King," and "Old Black Joe," and a shoebox with crushed sides that contains wooden red and black checkers pieces embossed with crowns, a notched Viewmaster reel called "Ali Baba and the Forty Thieves," tin play-money coins, a wooden slice of watermelon the size of a section of orange, a three-lobed puzzle piece showing rich blue sky, an edge of red roof, and a corner of yellow chimney, a small flip-book featuring a mouse who picks up a sledgehammer and cracks open a gigantic egg from which emerges a frowning chicken with a bump on its head that grows longer and longer, a green rubber grasshopper, a blue fifty-dollar Monopoly bill, and Professor Plum. Beyond the bookcases, in the dark part of the attic, Marian's old German school, a gift from her mother's mother, Rebecca Altgeld, lies under the slanting front wheel of a fallen bicycle. The teacher sits tilted at her desk with raised arms, the six pupils lean in different directions on three wooden benches. Deeper in the blackness, old wooden barrels stand among cardboard cartons and dress boxes. On the floor Pierrot sits with his head against a barrel, his blouse torn, his face stricken with sadness, dreaming of Columbine beside a trellis in moonlight.

Finale. It is late, and in the mansion a tiredness comes over things. The books in the LIBRARY bookcases have lost their depth, and in their flatness can no longer be removed. The billiard balls and the billiard table form one unbroken surface, smooth as paper to the stroking thumb. In the KITCHEN cupboard a mouse knocks over a fragile upright plate, which begins to fall slowly, as if through water, and dissolves in shadow. Miss Scarlet, alone on the window seat in the melancholy BALL-ROOM, feels a stiffening in her limbs: she is slowly turning to wood. Colonel Mustard will stop, his arm held out toward Mrs. White, who, already beginning to lean toward the consoling hand, will pause on the threshold of a momentous decision. Mrs. Peacock will enter the DINING ROOM and freeze in an attitude of disdain, Mr. Green will remain with one foot raised in a shadowy corridor, Professor Plum is already fading among his fading passageways.

Behind the Blue Curtain

On Saturday afternoons in summer my father took me to the movies. All morning long I waited for him to come down from his study, frowning at the bowl of his pipe and slapping the stairs with his slipper-moccasins, as though the glossy dark bowl, the slippers, the waiting itself were a necessary part of my long-drawn-out passage into the realm of dark. I savored every stage: the hot summer sunshine outside the ticket booth, the indoor sunlight of the entranceway with its glass-covered Coming Attractions and its velvet rope, the artificial glow of the red lobby, the mysterious dusk of the theater, the swift decisive darkening—and between the blue folds of the curtain, slowly parting, the sudden shining of the screen. Gravely my father had explained to me that the people on the screen were motionless photographs, passing quickly before my eyes. It was like my black-and-white flip-book from the candy store: a smiling mouse leaped from a diving board toward the water as a frowning shark rose up, opening its jaws wider and wider. And when you did it the other way, see!—the sinking jaws close, the upside-down mouse rises through the air and lands on his feet on the high board. My father was never wrong, but I felt he was trying to shield me from darker knowledge. The beings

behind the curtain had nothing to do with childish flip-books or
the long strips of gray negatives hanging in the kitchen from
silver clips. They led their exalted lives beyond mine, in some
other realm entirely, shining, desirable, impenetrable.

One Saturday afternoon when my father had to drive to the
university on business, and my mother lay on two pillows in
her darkened room, rasping with asthma, and my best friend
was spending the day at his cousin Valerie's, it was decided that
I could go to the movies alone. I knew that something forbidden was happening, but I greeted it with outward calm. After
the second feature I was to go directly to the front of the theater
and stand outside under the marquee, where my father would
be waiting. I felt that the decision had been arrived at too hastily, that the careful, repeated instructions only revealed the dan-
ger in this sudden violation of the usual. I wondered whether I
should warn my parents, but I remained silent and watchful.
My father dropped me off at the ticket booth, where a short line
had formed, and as I watched him drive away I felt an anxious
exhilaration, as if in the pride of his knowledge he had failed to
reckon with the powers of the dark.

Past the blue velvet rope on its silver post I stepped into the
well-lit lobby with its red rug and glass-covered candy counter.
The glossy wrappers brilliant under the counter lights, the high
popcorn machine with its yellow glass that turned the popcorn
butter-yellow, the crimson glow of a nearby exit sign, all these
expressed the secret presence of the dark, which here made itself
felt by the intensity of the effort to banish it. Behind me,
through the open door leading back to the entranceway, I could
see sunlight flashing on the glass of a Coming Attraction: in a
green-black jungle a man in a pith helmet was taking aim with
a rifle at something invisible in the blaze of obscuring light. I
turned to the darkening corridor leading away from the candy
counter. There the lights grew dim, as if they were candle-
flames bending in the wind of the gathering dark, there the
world was bathed in a reddish glow. I bought a box of popcorn

and made my way along the glowing night of the corridor. The aisle surprised me: it sloped down more sharply than I had remembered. As I passed the arms of seats I felt a slight tugging at my calves, as if I were being pulled forward against my will. Impulsively I chose a row. I slipped past four chair-arms and pulled down a red, sagging seat. I leaned back eagerly, waiting for artificial night to fall, whispers of ushers, the cone of a flashlight beam in the darkened aisle.

Soon the lights went out, on the luminous curtain bright letters danced, the blue folds began to part; and sliding down, far down, I rested my popcorn on my stomach and pressed the back of my head against the fuzzy seat.

And suddenly it was over, the lights came on, people rose to go. Legs pushed past my knees, a coin clinked and someone bent over sharply, slapping at the floor. A foot kicked a popcorn box, a seat came up with a bang. Was it really over? The rolling coin struck something and stopped. A heaviness came over me —I could scarcely drag myself to my feet. Outside my father would be waiting under the marquee: one arm across his stomach, the elbow of the other arm in the palm of the first, the bowl of his pipe supported with thick fingers. I felt that I had let something slip away from me, that I had failed in some way, but my thoughts were sluggish and kept sinking out of sight.

At the top of the aisle I hesitated, looking with disappointment toward the band of sun streaming in through the open door. I went over to the drinking fountain and took a long swallow. At the darkening end of the corridor I noticed a sign that said REST ROOMS, with a red arrow pointing down. Perhaps my father had not arrived yet; the out-streaming crowd was dense, oppressive; I would only be two seconds. Slowly I descended the speckled stone steps, sliding my hand along the dark brass rail. In the men's room a teenager with slicked-back yellow hair and a black leather jacket stood wiping his hands on a soiled roller-towel. I slipped into a stall and listened with relief to the departing footsteps, the banging door. Two people entered without speaking and left one after the other. I felt weary and restless. I didn't know what I wanted. I did not move.

I must have fallen into a stupor or reverie, for I was startled by a clanking sound. I opened the door of the stall and saw an old man in droopy pants standing with his back to me beside a bucket of soapy water. He was slowly pushing a mop whose long gray strings moved first one way, then the other. The mop left glistening patches on the white-and-black tiles. I tiptoed out of the bathroom as if I had been guilty of something and began climbing the stairway, which seemed darker than before. It was very quiet. At the top of the stairs I came to the corridor, now empty and still. At the other end the darkened candy counter was lit by a single bulb. The theater appeared to be deserted. I was nervous and calm, nervous and calm. Nearby I saw the row of closed doors leading to the entranceway; under the doors I could see a disturbing line of sunlight. And clattering around a turn in the spookhouse, suddenly you see a sliver of light at the bottom of the black walls. My father would be striding up and down, up and down, looking at his sunny watch. He would talk to the girl in the ticket booth. All at once a desire erupted in me with such force that I felt as if I had been struck in both temples.

I stepped onto a downward-sloping aisle and plunged into the soothing half-dark, penetrated by the odor of old dark red seat cushions, butter-stained cardboard popcorn boxes, the sticky sweetness of spilled soda. On one seat I saw a fat rubber nose with a broken elastic string. At the end of the aisle I stepped over to the wall and reached up my hand, but the bottom of the great curtain was high above my straining fingers. It was set back, leaving a ledge. The thick dark folds looked heavy as marble. It seemed to me that if only I could touch that curtain, if only I could push it aside and stare for one second at the fearful blankness of the screen, and perhaps graze the magic whiteness with my fingers, then my deep restlessness would be stilled, my heart would grow calm, I could turn away from the theater and hurry back, quickly quickly, to my waiting father, who at any moment was going to burst through the doors or drive away forever. I walked along the wall, desperately searching for something to stand on, say a popcorn box or one of those tall ashtrays with white sand that I had seen near the blue velvet rope. I saw nothing but an empty, carefully folded silver gum-wrapper with its phantom stick of gum. High overhead the curtain stretched away. As I approached the end of the curtain the lower wall curved slightly and I saw a narrow flight of six steps going up. The stairs were cut into the wall. The top stair was half concealed by the final fold of the curtain.

With a glance over my shoulder I climbed swiftly and began to push at the velvety thick folds, which enveloped my arm and barely moved. I had the sense that the curtain was slowly waking, like some great, disturbed animal. Somehow I pushed the final, sluggish fold aside and found myself before a flaking wooden door with a dented metal knob. The door opened easily. I stepped into a small room, scarcely larger than a closet. I saw dark brooms, mops in buckets, dustpans, a bulging burlap sack in one corner, an usher's jacket hanging from a nail; in the back wall I made out part of a second door.

Stepping carefully over buckets, cans, and bottles I felt for the knob. The door opened onto a narrow corridor carpeted in red. Glass candle-flames glowed in brass sconces high on the walls. There were no doors. At the end of the passage I came to a flight of red-carpeted stairs going down. I descended to a landing; over the polished wooden rail I saw landings within landings, dropping away. At the bottom of the seventh landing I found myself in another corridor. Through high, open doorways I caught glimpses of festive rooms. I heard footsteps along the corridor and stepped through one of the tall doors.

In the uncanny light of reddish gas lamps, many-branched candelabra, and chandeliers with flaming candles, I saw them taking their ease. They were splendidly costumed, radiantly themselves, expressing their natures through grand and flawless gestures. They lolled against walls, strolled idly about, displayed themselves on great armchairs and couches. I wasn't surprised by their massiveness, which suited their extravagant natures, and I looked up at them as if gazing up at the screen from the second row. Even the furniture loomed; my head barely came over the cushions of armchairs.

They seemed to pay no attention to me as I made my way among the great chairs and couches and came to an open place with a high table. Beside it strode a figure with flowing black hair, a great crimson cape, and a glittering sword. He seized a gold goblet and took an immense swallow, while beside him a bearded figure with a leather helmet bearing two sharp silver horns burst into rich laughter, and a lady with high-piled hair and a hoop dress covered with ruffles turned to look over her rapidly fluttering fan. Passing under the table I came to a great couch where a queen with ink-black hair and blue eyelids lay on her side looking coldly before her as she stroked a white cat. Beside her stood a grim figure with a skull and crossbones on his three-cornered hat, a red scarf at his throat, a long-barreled pistol thrust through his belt, and loose pants plunging into thick, cracked boots. I passed the couch and saw on the other side a jungle girl dressed in a leopardskin loincloth and a vineleaf halter, standing with her hands on her hips and her head flung back haughtily as two gray-haired gentlemen in white dinner jackets bent forward to peer through monocles at a jewel in her navel. Farther away I saw a figure in green with a quiver of cloth yard arrows on his back and a stout quarterstaff in one hand, standing beside a tall, mournful ballerina whose shiny dark hair was pulled so tightly back that it looked like painted wood; and far across the room, through high, open doorways, I saw other rooms and other figures, stretching back and back.

Though shy of their glances, I soon realized I had nothing to fear from them. At first I thought they failed to notice me, or, noticing me, shrugged their shoulders and returned to their superior lives. But gradually I recognized that my presence, far

from being ignored, inspired them to be more grandly themselves. For weren't they secretly in need of being watched, these
lofty creatures, did they not become themselves through the act
of being witnessed?

Through a wide doorway I wandered into another room, and
then into a third—and always through open doorways I saw
other figures, other rooms. The very abundance that drew me
proved quickly tiring, and I looked for a quiet place to sit before
returning to my father, who perhaps at this very moment was
pushing open the glass doors and striding toward the blue velvet rope. He would step into the empty theater and stare at the
dark seats, the closed curtain, the red-glowing exit signs.
Downstairs in the rest room he would find an old man in
droopy pants who would look up with red-rimmed eyes and
shake his head slowly: no, no. On the rung of a tall wooden
chair I sat down, hooking one arm around the thick leg. Almost
at once I became aware of someone pacing up and down before
me. She walked close to my chair in a great swirl of petticoats,
her ruffled skirts shaking as she walked. She sighed deeply and
petulantly, over and over again, and from time to time I caught
snatches of muttered monologue: ". . . have to do something
. . . impossible . . . unbearable . . ." Suddenly she sat down
on a chair opposite; I saw a flowery burst of petticoats settling
against white stockings; but she sprang up and continued her
odd pantomime, gradually moving away so that I was able to
catch a glimpse of her: a tumult of bouncing blond curls shaped
like small tubes, a pouting red mouth and round blue eyes, a
neckline that exposed the top third of high, very white breasts,
which appeared to be pressed tightly upward. When she
walked, all her curls shook like bells, the tops of her breasts
shook, her skirts bounced up and down, her eyelids fluttered,
her plump cheeks trembled; only her little nose was still. Sometimes she glanced in my direction, but not at me. All at once
she stamped her foot, pushed out her bottom lip, and swished
away, glancing for a moment over her shoulder. It was clear

that she expected to be followed, that she always expected to be
followed, and without hesitation I slipped from my rung.

　She pushed open a door and I followed her into a red room
brilliant with mirrors and the flames of many candles. I saw a
high white armchair, a great dressing table with a soaring mirror. Smaller mirrors hung on each wall; the dark red wallpaper
was patterned with little pale princesses leaning out of silver
towers with their long flaxen hair. She stepped onto a stool
before a swivel mirror and clapped her hands sharply twice. An
elderly woman in a black dress appeared and began removing
her ball gown with its flounced skirts and blue bows. Then she
removed another skirt under that, and several petticoats, leaving
a billowy, frilled petticoat and a satiny white corset with criss-
cross laces in back. "Thank you, Maria, now go away, go
away, go away now . . ." For a while she stared at herself in
the tall mirror, then hopped from the stool and began pacing
about, glancing at herself in the swivel mirror, in the mirror
over the dressing table, in the mirrors on the walls, in a silver
bowl. The room filled with images of her, turning this way and
that. As she paced and turned she heaved great sighs, and
pushed out her bottom lip, and tossed her curls, and muttered
to herself: "get away with . . . just who does he . . . can't
breathe in here . . ." Though she paid not the slightest attention
to me, I felt that my presence permitted her to display her
petulance with the richness she required; and as she pranced and
pouted she tugged at a fastening at the front of her corset, she
kicked off her shoes, she unbound her high-piled hair, which
spilled down her flame-lit shoulders and shook as she moved.
And as she flickered and shook before me I felt a vague excitement, my skin began to tingle, as if she were brushing against
me with her thick, shaking curls, her trembling skin, her white
silk stockings. All at once the shaking stopped and I saw her
raise the back of a hand to her forehead. Slowly, like a falling
leaf, she swooned onto the dark red rug.

　I had no thought of calling for help, for the swoon had been

executed with such elegance that I felt certain she had intended
it to be admired. She lay on the floor between the lion-paw legs
of the chair and the red wallpaper. Her heavy yellow ringlets
were strewn about her face and shoulders, her lips were partly
open, her stomach moved gently up and down, the lines and
bands of her corset went in and out, in and out. I stepped over
to her and looked down. An unaccountable desire seized me: I
wanted to feel the satiny material of her corset, I wanted to
place my hand against the fire-lit white breathing cloth. In her
white slip my mother had sat at the edge of the bed, drawing
on a stocking. Slowly the corset bands went in and out. I bent
over, careful not to touch the breathing form in any way; the
skin of my palm prickled; I felt tense and anxious, as if I were
about to transgress a law. And as I lowered my palm against the
forbidden white cloth with its stretching and contracting bands
I felt my hand sinking through melting barriers, as when, on a
trip to New Hampshire with my parents, one morning I had
walked through thick white cottony mist that lay heavy on the
grass and parted like air as I passed. So my hand fell through
the whiteness of that cloth. My sinking hand struck the velvety
hard rug—I felt myself losing my balance—suddenly I was falling through her, plunging through her corset, her breasts, her
bones, her blood. For a fearful instant I was inside her. I had a
sensation of whiteness or darkness, a white darkness. On the
sudden rug I rolled wildly through her, wildly out of her, and
sprang up. Blood beat in my temples. She lay there drowsily.
My whole body tingled, as if I had dried myself roughly with a
towel.

I stared at my hands and shirt and pants as if fearing to see
little pieces of cloth and flesh stuck to them, but I saw only
myself.

A moment later she sat up, shook her headful of thick,
springy curls, and pulled herself lightly to her feet. "Why, I
must have . . . fainted or . . . Maria! Oh, where is that
woman?" She began pacing up and down, sighing, pouting,

flinging back her hair; a corner of her flying petticoat rippled through my hand, which I snatched away; and in the many mirrors her many images appeared and reappeared, thrusting out their bottom lips, darting glances, fluttering their many eyelids.

I didn't know whether I was relieved or bitterly unhappy. Would I have guessed her secret? I knew only that I wanted to go.

In the doorway I stopped and half turned to look at her. Fiercely she paced, exuberantly she sulked, in the full radiance of her being. I was tempted to say something, to shout, to draw attention to myself in some way, but the desire drained swiftly out of me. A shout, a scream, a knife in the throat, a plunge to the death, all were quite useless here.

I stepped through the door and looked for the room I had come from, but found myself in an alien room filled with harsh laughter. I was careful not to touch any of them as I passed. Through a nearby doorway I emerged in a corridor that led to another room, another doorway, another room. I came to an upward-sloping corridor lined with shimmering mirrors; the sudden repetition of my anxious face gave me the sensation that my anxiety had increased in a burst. At the end of the corridor I climbed three steps to a closed door. I opened it and found myself in a dusky room I had never seen before, with many seats and a dark wall-hanging that resembled a curtain; gradually I recognized the theater.

I had entered by another door, beside one of the red-glowing exit signs. I hurried up the sloping aisle, stopped for a moment in the lobby to glance toward the sign that said REST ROOMS, then pushed open one of the metal doors and stepped into the sun-flooded entranceway.

A kneeling usher was sweeping a pile of candy wrappers and cigarette butts into a dustpan. In the white sand of a standing ashtray a slanting white straw cast a rippling shadow across a piece of bright yellow cellophane. The man in the pith helmet was taking aim at a tree concealing an orange tiger upon whose back sat a woman in a black fur loincloth. Through the brilliant glass doors I saw my father frowning at his watch. His look of stern surprise, when he saw me burst through the door into the late-afternoon sun, struck me as wildly funny, and I forgot to chasten my features into repentance as I seized his warm hand.

The Barnum Museum

1

The Barnum Museum is located in the heart of our city, two blocks north of the financial district. The Romanesque and Gothic entranceways, the paired sphinxes and griffins, the gilded onion domes, the corbeled turrets and mansarded towers, the octagonal cupolas, the crestings and crenellations, all these compose an elusive design that seems calculated to lead the eye restlessly from point to point without permitting it to take in the whole. In fact the structure is so difficult to grasp that we cannot tell whether the Barnum Museum is a single complex building with numerous wings, annexes, additions, and extensions, or whether it is many buildings artfully connected by roofed walkways, stone bridges, flowering arbors, booth-lined arcades, colonnaded passageways.

2

The Barnum Museum contains a bewildering and incalculable number of rooms, each with at least two and often twelve or even fourteen doorways. Through every doorway can be seen further rooms and doorways. The rooms are of all sizes, from the small chambers housing single exhibits to the immense halls rising to the height of five floors. The rooms are never simple, but contain alcoves, niches, roped-off divisions, and screened corners; many of the larger halls hold colorful tents and pavilions. Even if, theoretically, we could walk through all the rooms of the Barnum Museum in a single day, from the pyramidal roof of the highest tower to the darkest cave of the third subterranean level, in practice it is impossible, for we inevitably come to a closed door, or a blue velvet rope stretching across a stairway, or a sawhorse in an open doorway before which sits a guard in a dark green uniform. This repeated experience of refused admittance, within the generally open expanses of the museum, only increases our sense of unexplored regions. Can it be a deliberately calculated effect on the part of the museum directors? It remains true that new rooms are continually being added, old ones relentlessly eliminated or rebuilt. Sometimes the walls between old rooms are knocked down, sometimes large halls are divided into smaller chambers, sometimes a new extension is built into one of the gardens or courtyards; and so constant is the work of renovation and rearrangement that we perpetually hear, beneath the hum of voices, the shouts of children, the shuffle of footsteps, and the cries of the peanut vendors, the faint undersound of hammers, pickaxes, and crumbling plaster. It is said that if you enter the Barnum Museum by a particular doorway at noon and manage to find your way back by three, the doorway through which you entered will no longer lead to the street, but to a new room, whose doors give glimpses of further rooms and doorways.

3

The Hall of Mermaids is nearly dark, lit only by lanterns at the tops of posts. Most of the hall is taken up by an irregular black lake or pool, which measures some hundred yards across at its widest point and is entirely surrounded by boulders that rise from the water. In the center of the pool stands a shadowy rock-island with many peaks and hollows. The water and its surrounding boulders are themselves surrounded by a low wooden platform to which we ascend by three steps. Along the inner rim of the platform stand many iron posts about six feet apart, joined by velvet ropes; at the top of every third post glows a red or yellow lantern. Standing on the platform, we can see over the lower boulders into the black water with its red and yellow reflections. From time to time we hear a light splash and, if we are lucky, catch a sudden glimpse of glimmering dark fishscales or yellow hair. Between the velvet ropes and the boulders lies a narrow strip of platform where two guards ceaselessly patrol; despite their vigilance, now and then a hand, glowing red in the lantern-light, extends across the ropes and throws into the water a peanut, a piece of popcorn, a dime. There are said to be three mermaids in the pool. In the dark hall, in the uncertain light, you can see the faces at the ropes, peering down intently.

4

The enemies of the Barnum Museum say that its exhibits are fraudulent; that its deceptions harm our children, who are turned away from the realm of the natural to a false realm of the monstrous and fantastic; that certain displays are provocative, erotic, and immoral; that this temple of so-called wonders draws us out of the sun, tempts us away from healthy pursuits, and renders us dissatisfied with our daily lives; that the presence of the musuem in our city encourages those elements which, like confidence men, sharpers, palmists, and astrologers, prey on the gullible; that the very existence of this grotesque eyesore and its repellent collection of monstrosities disturbs our tranquility, undermines our strength, and reveals our secret weakness and confusion. Some say that these arguments are supported and indeed invented by the directors of the museum, who understand that controversy increases attendance.

5

In one hall there is a marble platform surrounded by red velvet ropes. In the center of the platform a brown man sits cross-legged. He has glossy black eyebrows and wears a brilliant white turban. Before him lies a rolled-up carpet. Bending forward from the waist, he unrolls the carpet with delicate long fingers. It is about four feet by six feet, dark blue, with an intricate design of arabesques in crimson and green. Each of the two ends bears a short white fringe. The turbaned man stands up, steps to the center of the carpet, turns to face one of the fringed ends, and sits down with his legs crossed. His long brown hands rest on his lap. He utters two syllables, which sound like "ah-lek" or "ahg-leh," and as we watch, the carpet rises and begins to fly slowly about the upper reaches of the hall. Unlike the Hall of Mermaids, this hall is brightly lit, as if to encourage our detailed observation. He flies back and forth some thirty feet above our heads, moving in and out among the great chandeliers, sometimes swooping down to skim the crowd, sometimes rising to the wide ledge of a high window, where he lands for a moment before continuing his flight. The carpet does not lie stiffly beneath him, but appears to have a slight undulation; the weight of his seated body shows as a faint depression in the carpet's underside. Sometimes he remains aloft for an entire afternoon, pausing only on the shadowy ledges of the upper windows, and because it is difficult to strain the neck in a continual act of attention, it is easy to lose sight of him there, high up in the great spaces of the hall.

6

In the rooms and halls of the Barnum Museum there is often an atmosphere of carnival, of adventure. Wandering jugglers toss their brightly colored balls in the air, clowns jump and tumble, the peanut vendors in their red-white-and-blue caps shout for attention; here and there, in roped-off corners, an artist standing at an easel paints a picture of a bird that suddenly flies from the painting and perches on a window ledge, a magician shakes from his long black hat a plot of grass, an oak tree hung with colored lanterns, and white chairs and tables disposed beneath the branches. In such a hall it is difficult to know where to turn our eyes, and it is entirely possible that we will give only a casual glance to the blue-and-yellow circus cage in the corner where, tired of trailing his great wings in the straw, the griffin bows his weary head.

7

One school of thought maintains that the wonders of the Barnum Museum deliberately invite mechanical explanations that appear satisfactory without quite satisfying, thereby increasing our curiosity and wonder. Thus some claim that the flying carpet is guided by invisible wires, others argue that it must conceal a small motor, still others insist that it is controlled electronically from within the marble platform. One branch of this school asserts that if in fact the explanation is mechanical, then the mechanism is more marvelous than magic itself. The mermaids are readily explained as real women with false fish-tails covering their bottom halves, but it must be reported that no one has ever been able to expose the imposture, even though photographs are permitted on Sundays from three o'clock to five. The lower halves, which all of us have seen, give every appearance of thickness and substance, and behave in every way like fish bodies; no trace of concealed legs is visible; the photographs reveal a flawless jointure of flesh and scale. Many of us who visit the Hall of Mermaids with a desire to glimpse naked breasts soon find our attention straying to the lower halves, gleaming mysteriously for a moment before vanishing into the black pool.

8

There are three subterranean levels of the Barnum Museum. The first resembles any of the upper levels, with the exception that there are no windows and that no sunlight dilutes the glow of the fluorescent ceiling lights. The second level is darker and rougher; old-fashioned gas lamps hiss in the air, and winding corridors lead in and out of a maze of chambers. Crumbling stone stairways lead down to the third level. Here the earthen paths are littered with stones, torches crackle on the damp stone walls, bands of swarthy dwarfs appear suddenly and scamper into the dark. Moldering signs, of which only a few letters are legible, stand before the dark caves. Few venture more than a step or two into the black openings, which are said to contain disturbing creatures dangerous to behold. Some believe that the passageways of the third level extend beyond the bounds of the upper museum, burrowing their way to the very edges of the city. Now and then along the dark paths an opening appears, with black stairs going down. Some say the stairways of the third level lead to a fourth level, which is pitch black and perilous; to descend is to go mad. Others say that the stairways lead nowhere, continuing down and dizzyingly down, beyond the endurance of the boldest venturer, beyond the bounds of imagination itself.

9

It may be thought that the Barnum Museum is a children's museum, and it is certainly true that our children enjoy the flying carpet, the griffin in his cage, the winged horse, the homunculus in his jar, the grelling, the lorax, the giant in his tower, the leprechauns, the Invisibles, the great birds with the faces and breasts of women, the transparent man, the city in the lake, the woman of brass. But quite apart from the fact that adults also enjoy these exhibits, I would argue that the Barnum Museum is not intended solely or even primarily for children.

For although there are always children in the halls, there are also elderly couples, teenagers, men in business suits, slim women in blue jeans and sandals, lovers holding hands; in short, adults of all kinds, who return again and again. Even if one argues that certain exhibits appeal most directly to children, it may be argued that other exhibits puzzle or bewilder them; and children are expressly forbidden to descend to the third subterranean level and to enter certain tents and pavilions. But the real flaw in the suggestion that the Barnum Museum is a children's museum lies in the assumption that children are an utterly identical tribe consisting of simple creatures composed of two or three abstract traits, such as innocence and wonder. In fact our children are for the most part shrewd and skeptical, astonished in spite of themselves, suspicious, easily bored, impatient for mechanical explanations. It is not always pleasing to take a child to the Barnum Museum, and many parents prefer to wander the seductive halls alone, in the full freedom of adult yearning, monotony, and bliss.

10

Passing through a doorway, we step into a thick forest and make our way along dark winding paths bordered by velvet ropes. Owls hoot in the nearby branches. The ceiling is painted to resemble a night sky and the forest is illuminated by the light of an artificial moon. We come out onto a moonlit grassy glade. The surrounding wood is encircled by posts joined by velvet ropes; here and there an opening between posts indicates a dark path winding into the trees. It is in the glade that the Invisibles make themselves known. They brush lightly against our arms, bend down the grass blades as they pass, breathe against our cheeks and eyelids, step lightly on our feet. The children shriek in joyful fear, wives cling to their husbands' arms, fathers look about with uncertain smiles. Now and then it happens that a visitor bursts into sobs and is led quickly away by a mu-

seum guard. Sometimes the Invisibles do not manifest themselves, and it is only when the visitor, glancing irritably at
his watch, begins to make his way toward one of the roped
paths, that he may feel, suddenly against his hair, a touch like
a caress.

11

It is probable that at some moment between birth and death,
every inhabitant of our city will enter the Barnum Museum. It
is less probable, but not impossible, that at some moment in the
history of the museum our entire citizenry, by a series of over-
lapping impulses, will find themselves within these halls: moth-
ers pushing their baby carriages, old men bent over canes, *au
pair* girls, policemen, fast-food cooks, Little League captains.
For a moment the city will be deserted. Our collective attention,
directed at the displays of the Barnum Museum, will cause the
halls to swell with increased detail. Outside, the streets and
buildings will grow vague; street corners will begin to dissolve;
unobserved, a garbage-can cover, blown by the wind, will roll
silently toward the edge of the world.

12

The Chamber of False Things contains museum guards made
of wax, trompe l'oeil doorways, displays of false mustaches and
false beards, false-bottomed trunks, artificial roses, forged
paintings, spurious texts, quack medicines, faked fossils, cinema
snow, joke-shop ink spills, spirit messages, Martian super-bees,
ectoplasmic projections, the footprints of extraterrestrials, Professor Ricardo and Bobo the Talking Horse, false noses, glass
eyes, wax grapes, pubic wigs, hollow novels containing flasks
of whiskey, and, in one corner, objects from false places: por-
phyry figurines from Atlantis, golden cups from El Dorado, a
crystalline vial of water from the Fountain of Youth. The mean-

ing of the exhibit is obscure. Is it possible that the directors of the museum wish to enhance the reality of the other displays by distinguishing them from this one? Or is it rather that the directors here wittily or brazenly allude to the nature of the entire museum? Another interpretation presents itself: that the directors intend no meaning, but merely wish to pique our interest, to stimulate our curiosity, to lure us by whatever means deeper and deeper into the museum.

13

As we wander the halls of the Barnum Museum, our attention is struck by all those who cannot, as we can, leave the museum whenever they like. These are the museum workers, of whom the most striking are the guards in their dark green uniforms and polished black shoes. The museum is known to be strict in its hiring practices and to demand of all workers long hours, exemplary performance, and unremitting devotion. Thus the guards are expected to be attentive to the questions of visitors, as well as unfailingly courteous, alert, and cheerful. The guards are offered inexpensive lodgings for themselves and their families on the top floor of one wing; few are wealthy enough to resist such enticements, and so it comes about that the guards spend their lives within the walls of the museum. In addition to the guards, whom we see in every room, there are the janitors in their loose gray uniforms, the peanut vendors, the gift-shop salesgirls, the ticket sellers, the coat-check women, the guides in their maroon uniforms, the keepers of the caged griffin, of the unicorn in the wooded hill, of the grelling in his lair, the wandering clowns and jugglers, the balloon men, the lamplighters and torchlighters of the second and third subterranean levels, as well as the carpenters, plasterers, and electricians, who appear to work throughout the museum's long day, from nine to nine. These are the workers we see, but there are others we have heard about: the administrators in small rooms in remote corridors on the upper floors, the researchers and historians, the archivists, the typists, the messengers, the accountants and legal advisers. What is striking is not that there are so many workers, but that they spend so much of their lives inside the museum—as if, absorbed by this realm of enchantments, they are gradually becoming a different race, who enter our world uneasily, in the manner of revenants or elves.

14

Hannah Goodwin was in her junior year of high school. She was a plain, quiet girl with lank pale-brown hair parted in the middle and a pale complexion marred by always erupting whiteheads that she covered with a flesh-colored ointment. She wore plain, neat shirts and drab corduroys. She walked the halls alone, with lowered eyes; she never initiated a conversation, and if asked a question would raise her startled eyes and answer quickly, shifting her gaze to one side. She worked hard, never went out with boys, and had one girlfriend, who moved away in the middle of the year. Hannah seemed somewhat depressed at the loss of her friend, and for several weeks was more reserved than usual. It was about this time that she began to visit the Barnum Museum every day after school. Her visits grew longer, and she soon began returning at night. And a change came over her: although she continued to walk the halls alone, and to say nothing in class, there was about her an inner animation, an intensity, that expressed itself in her gray eyes, in her partly open lips, in the very fall of her hair on her shoulders. Even her walk was subtly altered, as if some stiffness or constraint had left her. One afternoon at the lockers a boy asked her to go to the movies; she refused with a look of surprised irritation, as if he were interrupting a conversation. Although her schoolwork did not suffer, for discipline was an old habit, she was visibly impatient with the dull routines of the day; and as her step grew firmer and her gaze surer, and her bright gray eyes, burning with anticipation, swept up to the big round clock above the green blackboard, it was clear that she had been released from some inner impediment, and like a woman in love had abandoned herself utterly to the beckoning halls, the high towers and winding tunnels, the always alluring doorways of the Barnum Museum.

15

The bridges of the Barnum Museum are external and internal. The external bridges span the courtyards, the statued gardens, the outdoor cafés with their striped umbrellas, so that visitors on the upper floors of one wing can pass directly across the sky to a nearby wing simply by stepping through a window; while down below, the balloon man walks with his red and green balloons shaped like griffins and unicorns, the hurdy gurdy man turns his crank, a boy in brown shorts looks up from his lemon ice and shades his eyes, a young woman with long yellow hair sits down in the grass in a laughing statue's shade. The internal bridges span the upper reaches of the larger halls. At any moment, on an upper floor, we may step through an arched doorway and find ourselves not on the floor of an adjacent room, but on a bridge high above a hall that plunges down through five stories. Some of these bridges are plain wooden arches with sturdy rails, permitting us to see not only the floor below but pieces of rooms through open doorways with iron-work balconies. Other bridges are broad stone spans lined on both sides with toss-penny booths, puppet theaters, and shops selling jack-in-the-boxes, chocolate circus animals, and transparent glass marbles containing miniature mermaids, winged horses, and moonlit forests; between the low roofs, between the narrow alleys separating the shops, we catch glimpses of the tops of juggled balls, the pointed top of a tent, the arched doorway of a distant room.

16

There are times when we do not enjoy the Barnum Museum. The exhibits cease to enchant us; the many doorways, leading to further halls, fill us with a sense of boredom and nausea; beneath the griffin's delicate eyelids we see the dreary, stupefied eyes. In hatred we rage through the gaudy halls, longing for the entire museum to burst into flame. It is best, at such moments, not to turn away, but to abandon oneself to desolation. Gaze in despair at the dubious halls, the shabby illusions, the fatuous faces; drink down disillusion; for the museum, in its patience, will survive our heresies, which only bind us to it in yet another way.

17

Among the festive rooms and halls of the Barnum Museum, with their flying carpets, their magic lamps, their mermaids and grellings, we come now and then to a different kind of room. In it we may find old paint cans and oilcans, a green-stained gardening glove in a battered pail, a rusty bicycle against one wall; or perhaps old games of Monopoly, Sorry, and Risk, stacks of dusty 78 records with a dog and Victrola pictured on the center labels, a thick oak table-base dividing into four claw feet. These rooms appear to be errors or oversights, perhaps proper rooms awaiting renovation and slowly filling with the discarded possessions of museum personnel, but in time we come to see in them a deeper meaning. The Barnum Museum is a realm of wonders, but do we not need a rest from wonder? The plain rooms scattered through the museum release us from the oppression of astonishment. Such is the common explanation of these rooms, but it is possible to find in them a deeper meaning still. These everyday images, when we come upon them suddenly among the marvels of the Barnum Museum, startle us with their strangeness before settling to rest. In this sense the plain rooms do not interrupt the halls of wonder; they themselves are those halls.

18

It must be admitted that among the many qualities of the Barnum Museum there is a certain coarseness, which expresses itself in the stridency of its architecture, the sensual appeal of certain displays, and the brash abundance of its halls, as well as in smaller matters that attract attention from time to time. Among the latter are the numerous air ducts concealed in the floors of many halls and passageways. Erratically throughout the day, jets of air are released upward, lifting occasional skirts and dresses. This crude echo of the fun house has been criticized sharply by enemies of the museum, and it is certainly no defense to point out that the ducts were installed in an earlier era, when women of all ages wore elaborate dresses to the Barnum Museum—a fact advertised by framed photographs that show well-dressed women in broad-brimmed hats attempting to hold down their skirts and petticoats, which blow up above the knees as gallants in straw hats look on in amusement. For despite the apparent absurdity of air ducts in a world of pants, it remains true that we continue to see a fair number of checked gingham dresses, pleated white skirts, trim charcoal suits, belted poplin shirtwaists, jungle-print shifts, flowery wraparounds, polka dot dirndls, ruffled jumpers, all of which are continually blowing up in the air to reveal sudden glimpses of green or pink panty hose, lace-trimmed white slips, gartered nylon stockings, and striped bikini underpants amidst laughter and shrill whistles. Our women can of course defeat the ducts by refusing to wear anything but pants· to the Barnum Museum, but in fact the ducts appear to have encouraged certain women, in a spirit either of rebellion or capitulation, to dress up in long skirts and decorative underwear, a fad especially popular among girls in junior high school. These girls of twelve and thirteen, who often visit the museum in small bands, make themselves up in bright red or bright green lipstick and false eyelashes, carry shiny leather pocketbooks, and wear flowing ankle-length skirts over glossy plastic boots. The skirts rise easily in the jets of air and reveal a rich array of gaudy underwear: preposterous bloomers with pink bows, candy-colored underpants with rosettes and streamers, black net stockings attached to black lacy garter belts over red lace underwear, old-fashioned white girdles with grotesque pictures of winking eyes and stuck-out tongues printed on the back. Whatever we may think of such displays, the presence of fun-house air ducts in the Barnum Museum is impossible to ignore. To defend them is not to assert their irrelevance; rather, it is to insist that they lend to the museum an air of the frivolous, the childish, the provocative, the irresponsible. For is it not this irresponsibility, this freedom from solemnity, that permits the museum to elude the mundane, and to achieve the beauty and exaltation of its most daring displays?

19

The museum researchers work behind closed doors in small rooms in remote sections of the uppermost floors. The general public is not admitted to the rooms, but some visitors, wandering among the upper exhibits, have claimed to catch glimpses of narrow corridors and perhaps a suddenly opened door. The rooms are said to be filled with piles of dusty books, reaching from floor to ceiling. Although the existence of the researchers is uncertain, we do not doubt its likelihood; although the nature of their task is unknown, we do not doubt its necessity. It is in these remote rooms that the museum becomes conscious of itself, reflects upon itself, and speaks about itself in words that no one reads. The results of research are said to be published rarely, in heavy volumes that are part of immense multivolume collections stored in upper rooms of the museum and consulted only by other researchers. Sometimes, in a narrow corridor on an upper floor, a door opens and a chalk-pale man appears. The figure vanishes so swiftly behind the door that we can never be certain whether we have actually seen one of the legendary researchers, elusive as elves, or whether, unable to endure the stillness, the empty corridors, and the closed doors, we have summoned him into existence through minuscule tremors of our eye muscles, photochemical reactions in our rods and cones, the firing of cells in the visual cortex.

20

In the gift shops of the Barnum Museum we may buy old sepia postcards of mermaids and sea dragons, little flip-books that show flying carpets rising into the air, peep-show pens with miniature colored scenes from the halls of the Barnum Museum, mysterious rubber balls from Arabia that bounce once and remain suspended in the air, jars of dark blue liquid from which you can blow bubbles shaped like tigers, elephants, lions, polar bears, and giraffes, Chinese kaleidoscopes showing ceaselessly changing forms of dragons, enchanting pleniscopes and phantatropes, boxes of animate paint for drawing pictures that move, lacquered wooden balls from the Black Forest that, once set rolling, never come to a stop, bottles of colorless jellylike stuff that will assume the shape and color of any object it is set before, shiny red boxes that vanish in direct sunlight, Japanese paper airplanes that glide through houses and over gardens and rooftops, storybooks from Finland with tissue-paper-covered illustrations that change each time the paper is lifted, tin sets of specially treated watercolors for painting pictures on air. The toys and trinkets of the Barnum Museum amuse us and delight our children, but in our apartments and hallways, in air thick with the smells of boiling potatoes and furniture polish, the gifts quickly lose their charm, and soon lie neglected in dark corners of closets beside the eyeless Raggedy Ann doll and the dusty

Cherokee headdress. Those who disapprove of the Barnum Museum do not spare the gift shops, which they say are dangerous. For they say it is here that the museum, which by its nature is contemptuous of our world, connects to that world by the act of buying and selling, and indeed insinuates itself into our lives by means of apparently innocent knickknacks carried off in the pockets of children.

21

The museum eremites must be carefully distinguished from the drifters and beggars who occasionally attempt to take up residence in the museum, lurking in dark alcoves, disturbing visitors, and sleeping in the lower passageways. The guards are continually on the lookout for such intruders, whom they usher out firmly but discreetly. The eremites, in contrast, are a small and rigorously disciplined sect who are permitted to dwell permanently in the museum. Their hair is short, their dark robes simple and neat, their vows of silence inviolable. They drink water, eat leftover rolls from the outdoor cafés, and sleep on bare floors in roped-off corners of certain halls. They are said to believe that the world outside the museum is a delusion and that only within its walls is a true life possible. These beliefs are attributed to them without their assent or dissent; they themselves remain silent. The eremites tend to be young men and women in their twenties or early thirties; they are not a foreign sect, but were born in our city and its suburbs; they are our children. They sit cross-legged with their backs straight against the wall and their hands resting lightly on their knees; they stare before them without appearing to take notice of anything. We are of two minds about the eremites. Although on the one hand we admire their dedication to the museum, and acknowledge that there is something praiseworthy in their extreme way of life, on the other hand we reproach them for abandoning the world outside the museum, and feel a certain contempt for the exaggeration and distortion we sense in their lives. In general they make us uneasy, perhaps because they seem to call into question our relation to the museum, and to demand of us an explanation that we are unprepared to make. For the most part we pass them with tense lips and averted eyes.

22

Among the myriad halls and chambers of the Barnum Museum we come to a crowded room that looks much like the others, but when we place a hand on the blue velvet rope our palm falls through empty air. In this room we pass with ease through the painted screens, the glass display cases, the stands and pedestals, the dark oak chairs and benches against the walls, and as we do so we stare intently, moving our hands about and wriggling our fingers. The images remain undisturbed by our penetration. Sometimes, passing a man or woman in the crowd, we see our arms move through the edges of arms. Here and there we notice people who rest their hands on the ropes or the glass cases; a handsome young woman, smiling and fanning herself with a glossy postcard, sits down gratefully on a chair; and it is only because they behave in this manner that we are able to tell they are not of our kind.

23

It has been said, by those who do not understand us well, that our museum is a form of escape. In a superficial sense, this is certainly true. When we enter the Barnum Museum we are physically free of all that binds us to the outer world, to the realm of sunlight and death; and sometimes we seek relief from suffering and sorrow in the halls of the Barnum Museum. But it is a mistake to imagine that we flee into our museum in order to forget the hardships of life outside. After all, we are not children, we carry our burdens with us wherever we go. But quite apart from the impossibility of such forgetfulness, we do not enter the museum only when we are unhappy or discontent, but far more often in a spirit of peacefulness or inner exuberance. In the branching halls of the Barnum Museum we are never forgetful of the ordinary world, for it is precisely our awareness of that world which permits us to enjoy the wonders of the halls. Indeed I would argue that we are most sharply aware of our town when we leave it to enter the Barnum Museum; without our museum, we would pass through life as in a daze or dream.

24

For some, the moment of highest pleasure is the entrance into the museum: the sudden plunge into a world of delights, the call of the far doorways. For others, it is the gradual losing of the way: the sense, as we wander from hall to hall, that we can no longer find our way back. This, to be sure, is a carefully contrived pleasure, for although the museum is constructed so as to help us lose our way, we know perfectly well that at any moment we may ask a guard to lead us to an exit. For still others, what pierces the heart is the stepping forth: the sudden opening of the door, the brilliant sunlight, the dazzling shop windows, the momentary confusion on the upper stair.

25

We who are not eremites, we who are not enemies, return and return again to the Barnum Museum. We know nothing except that we must. We walk the familiar and always changing halls now in amusement, now in skepticism, now seeing little but cleverness in the whole questionable enterprise, now struck with enchantment. If the Barnum Museum were to disappear, we would continue to live our lives much as before, but we know we would experience a terrible sense of diminishment.

We cannot explain it. Is it that the endless halls and doorways of our museum seem to tease us with a mystery, to promise perpetually a revelation that never comes? If so, then it is a revelation we are pleased to be spared. For in that moment the museum would no longer be necessary, it would become transparent and invisible. No, far better to enter those dubious and enchanting halls whenever we like. If the Barnum Museum is a little suspect, if something of the sly and gimcrack clings to it always, that is simply part of its nature, a fact among other facts. We may doubt the museum, but we do not doubt our need to return. For we are restless, already we are impatient to move through the beckoning doorways, which lead to rooms with other doorways that give dark glimpses of distant rooms, distant doorways, unimaginable discoveries. And is it possible that the secret of the museum lies precisely here, in its knowledge that we can never be satisfied? And still the hurdy-gurdy plays, the jugglers' bright balls turn in the air, somewhere the griffin stirs in his sleep. Welcome to the Barnum Museum! For us it's enough, for us it is almost enough.

The Sepia Postcard

I was tense, irritable, overworked; the city stifling, my nerves stretched taut; life was a foul farce with predictable punchlines; things were not going well between Claudia and me; one morning in early September I threw a suitcase in the back of the car, and toward dusk I came to the village of Broome. A single street wound down to the darkening cove. The brochure had shown sunny red-and-white buoys lying against piles of slatted lobster pots, with brilliant blue water beyond, but tomorrow would be time enough for that. I expected no miracles; I wasn't young enough for dreams; I knew in my bones that I couldn't escape my troubles by changing the view from my window. But I hoped for a little respite, do you know, a little forgetfulness, and perhaps a freshness of spirit, too. Was it asking so much? At the bottom of the street I rolled down my window and breathed the sharp chill air, drew it deep into my lungs. The brochure had shown a girl in a white bathing suit lying on a golden beach, but if the season was over, what was that to me? I needed the cleansing air, the purifying otherness, of Broome. The inn was a rambling many-gabled Victorian with a broad front porch and paired brackets under the eaves. It stood near the top of the hill, on a lane off the winding street of shops.

And if the lamplit sign on the sloping lawn said OCEAN GABLES, what was that to me? Claudia would have found the perfect words for the sign, with its black iron lighthouse screwed into the wood. Claudia would have had something to say about the rockers on the porch, the old brass chandelier over the mahogany dining table, the square stairpost with its dark globe, the carpeted creaking stairs, the framed engraving on the landing (a little girl in a bonnet embracing a Saint Bernard), the ruffled pink bedspread, but Claudia hadn't smiled at me in a month. I was here alone.

I slept well enough, not well, but well enough, and woke almost refreshed to a gray morning. Downstairs a brisk woman in a half apron was clearing the table in a small room off the main dining room. Her apron had a design of purple plums, red apples, and yellow pears, all with stems and little leaves. A white-haired couple sat at one table, sipping heavy-looking cups of coffee. "Am I late for breakfast?" I asked in surprise; it was 8:45. The brisk woman hesitated and glanced sharply at a blue wooden clock shaped like a teapot. "I can fix you up something," she said, banging a knife onto a saucer. I sat down at a table covered with a clean white tablecloth with crisp fold-lines. Despite the slightly unpleasant note, the breakfast when it came proved generous—a tall, fluted glass of orange juice, two eggs with bacon, two slices of toast with blackberry jam, a yellow porcelain pot of superb coffee—and I rose in a buoyant mood, determined to make the best of the gray day.

Outside it was drizzling lightly, barely more than a mist. I turned up the collar of my trench coat and walked along the lane to the steep street that curved down to the water. Most of the shops had the look of houses, with curtained windows above the converted main floors. Between the shops on the shore side of the street I caught glimpses of grass, cove, and stormy sky. Once, through a large window containing giraffes and trains, I saw an open doorway, and through the doorway another window, with a view of rushing clouds. It was as if the shop were flying through the sky, like Dorothy's house in the tornado. On the other side of the street I passed winding roads of white clapboard houses with bracketed porch posts, bay windows, and gingerbread along the gables. It was a village meant for brilliant sun and hard-edged shadow, for sharp rectangles of blue between the shingled shops. But what was it to me that the sun didn't shine, that a cold drizzle matted my lashes and trickled down my neck? I wasn't out for sun. I was here because it was not there, I was here because it was anywhere else, because Broome was—well, Broome; and I was set on taking it as it was, in dazzle or drizzle.

I stopped at every shop window, every one. I studied the realtor's corkboard display of slightly blurred black-and-white photographs of houses in sun-dappled woods, I browsed in the window of the garden shop with its baked-earth flowerpots and shiny green hoses and country-humor lawn ornaments, including a pink wooden piglet and a fat woman bending over and showing her polka-dot underpants, I paused under the awning of the stationer's to examine the table that offered half-price notepads stamped with treble clefs and called Musical Notes, gigantic pencils as thick as towel bars, pencil sharpeners shaped like typewriters, mice, and black shoes. I admired the striped pole turning in a misted tube of glass and the melancholy barber with heavy-lidded eyes who stared out the window at the rain and me. I studied the ice cream parlor, the grocery store, the drugstore with its display of rubber-tipped crutches, aluminum walkers, and back-to-school specials. I passed two gift shops and entered a third. I like gift shops; I like the variety of invention within a convention of rigorous triteness. I looked at the flashlight pens that said BROOME; the little straw brooms with wooden handles that said BROOME; erasers shaped like chipmunks, rabbits, and skunks; little slatted lobster pots containing miniature red plastic lobsters; tiny white-and-gray seagulls perched on wooden piles the size of cigarettes; porcelain thimbles painted with lighthouses; little wind-up kangaroos that flipped over once and landed on their feet; foot-high porcelain fishermen with pipes and yellow slickers; red wax apples with wicks for stems; a rack of comic postcards, one of which bore the legend LOBSTER DINNER FOR TWO and showed two lobsters in bibs seated at a table before plates of shrimp; black mailboxes with brass lobsters on them; sets of plastic teeth that clacked noisily when you wound them up; a bin of porcelain coin banks shaped like lobster pots, Victorian houses with turrets, and mustard-covered hot dogs in buns; and a basket of red, blue, and green brachiosauruses. When I stepped out of the gift shop I saw that the sky had darkened. I was more than halfway down the main street of Broome and it was not yet eleven in the morning. I didn't know what to do. I passed a window filled with watches, two of which formed the eyes of a cardboard mouse. I passed a window with a white crib in which slept a red cotton lobster and a polar bear. The rain began to fall harder. The steep sidewalk turned sharply, and at the end of the street I saw wet grass, a stretch of slick dirt with pools of trembling rainwater, a gray pier leading into gray water.

The shops were more thickly clustered here, as if backing away from the muddy bottom of the street. They seemed darker and shabbier than the shops above, and the steepness of the descent gave everything a tilted and precarious look. I passed a red-lit window crowded with the glimmering lower halves of sawed-off women in panty hose; some appeared to be dancing wildly, some were lounging about, and some were upside down, their legs straining desperately upward, as if at any moment they would be pulled underground. There was a window with a handwritten sign that said BOOTS BAIT TACKLE. There was an empty dark window with a telephone number written across it in white soap, and another dark window that said PLUMSHAW'S RARE BOOKS. A dim light burned inside. Here the sidewalk was so steep that the left-hand edge of the window began at my knees, the right-hand edge at my stomach. I felt oddly unbalanced, but something about the place drew me, and I lingered uncertainly under the narrow green awning.

It was a crowded, scattered sort of display, with here an open children's book showing a boy trundling a hoop, there a set of twelve cracked leather volumes called *Barnsworth's Geographic Cyclopaedia*. In one corner a doll dressed like Little Boy Blue was leaning with his eyes closed against a globe on a dusty stand, not far from a large atlas open to a faded map of the Roman Empire in 200 A.D. It was difficult to know what to make of this shop, where a Victorian toy theater with a red paper curtain sat next to a book of fairy tales open to a color print of a princess drawing a bucket out of a well, where a stereoscope mounted on a wooden bar lay aslant on its wooden handle in front of a glass-covered engraving of the Place de la Concorde, and thirteen volumes of a sixteen-volume set of Hawthorne rose like a crooked red chimney behind an old top hat and a pair of opera glasses. Plumshaw's taste was odd and eccentric, but I seemed to detect in the display a secret harmony. The rain had begun to fall in earnest. I stepped inside.

A bell tinkled faintly over the door. The room was small and gloomy, lit by a single bare bulb at the bottom of a green-stained brass ceiling fixture shaped like flower petals. A dark passage led to a room beyond. On the counter stood an old black cash register and a small wire rack hung with cellophane bags of butterscotch squares, jelly beans, and gumdrops. Behind the counter was a tall woman with high hair who looked at me without smiling. Plumshaw, I decided. Her voluminous gray hair was pulled tightly upward and piled on top of her head in masses of sharp-looking little curls. She wore a high-necked black dress with long sleeves ending in stiff bursts of faded lace. A pearl circle pin was fastened at her throat, and on one wrist she wore a yellowed ivory bracelet composed of a ring of little elephants each holding in its trunk the tail of the elephant in front. Plumshaw, without a doubt. Oh, maybe some other Plumshaw had started the shop, maybe she was the unmarried daughter of Plumshaw the First, but she had taken it over and had stood motionless and unsmiling behind that cash register for forty years. The dark walls were lined with books, but here and there stood knickknacks of brass or ivory and boxes of stereoscopic views, and in one corner stood an umbrella stand containing three walking sticks with ivory handles, one of which was shaped like a hand curved over a ball. Evidently PLUMSHAW'S RARE BOOKS had fallen on hard days and was forced to drum up extra trade in antiques. Or perhaps—the thought struck me—perhaps these odds and ends were Plumshaw's own possessions, brought down one by one from the backs of closets and the depths of attic trunks to be offered for sale. The books themselves, arranged carefully by category, were the mediocre used books of any second-rate bookshop (sets of Emerson, sets of Poe), and among them were library discards, with the Dewey Decimal number printed in white ink on the spine and the melancholy DISCARDED stamped across the card pocket in back. I lingered politely under Plumshaw's severe gaze for as long as I could stand it and then escaped through the dark passage into the next room.

I saw at once that there were other rooms; PLUMSHAW'S RARE BOOKS was a warren of small rooms connected by short dark passages lined with books. The invasion of alien objects was more noticeable as I moved deeper into the back, where entire shelves had been cleared to make way for stacks of maroon record albums containing heavy, brittle 78's as thick as roof slates, boxes of old postcards, empty cardboard cylinders the size of soup cans each bearing the words EDISON GOLD MOULDED RECORD and an oval photograph of Thomas A. Edison, daguerreotypes, tintypes, stacks of pen-and-ink illustrations torn from old books, a moldering gray Remington typewriter with dark green keys, a faded wooden horse with red wheels, little porcelain cats, a riding crop, old photograph albums containing labeled black-and-white photographs (Green Point, 1926) with upcurled corners showing traces of rubber cement, a cribbage board with ivory pegs, a pair of high cracked black lace-up shoes. Here and there I saw brass standing lamps with cloth shades and yellowed ivory finials, and armchairs with faded doilies; I wondered whether they were for sale. All the rooms were gloomily lit by dim yellow bulbs with tarnished brass chains.

I had slipped into one room to examine a little music box with a red-jacketed monkey on top, who turned slowly round and round and raised and lowered his cup as the melody played, when I happened to look up to see a figure standing in the doorway. At first she said nothing, but only looked at me from the shadows. I placed the music box back on the shelf—the tinkling music was playing, the monkey was turning and raising its cup. "May I be of help?" Plumshaw said at last, decisively. "I was just browsing—a nice little fellow!" I answered, wanting to strangle the little monster. I turned to push it deeper into the shelf, as if to conceal a crime; when I looked up, Plumshaw was gone. I cursed her suspicions—did she think I'd pocket him?— but felt obscurely obliged to purchase some trifle, as if my visit to the shop were an intrusion that required apology. With this in mind I began looking at engravings, stereoscopic views, a box of black-and-white photographic portraits on glass. It seemed there was nothing here for me, nothing in all of Broome for me, or in all the gray universe, and with a dull sort of curiosity I came to a table on which stood a black wire rack filled with old postcards.

They were black-and-white and sepia and tinted postcards, showing topiary gardens, and Scottish castles, and boats on the Rhine, and public buildings in Philadelphia. Some bore stamps and postmarks and messages in ink: *Dear Robert, I cannot tell you how lovely our rooms are*—but then, I've never been interested in other people's mail. The pictures had a faded and melancholy air that pleased me; there is a poetry of old postcards, which belong in the same realm as hurdy-gurdy tunes, merry-go-round horses, circus sideshows, silent black-and-white cartoons, tissue-paper-covered illustrations, old movie theaters, kaleidoscopes, and storm-faded figureheads of women with their wooden hair blown back. I examined the postcards one by one, turning now and then to look at the doorway, which remained ominously empty, and after a while I found myself lingering over a sepia postcard. The back was clean; it had never been sent. The melancholy brown photograph showed a rocky point extending into a lake or river; on the other side of the water was a brown forest of pines, and above the trees were long thin brown clouds and a setting brown sun. In the upper left-hand corner of the sky, in small brown capital letters, was the single word INNISCARA. On the farthest rock two small figures were seated, a man and a woman, looking out at the water. Beside the man I could make out a straw hat and a walking stick. The woman was bareheaded, her hair full and tumbling. The details were difficult to distinguish in the dim light, but the very uncertainty seemed part of the romantic melancholy of the brown scene. I decided to purchase it. Perhaps I would send it to Claudia, with a terse, ambiguous message.

There was no price on the rack of cards, no price penciled on the backs. It occurred to me that I hadn't seen a price anywhere in PLUMSHAW'S RARE BOOKS. I wandered back through the jumble of ill-lit rooms and when I reached the cash register I presented my postcard with a flourish to Plumshaw. Majestically, with her torso flung back, she took it from me. She looked at the picture, turned the card over and studied the blank side, and gave me a sharp glance, as if estimating my bank account. She held the card up and appeared to examine one corner. At last she lowered the postcard to the counter, where she rested it on its edge and supported it lightly with both hands. She drew her shoulders back and looked directly at me.

"That will be three dollars," she said.

"Three dollars! For a postcard!" I couldn't stop myself.

She hesitated; looked at the card again; reached her decision. "Some postcards are two dollars, some are three, and some are five. It depends on the condition. This is in very good condition, as you can see—no postmark, no stains, no creases. Only here, at the corner"—she held the card toward me—"it is bent a little. It hardly touches the picture itself, but the card is not in mint condition. I can let you have it for two dollars and fifty cents, but I cannot possibly—"

"Please," I said, holding up my hand. "I'll take it for three. I was just curious."

"My customers never complain. If you think three is too high—"

"I think three is perfect—perfect." Quickly, one after the other, I placed three dollar bills on the counter. She slipped them one by one into her hand and rang open the cash register.

"If you would care to see other cards, I have a number of unopened boxes—"

I assured her that I wanted only the one card. She picked it up, glanced at it once more, and slipped it into a small flat paper bag. She folded the top over once and flattened the fold with a single slow stroke of her long thumb. She held it out to me and said, "A very nice postcard."

"Thank you," I replied; it seemed the only thing to say. She banged the drawer of the cash register shut. No smile from Plumshaw—no flicker of friendliness—only, for a moment, she turned to look at the streaming window, as if imagining my misfortune.

Through cold, gusting rain I trudged uphill, keeping under the occasional awnings. Rain coursed down my face and neck and trickled onto my collarbone; the bottoms of my pants darkened. I walked with bent head, my hands thrust deep in my trench coat pockets. Between the shops the gray of the water met the darker gray of the sky. Somewhere on the water a bell clanged, and I heard ropes creaking and a faint tinkling sound. It struck me that Columbus had been wrong. The earth was flat, and ended right here, at Broome—you could fall over the edge into grayness, and be lost forever.

In my room I rubbed my hair with a towel and changed into dry clothes and slippers. Despite the chill the radiator was cold, and I put on my summer bathrobe, wishing I had brought my winter one. I had placed the paper bag on the night table and I now drew out the postcard and propped it up against the white porcelain base of the lamp. I had chosen well. The sepia sun, the sepia lovers on their rock, the gloomy reflections in the lake, all these pleased me. In the light of the lamp I saw details I had failed to notice in Plumshaw's cavern: the tips of grasses rising through the shallow water in front of the pines, a pine root twisting through the bank and hanging over the water, a ribbon in her hair; and it was now plain that the figures were not looking out over the water, but were turned slightly toward each other. I could make out part of his face, and she was turned almost in profile. Her miniature features were sharply caught by the camera: I could see her eyelashes, her slightly open lips, a brown shadow of cheekbone. She was beautiful, but it was difficult to read her expression; I seemed to detect something questioning or uncertain in her face.

Lunch was served in the chilly room of small tables. There were seven other guests at OCEAN GABLES, all of them elderly except for a thin, fragile-looking, thirtyish woman with eyeglasses and sharp elbows, who sat hugging herself as she leaned over a book held open by a saucer at one edge and the top of a sugar bowl at the other and who looked up now and then with large, startled eyes. Even among the three couples there was no conversation, as if the presence of others compelled secrecy. After a hefty lunch I sought out the manager, John Kearns. I found him sitting in the living room reading a newspaper: a boyish gray-haired man with round, clear-rimmed eyeglasses and shiny cheeks, wearing a corduroy jacket with leather elbow patches over a buttoned sweater that revealed at the throat a red-and-black lumberjack shirt. He continued to hold open the paper while looking up with a big, hearty smile. "A cold snack," he said, and shook his paper sharply once. I realized that I must have heard incorrectly: a cold snap. "We never turn the heat on before the first of October. By law I can wait till the fifteenth." He paused and lowered his voice. "There's a man coming to look at the furnace next week. Unusual weather for this time of year. Bracing. You'll see: in two, three days people will be complaining about the heat and humidity. Never fails, does it." The last sentence seemed not quite to fit, but I was certain there would be no heat at OCEAN GABLES.

I sat for a while in a small room off the living room, in a plump, flowered armchair beside a bay window dripping with rain. The room contained a small bookcase filled with faded forty-year-old best-sellers and back issues of an architectural journal. I felt myself falling into a black mood and I suddenly sprang up and went upstairs for my coat and umbrella. Outside the rain ran in black rivulets along the sides of the lane. When I reached the main street I walked down the other side, stopping in a warm store to look at bamboo napkin holders, lacquered wicker picnic baskets lined with red-and-white-checked cloth, and white wicker wine carriers each with an empty green wine bottle, and then stopping in an even warmer store to examine a perforated wall hung with big shiny brass numerals, brass knockers, barrel bolts, cabinet catches, and double-pronged door hooks. Toward the bottom of the hill I looked across the street for PLUMSHAW'S RARE BOOKS, but it had disappeared. I imagined Plumshaw folding it all up like a cardboard box and walking away with it under a black umbrella. A moment later I caught sight of a white telephone number in a dark window; beside it Plumshaw's dripping black window reflected a white storefront, through which a dim book was visible. At the bottom of the street I walked through the muddy field past a gray rowboat half-filled with water. On the slippery pier I stood looking at a lobster boat with its piles of wet buoys, its slick tarpaulin spread over something with sharp edges, and its dark crate with a slightly open lid from which emerged a single brown-green pincer.

Back in my chilly room I wrapped myself in my bathrobe and walked back and forth rubbing my arms. The windows rattled. I began turning the sash locks, and discovered that one

was missing—there were four little holes for screws. Still in my
bathrobe I got into bed and lay reading one page in turn of the
three impossible books I had brought with me: a history of the
United States beginning with the Bronze Age, a complete
Shakespeare in double columns, and a novel set in ancient
Rome. I tossed the books aside and tried to sleep, but I was too
bored for sleep. Rain lashed the windows—hammer-blows of
rain. At any moment the panes were going to crack like egg-
shells. Then the rain would fall on the cold radiator, on the
bedspread, on the open suitcase sitting on the wooden chair.
Slowly the room would fill with water, slowly my bed would
rise—and turning and turning, I would float out through the
window into the angry sky. In the lamplit dusk of midafternoon
I reached for my postcard. Despite a first, general impression of
brown softness, I was struck again by the sharpness of the image
as I drew the card close. I could distinguish the woman's brown
iris from her darker brown pupil, and I could see her individual
eyelashes. With surprise I now saw that the man faced her directly: his forehead, the straight line of his nose, even his lips,
were distinctly visible. I detected a harshness about his expression; she for her part appeared sorrowful, the set of her lips
mournful. On the rock beside him I could see the interwoven
pattern of straw on his boater and the tiny ivory monkey, his
hands pressed over his eyes, on top of the walking stick.

I replaced the card against the lamp and tried to nap, but the
rain splattering against the windows, and the rattling sashes
with the missing lock, and the rattling gray universe, all ban-
ished sleep, and I lay with my arm over my eyes waiting for
dinner in my darkening room.

Dinner at OCEAN GABLES was served from six to eight. At one
minute past six I stepped into the room of small tables covered
with fresh white tablecloths and lit by fat candles in colorless
glass globes. A small electric heater with a black rubber cord
rattled in the center of the room. I wondered what occasion
called forth the use of the main dining room and chose a corner

table beside a curtained window. As I sat down the woman
with sharp elbows appeared in the doorway, wearing a heavy
baggy sweater that came down to her thighs and clutching her
book against her stomach. She cast an alarmed look in my direction and chose a table in a far corner, where she sat down
with awkward suddenness and bent her head over her book.
Slowly the other couples came in and took their silent places.
"Still raining," one man said, perhaps to his wife, perhaps to no
one in particular, and "Yes," a woman from another table answered, "it certainly is coming down," before we subsided into
silence. Dinner dazzled us: duck à l'orange with wild rice, hot
homemade bread, hot apple crisp for dessert. I lingered over a
superb cup of coffee and wondered how on earth I would pass
the time till bed. The expression struck me: how on earth. Was
it possible I needed some other place? Slowly the room emptied,
leaving only me and my destined companion. She had the look
of a librarian or a third-grade teacher. We would be married in
a white church on a green hill and open a gift shop in Broome.
I stared at the bowed top of her head and began counting
slowly, but at two hundred thirty she had not looked up. I
finished a second cup of coffee and rose, but my fading bride
remained rigidly bent over her book. In the living room a number of guests and John Kearns sat on flowered armchairs and
couches and watched television. The screen showed rolls of
smiling antacid tablets, dancing. Kearns wore a heavy, ribbed
sweater and thick shoes with spongy soles; he looked like a
happy bear. At the reception desk in the front hall I found a boy
of ten reading a toy catalogue open to a page of robots. When I
asked about movie theaters he said there was one over in Rock
Ridge, at which moment a door opened and Mrs. Kearns came
out, holding a tissue to her reddish nostrils and suddenly turning her face away to give a delicate, suppressed sneeze. Rock
Ridge was twenty-five miles away through heavy rain. There
was a drive-in theater ten miles away but sometimes the bridge
was washed out and you had to go through Ashville. I recom-

mended tea with lemon juice and three thousand milligrams of Vitamin C and returned upstairs, where I took a hot bath in a claw-foot tub. In my room I sat in pajamas, shirt, and bathrobe on a hard wooden chair at a small writing table and held my ballpoint poised above the back of a postcard I had found in the drawer, showing on the front a pen-and-ink sketch of OCEAN GABLES. I wrote the *C* of *Claudia*, brooded for ten minutes, and went to bed.

Before turning off the lamp I took my sepia postcard from the table and lay holding it upright on my chest. With surprise I realized that I had been looking forward impatiently to this moment, as if in the brown rectangle of the postcard I could forget for a while the rain and the room and the town and my restless, oddly askew life. In the light of the close-pulled lamp the sharpness of the image was almost startling. I could see the needles in the pine trees and the wingtip of a bird on a branch; in a tiny opening in the pines the spotted back of a fawn was visible. I could see the knot in the ribbon in the woman's hair and the minuscule lines streaming outward from the knot. The hardness of the man's expression was unmistakable, the tension in lip and nostril sharp and clear. For the first time I noticed that his face was tilted toward hers, which was pulled back slightly, as if from a fire. A long brown cloud was reflected with a single ripple beneath the reflected pines. Uncomfortably I returned the postcard to the base of the lamp and turned out the light.

Perhaps it was the unnatural earliness, perhaps it was the second cup of coffee, perhaps it was only my life, my life, but I could not fall asleep. I listened to the rain, the dark rain of Broome, to the heavy creak and crack of footsteps on the stairs, to the always opening and closing bathroom door—and long after the floor had grown quiet, and I was drifting off to sleep, again I heard the creaking of the stairs as someone climbed slowly, very slowly, pausing as if abashed at each loud crack of wood, until I wanted to shout into the night: and still the steps ascended, timidly, crashingly, and suddenly stopped forever. I

fell into a restless sort of half-waking sleep and dreamed that I
was wandering ankle-deep in water in a dark tangle of decaying
rooms. I came to a massive door with a handle so high I could
not reach it. The wood of the door was slippery and covered
with greenish slime, and when the door sprang open I saw
Plumshaw before me, but she was grinning wildly and her hair
was blowing in the wind. I turned over and Plumshaw vanished
but the rooms remained, filled now with small tables heaped
with bowls of soup. Claudia was complaining about the soup,
knocking one bowl after another from the tables, and when I
crouched down to pick up a bowl I saw a woman seated on the
floor with her head bowed, who looked up with startled eyes as
I woke in the dark. My windows were rattling. I turned on the
lamp. It was 11:46. Grimly I threw off the covers and marched
to the writing table, where I folded the OCEAN GABLES postcard
in half and in half again before thrusting it between the clattering pair of unlocked sashes. Back in my bed I lay in lamplight
listening to the rain. As I turned on my side and reached up to
turn off the lamp I glanced at the postcard.

There was no possibility of misreading their expressions: she
was in anguish, his face was twisted in anger. The dark sun
seemed to have slipped lower, it was barely visible above the
pines. His body leaned harshly toward her and she was straining
away. The dark brown sun half-sunk behind the trees, the un-
peaceful lovers, the sharp rocks, the brown clouds, all were
burdened with sorrow, and with a sense of oppression I thrust
the picture back against the lamp.

I must have fallen into a light, uneasy sleep, for I was wakened by what sounded like a faint gasp or cry. I lay listening,
but heard only the harsh rain. In that black room my chest felt
heavy, my lungs labored, I could barely breathe. With a feeling
of anxiety I sat up and switched on the lamp, which instantly
sprang up in a black window. I snatched the postcard and
looked in anguish at her face stricken with terror, his face taut
with fury. A tendon stood out sharply on his neck and I saw

that his slightly raised right hand grasped a small sharp rock. I could see the tense knuckles and the tiny, carefully manicured nails.

I tore my eyes away and saw on the lamp table the small, flat paper bag. Quickly I thrust the postcard into the bag.

I turned off the lamp and could not sleep. The oppressive postcard, the clattering rain, the labyrinth of tangled bedclothes, my racing mind, all lashed me into heavy wakefulness. Sometime in that hellish night I heard a dim cry, a thud, a splash, but I was sick to death of Broome, I was sick to death of it all, and lay with clenched fists in the streaming dark, imagining the bloody stone, the circle of spreading ripples, the floating hair. Toward dawn I slept, and was wakened not long after by the banging of the bathroom door.

I was the first one down for breakfast, and I rose wiping my lips as two silent couples were studying the menu. Through the cold morning rain I made my way down the steep street, leaning forward in the wind and holding my umbrella with two hands, one on the curving handle and one under the spokes. Though it was ten of eight, Plumshaw was there. I had known she would be. The look she gave me, when I entered under the tinkling bell, seemed to say: no returns accepted. I balanced my dripping umbrella carefully against the counter and strode toward the passage as the handle began to slide in a dream-slow arc. In the warren of rooms and passages I lost my way and came to a room filled with old furniture: a flattish rolled-up carpet lay bent across an armchair, and a dressmaker's dummy, wearing nothing but a wide-brimmed black hat, rose up from behind an upside-down bicycle. After that I found myself in a room with a boarded-up window, and then I stepped through a narrow passage into the room with the rack of postcards. At the table I kept looking at the entrance, but Plumshaw didn't appear. Furtively I pulled the paper bag from my pocket and slipped out the postcard, pausing for an instant before thrusting it into the middle of a cluster of cards. In that pause I glanced at it, but in the poor light I saw only a vague brown scene, with something dim, perhaps a figure, at the end of the rocky point. Wildly I spun the teetering rack and turned away. At that moment I was seized by a violent curiosity, like a hand gripping my throat, and stepping back to the rack I began searching desperately through postcards of baroque fountains and Alpine huts and old railroad trains. It was Plumshaw who saved me: she walked into the room and I whirled around. She was carrying a shoebox under one arm.

"I thought you might like to see these," she said, taking off the lid and holding out a box tightly stuffed with postcards. "There are some very nice views."

"Not today, no, not right now. Here, allow me." I took the box from her, tucked it under my arm, and followed her to the front of the shop. My umbrella hung by its handle from the side of the counter. I set down the box next to the cash register and pulled from the candy rack a cellophane bag of gumdrops. "One of these instead." There was no price on any of the candy; I looked forward to being amazed. Plumshaw disappointed me by ringing up seventy-five cents. "More rain," I said, gesturing vaguely toward the window.

"It rains often, here in Broome." She paused a moment, drew herself up, and added, "The jellybeans are also very good."

In my room I ate two gumdrops and packed my bag, which seemed to contain nothing but damp clothes. As I swung across the landing I nearly knocked into the woman with the book, who looked at me in alarm and stepped back against a wall. "Wonderful weather!" I said. She blinked at me through her glasses and said quietly, as if reproachfully, "I love it when it rains." She looked disapprovingly at my suitcase. I reached into my pocket and held out the open bag of gumdrops. She shook her head quickly. I imagined staying at Broome, taking her out to dinner, marrying her. "I don't like gumdrops," she said. "Goodbye," I said, and bounded down the stairs. At the desk in the front hall Mrs. Kearns looked at my suitcase with red, rheum-glittering eyes. I had paid for three nights; she said nothing at all as I nodded at her and stepped onto the front porch.

Rain splashed on the flagstone path and ran from the roof gutters. I turned up the collar of my trench coat and made my way through cuff-high wet grass to the gravel parking lot pooled with rain. My windshield was covered with large wet leaves. I threw my dripping suitcase in the car and backed out onto the muddy lane, remembering suddenly the black-and-silver ballpoint I had left on the writing table, and making a mental gift of it to John Kearns. It would look good in the pocket of his corduroy jacket. As I turned onto the steep street, in the uphill direction, I saw the shops plunging downhill in the rearview mirror, and I was seized by the certain feeling that the moment the street vanished from view, suddenly the clouds above the shops would part, a big yellow sun would burst forth, the sky would turn bright, dazzling blue.

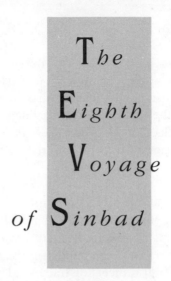

The Eighth Voyage of Sinbad

For Mark Lehman

L ate afternoon, the slant sun bright and the sky blue fire, Sinbad the merchant sits in the warm shade of an orange tree, in the northeast corner of his courtyard garden. Through half-closed eyes he sees spots of sun in leafshade, the white column of the marble sundial, the flash of light on a far white fountain's rim. The voyages flicker and tremble like sunlight on fountain water, and Sinbad cannot remember on which of the seven voyages he arrives at a shore where the trees have ripe yellow fruit and the streams flow crystal clear, he cannot remember, he cannot remember whether the old man clinging to his back comes before or after the hairy apelike creatures who swarm upon the ship, gnawing the ropes and cables with their sharp teeth.

The first European translation of *The Arabian Nights* was made by the French orientalist Antoine Galland, in twelve volumes published between 1704 and 1717. Galland's *Les Mille et*

Une Nuit [*sic*], *Contes Arabes,* contains only twenty-one stories, including the *Histoire de Sindbad le Marin.* It is interesting to consider that neither Shakespeare, nor Milton, nor Dante, nor Rabelais, nor Cervantes knew the story of Sinbad the Sailor, or indeed of *The Arabian Nights,* which did not exist in the imagination of Europe until the eighteenth century.

I abode awhile in Baghdad-city savoring my prosperity and happiness and forgetting all I had endured of perils and hardships and sufferings, till I was again seized with a longing to travel and see strange sights, whereupon I bought costly merchandise meet for trade, and binding it into bales, repaired to Bassorah. There I found a tall and noble ship ready to sail, with a full crew and a company of merchants. I took passage with them and set forth in all cheer with a fair wind, sailing from island to island and sea to sea, till one day a great darkness came over the sun, whereat the captain cried out, "Alas! Alas!" and cast his turban to the deck. Then the merchants and the sailors crowded around him and asked in great fear, "O master, what is the matter?" Whereupon he answered, "Know, O my brethren (may Allah preserve you!), that we have come to the sea of whirling waters. There is no might save in Allah the Most High, who alone can deliver us from destruction." Hardly had he made an end of speaking when the ship struck a great swirling and tumbling of waters, which carried it round and round. Some of the merchants were thrown from the ship and drowned, and others made shift to shelter themselves; I seized a rope and lashed myself to the mast, from which post I saw our ship plunge down in the turning water-funnel till the walls of ocean reached high overhead. Then as I fell to weeping and trembling, and besought the succor of Allah the Almighty, behold, a great force smote the ship and broke it into planks, throwing me into the sea where I seized a piece of mast and continued to be carried down by the turning water; and I was as a dead man for weariness and anguish of heart.

From the pillowed divan in the northeast corner of the court-yard garden, under the shady orange tree, Sinbad can see, through leafshade and sunshine, the white column of the marble sundial that stands in a hexagon of red sand in the center of the courtyard. He cannot see the black shadow on top of the sun-dial, cast by the triangle of bronze, but he can see the slightly rippling shadow of the column on the red sand. The shadow is twice the length of the column and extends nearly to the edge of the hexagon. Sometimes he remembers only what he has spoken of, say the tall white dome soaring above him and how he walked all around it, finding no door. But sometimes he remembers what he has never spoken of: the stepping from sun to shadow and shadow to sun as he circled the white dome of the roc's egg, the grass, crushed by his footsteps, rising slowly behind him, the sudden trickle of perspiration on his cheek, the itching of his left palm scraped on a branch of the tree he had climbed shortly before, his head among the leaves, and there, beyond the great white thing in the distance, a greenish-blue hill shaped like a slightly crushed turban, a slash of yellow shore, the indigo sea.

There are two different versions of the Sinbad story, each of which exists in several Arabic texts, which themselves differ from one another. The A version is "bald and swift, even sketchy" (Gerhardt, *The Art of Story-Telling: A Literary Study of the Thousand and One Nights,* 1963); the B version is "much more circumstantial." The B redaction may be an embellished version of A, as Gerhardt thinks likely, or else A and B may both derive from an earlier version now lost. The matter of embellishment deserves further attention. B does not simply supply an additional adjective here and there, but regularly pro-vides details entirely lacking in A. In the first voyage, for ex-ample, when Sinbad is shipwrecked and reaches an island by floating on a washtub, he reports in the B version that "I found my legs cramped and numbed and my feet bore traces of the nibbling of fish upon their soles" and that, waking the next morning, "I found my feet swollen, so made shift to move by shuffling on my breech and crawling on my knees" (Burton)— details not present in A. In this sense, B is a series of different voyages, experienced by a different voyager.

So clinging to my piece of broken mast and turning in the sea I bemoaned myself and fell to weeping and wailing, blaming myself for having left Baghdad and ventured once again upon the perils of voyages; and as I thus lamented, lo! I was flung forth from the whirling waters, and felt land beneath my side. And marveling at this I lifted my head and saw the sides of the sea rising far above me and at the top a circle of sky. At this my fear and wonder redoubled and looking about me I saw many broken ships lying on the ocean floor, and in the mud of the floor I saw red and green and yellow and blue stones. And taking up a red stone I saw it was a ruby, and taking up a green stone I saw it was an emerald; and the yellow stones and blue stones were topazes and sapphires; for these were jewels that had spilled from the treasure chests of the ships. Then I went about filling my pockets with treasure until I could scarcely walk from the heaviness of the jewels I had gathered. And looking up at the water-walls all about me I berated myself bitterly, for I knew not how I could leave the bottom of the sea; and I felt a rush of wind and heard a roar of waters from the ocean turning in a great whirlpool about me. And seeing that the walls of the sea were coming together, my heart misgave me, and I looked where I might run and hide, but there was no escape from drowning. Then I repented of bringing destruction on myself by leaving my home and my friends and relations to seek adventures in strange lands; and as I looked about, presently I caught sight of a ring of iron lying in the mud and seaweed of the ocean floor. And lifting the ring, which was attached to a heavy stone, I saw a stairway going down, whereat I marveled exceedingly.

Odor of oleander and roses. From a window beyond the garden a dark sound of flutes, soft slap of the black feet of slave girls against tiles. The shout of a muleteer in the street. Although he can no longer reconstruct the history of each voyage, although he is no longer certain of the order of voyages, or of the order of adventures within each voyage, Sinbad can summon to mind, with sharp precision, entire adventures or parts of adventures, as well as isolated images that suddenly spring to enchanted life behind his eyelids, there in the warm shade of the orange tree, and so it comes about that within the seven voyages new voyages arise, which gradually replace the earlier voyages as the face of an old man replaces the face of a child.

According to Gerhardt (*The Art of Story-Telling*), the story of Sinbad was probably composed at the end of the ninth or beginning of the tenth century. According to Joseph Campbell (*The Portable Arabian Nights,* 1952), the story probably dates from the early fifteenth century. According to P. Casanova (*Notes sur les Voyages de Sindbâd le Marin,* 1922), the story dates from the reign of Haroun al Raschid (786–809). According to the translator Enno Littmann (*Die Erzählungen aus den Tausendundein Nächten,* 1954), the story probably dates from the eleventh or twelfth century.

Now when I had descended four of the stairs I replaced the stone over my head, for fear the waters of the sea would rush down on me; after which I continued down the stairway, till the steps of stone grew wet and I came to a dark stream, into which the steps passed. Presently I saw floating on that stream a raft whereon sat an old man of reverend aspect who wore black robes and a black turban, and I cried out to him, but he spake not a word; and stopping at the steps he waited till I sat down behind him. Then we two set forth along the dark stream, which flowed between walls of black marble. Though I accosted him, he turned not his head toward me, nor uttered a word; so in silence we passed along that stream for two days and two nights, till waking on the third day I saw that our way was along the banks of a broad river in sunlight, past date groves and palm groves and stately gardens that came down to the river. Then I saw white minarets and the gilded domes of mosques, and I cried out in astonishment and wonder, for it was Baghdad-city. So I called out to people passing over a bridge, but no one took notice of me; and seizing the pole from the old man, who made no motion to resist, I pushed to shore. Then I passed along the riverbank till I came to the bridge-gate that led into the market street, where I saw people passing; and though I cried out to them, none answered me, nor looked at me; nor did I hear any sound of voices or of passing feet, but all was still as stone. And a great fear coming over me, I wept over myself, saying, "Would Heaven I had died at the bottom of the sea."

Above the rows of orange trees that border the south and west sides of the courtyard, Sinbad sees the tops of pink marble pillars. The deep, pillared corridor runs along all four sides of the courtyard and is surmounted by a gallery upon which all the rooms of the upper story open. Beyond the south wall is a second courtyard with a corridor of pillars, and beyond that a garden, and beyond the garden wall a grove of date palms and orange trees, leading down to the Tigris. The seven voyages have enriched him. In the warm shade and stillness of the garden, it seems to Sinbad that the dreamlike roc's egg, the legendary Old Man of the Sea, the fantastic giant, the city of apes, the cavern of corpses, all the shimmering and insubstantial voyages of his youth, have been pressed together to form the hard marble of those pillars, the weight of that orange bending a branch, that sharp-edged shadow. Then at times it is quite different: the pillars, the gallery, the slave girls and concubines, the gold-woven carpets, the silk-covered divans, the carved fruits and flowers on the ceilings, the wine-filled flagons shimmer, tremble, become diaphanous, and dissolve to reveal the unwound turban binding his waist to the leg of the roc, the giant's sharp eyeteeth the size of boar's tusks, the leg bone of the corpse with which he smashes the skulls of wives and husbands buried alive in the cavern, the shadow of the roc darkening the sun, the jewels torn from the necks of corpses, the legs of the clinging old man black and rough as a buffalo hide.

The three major English translations of *The Arabian Nights* are by Edward William Lane (three volumes, 1839–41), John Payne (nine volumes, 1882–84), and Richard Burton (ten volumes, 1885; six supplemental volumes, 1886–88). The translation by Lane contains roughly two fifths of the original material; the tales he does include are heavily bowdlerized. In the story of Sinbad, for example, the episode of the mating horses in the first voyage is omitted. The translation by John Payne is the first complete and unexpurgated version in English. Burton's translation is likewise complete and unexpurgated; it relies so heavily on Payne, borrowing entire sentences and even paragraphs, that Burton cannot escape the charge of plagiarism. "Burton's translation," Gerhardt states, "really is Payne's with a certain amount of stylistic changes." Burton, in his Terminal Essay (vol. X), defines the difference between Payne's translation and his own thus: "Mr. Payne's admirable version appeals to the Orientalist and the 'stylist,' not to the many-headed; and mine to the anthropologist and student of Eastern manners and customs." He is here calling attention to his voluminous footnotes. Burton, who never fails to praise Payne's style, is less kind to Lane, referring to his "curious harsh and latinized English, at once turgid and emasculated." Gerhardt finds Lane's style "plodding but honest"; he says of Payne's translation that it is written in "a tortured and impossible prose, laboriously constructed out of archaic and rare words and turns." Campbell finds Payne's translation "superb" and calls it the "most readable" version in English, which "omits, moreover, not a syllable of the vigorous erotica." Gerhardt judges Burton's translation to be generally reliable but adds: "The English prose in which it is written, however, is doubtless still worse than Payne's."

So as I walked about the streets of the city I came to the gate of a great house, with a stone bench beside the door, and within the gate I saw a flower garden. Now at this sight my wit became dazed, and a trembling came over me; and I passed within the gate and through the garden. Then I entered the house and passed from room to room, wherein I saw pages and slave girls and servants and attendants, but none took notice of me, till coming to a wide door I stepped forth from the house into the inner courtyard. There I saw orange trees and date trees, and an abundance of sweet-smelling flowers, and marble fountains, and a sundial in red sand; and beneath an orange tree sat a man whose eyes were closed and whose beardsides were streaked with white. Then I was confounded, and I fell to trembling, and knew not what to do; and all was silent in that place. So after a time I cried out "Sinbad!" but he stirred not. Then I fled from that garden, and passing through many rooms I came to an orchard of date trees, which led down to the river. And finding a boat at the riverbank I seized the oars and rowed along the water, till my arms ached and my hands were sore; and as my course continued, the channel grew straiter and the air darker, and I saw banks of stone rising high on both sides. Then a voice called out to me from the bank, and I saw an opening in the stone, where an old man squatted on a rock; and he said, "Who art thou and whence farest thou? How camest thou into this river?" Then I answered him, "I am the merchant Sinbad, whose ship went down to the bottom of the sea, and there I found a stairway leading to this place. What city is that behind me, which I have seen?" Quoth he, "Unhappiest of mortals, that is a demon-city. Better it is, never to have seen that city, than to find a ship filled with pearls." Then seeing my unhappiness, and seeing that I was weak from thirst and hunger, he offered to lead me to his city, that I might rest and refresh me, whereat I thanked him; after which he hopped from the rock into my boat beside me, which was great wonder to see, for his legs were as the legs of frogs; and squatting beside me he bade me enter the opening in the cliff.

In the warm shade of the orange tree, leaning back against the silk pillows of the divan, Sinbad half dreams of the telling of the voyages. At first the telling had made the voyages so vivid to him that it was as if the words had given them life, it was as if, without the words, the voyages had been slowly darkening or disappearing. Thus the voyages took shape about the words, or perhaps took shape within the words. But a change had been wrought, by the telling. For once the voyages had been summoned by the words, a separation had seemed to take place, as if, just to one side of the words, half-hidden by their shadows, the voyages lay dreaming in the grass. In the shade of the orange tree Sinbad tries to remember. Are there then two septads of voyages, the seven that are told and the seven that elude the telling? Before the telling, what were the voyages? Unspoken, did they exist at all? Are there perhaps three septads: the seven voyages, the memory of the seven voyages, and the telling of the seven voyages? Sinbad shifts in his seat. From a bough a blackbird shrills.

The seven voyages of Sinbad are cast as first-person narratives, told by the protagonist (Sinbad). But it is important to remember that Sinbad himself is a character in a story narrated

"in time long gone before" (Burton) by Scheherazade to King
Shahriyar of Persia. Scheherazade in turn is a character in *The
Arabian Nights*. The unnamed omniscient narrator of *The Arabian
Nights* recounts the story of Scheherazade, the well-read
daughter of the King's vizier, who over the course of one thousand
and one nights tells nearly two hundred stories to the King
to prevent him from killing her; during the course of the thousand
and one nights, she bears him three children. In what sense
therefore may we say that Sinbad narrates his voyages? Scheherazade,
who reports his words, has a strong motive for her
storytelling, which has nothing whatever to do with Sinbad and
his storytelling. Perhaps she inserts words in his mouth that
serve her own purposes. Each night of storytelling begins with
the words: "She said, It hath reached me, O auspicious King,
that . . ."—a formula that invites speculation. We may wonder
whether Sinbad's words are his own or Scheherazade's, we may
wonder whether Scheherazade has omitted details for the sake
of shaping her tale effectively, we may wonder whether there
are episodes from the seven voyages, or even entire voyages,
that did not reach her.

Then we passed along the stream and came to a town built
on one side of the water, and on the other side was a great
marsh; and I was received courteously by the folk of that town,
and ate and drank till my strength returned. Now the inhabitants
of that place lived there by day, but by night they swam
across the water to the marsh, for they were frog folk with
sinewy and slick legs like the legs of marsh frogs; and they
moved by hopping from one place to another. Yet by day they
lived in fine houses and drank wine from cups and listened to
the music of flutes and had servants and slaves and were in all
ways courteous and kind. These folk fed on fish, which they
hunted in strange wise. They concealed themselves in hollow
dwellings at the bottom of the river, for they were amphibious

folk that could breathe under water, and they swam out through a cunning door hidden in the side of the dwelling and thrust sharp sticks at fish that swam there. And though they were exceeding kind, yet when I enquired how I might return to Baghdad, they knew naught of it, nor how I might return there. I abode with the frog folk for many days and nights, remaining alone in the town when they swam across the river to the marsh, till one night, when I could not sleep for sorrow, I rose from the floor and walked for solace into the meadow behind the town. There I sat down and bemoaned myself, saying, "Would Heaven I had been drowned in the sea! That were better than to live among frog folk to the end of my days. But what the Lord willeth must come to pass, for there is no Majesty and there is no Might save in Allah the Glorious." Scarcely had I spoken when I heard a fluttering in that field and saw not far distant a flock of low-flying birds. Then I rose and went over to those birds, to see what sort they were, and behold, they were no birds, but strange creatures such as I knew not, for they had no wings, nor tails, nor feathers, nor faces, yet they flew in the air. So as I drew near I saw some settling in the grass, and I approached them warily, for fear they might attack me and put out my eyes.

Through half-closed eyes heavy with heat and shadow, Sinbad watches the brilliant column of the sundial in its hexagon of red sand. Dim cries sound from the river beyond the date grove. Murmur of insects, sweet smell of rotting orange blossoms. Dark blue shadows of leaves on the white rim of the fountain. Slowly a great bird descends. It settles on the sundial and folds its dark blue wings. Its long tail touches the sand. Sinbad has never seen such a bird before and rising from the divan he steps over to touch its shimmering, warm side. The bird lifts a wing, sweeping Sinbad onto its back, and at once rises into the air. Sinbad clutches the thick oily feathers as the

bird flies over the city. Far below he can see the brown river
with its boats and barges, the shadow of the bridges on the
water, the palm trees the size of date stones, the slender white
towers, the gilded onion domes like scattered gold dinars, the
little green gardens, the little dromedaries in the little streets.
Slowly the bird descends, the garden rises, Sinbad slides from
the back of the bird and watches as it lifts its wings and soars
into the fierce blue sky. In the warm shade of the orange tree he
watches the brilliant column of the sundial in its hexagon of red
sand. The mysterious, the magical, the unexpected do not happen in his garden, and after deep thought he concludes that the
bird was a dream or illusion, summoned by the heat, the flicker
of leafshade, an old man's weariness.

The frontispiece of Burton's Volume VI (Illustrated Benares
Edition) shows an engraving of two rocs attacking a ship. These
are not the rocs of the second voyage, who nest above the
Valley of Diamonds, but the two rocs of the fifth voyage, who
drop great boulders on Sinbad's ship. The female roc is shown
grasping a boulder in her claws. One of her wings is as long as
the two-masted ship below, and the boulder is as thick as the
height of the men cowering on deck. The roc resembles a great
eagle, but with a long neck; at the top of the hooked beak,
between the eyes, is a disturbing hump. The male roc, at the
top of the engraving, is closer to the viewer and is visible only
as a pair of immense talons and some half-dozen feathers. The
talons resemble the feet of roosters and have sharp, curved nails
on each long toe. They have just released their boulder, as indicated by a splash beside the ship's bow in the lower left-hand
corner of the engraving. We know from the story that the second boulder will strike the ship. One little man holds up his
arms as if to ward off a blow; another lies face down on the
deck; a third is diving over the side. The water about the ship is
mostly white, with several curving lines indicating agitation; in

the background the water is darker, drawn with many lines, and appears thick.

Now when I drew close to those creatures in the grass, suddenly they rose up and flew a little distance away, whereat I followed; and in this manner I drew farther and farther from the town, till looking about me I saw I had lost my way. I was among steep hills, which rose up on all sides; and I was as a dead man for weariness, and knew not what to do. So looking about, I saw those creatures rise from the grass, and I followed them into a nearby valley, where I beheld a marvelous sight. The valley was filled with flying creatures, which made a noise as of many winds. Then I saw that one lay in the grass not far from where I stood, and when I descended a small way to see what it was, all unknowing I stumbled on one hidden in the grass, and fell upon it fearfully, and lo! it rose in the air bearing me on its back. And I saw that it was a carpet, that flew like a bird; and I was in a valley of flying carpets, that flew to and fro. So lying on my stomach and quaking in great fear, for I knew not whether I would plunge to destruction, I gripped the sides of my carpet and flew down into the valley. And the valley was so thick with those flying creatures that I felt them brush against my cheeks and fingers; and I held tight with one hand, and covered my face with the other. At the bottom of the valley there was an opening in the hillside, and thither my carpet carried me; and I entered a great dark cavern. Now at the bottom of the cavern sat three men with beards who worked at three looms. And one, seeing me, cried out as if in anger; and that old man picked up a stone and threw it at me, striking the underside of the carpet, so that I felt a blow in my ribs. Then another called up to me coaxingly, saying, "Come down, and we will reward you"; but I trusted them not.

▪

Old man's hour: heat and shade of late afternoon. Green hands, blue shadows, a slight oppression in the chest. Behind the eyelids rings of light, red-yellow, dancing. Bone-weariness and a dull drumming in the ears. The voyages are rings of red light dancing. There are no voyages, only the worm-thick veins on the back of the hand. Only the heavy body, the laboring heart, blossoms rotting under the sun. Dead hour: his hands green corpses. The stench of corpses, the groans of the dying in the cavern under the mountain. His dead wife beside him, rotting in her jewels. A pitcher of water and seven cakes of bread. He swings the leg bone and crushes the skull. He lifts the stone and crushes the skull of the old man with buffalo-hide legs. A shrill cry cuts him like a blade. Bright blue sky, the cry of the blackbird. Heat, shade: old man's hour.

Sinbad addresses his tales to a double audience: a company of lords and nobles, who are his friends, and a poor porter, also named Sinbad, who is a stranger and whose melancholy verses recited outside the gate have incited Sinbad the merchant to narrate his seven voyages. Sinbad's immediate purpose is to persuade the poor porter that he became wealthy only after hardship and misfortune, as represented by the voyages; that is, to persuade the poor man that the merchant's immense wealth is deserved. To put it another way, Sinbad is attempting to justify his life. His purpose in narrating the voyages to the lords and nobles is less clear. We know that Sinbad has been struck by the identity of his name and that of the poor porter, because he asserts it for all to hear; a moment later he greets the porter as "brother." Perhaps, then, in the presence of the poor man Sinbad feels a need to set himself apart from his wealthy friends, to insist on his difference. It is evident that he has never spoken to them of his voyages before; they are his secret. In this sense the narration of the voyages to the lords and nobles is a form of confession. It is difficult to state precisely the nature of this confession, but surely it has to do with Sinbad's restlessness, his craving for violent adventure, his inner wildness and boredom —everything, in short, that separates him from the sober and respectable, everything that secretly undermines his shrewd merchant's nature. In any case, Sinbad requires for the recital of his story the presence of both the wealthy company and the poor porter; each morning the porter arrives early at Sinbad's house and is made to wait for the rest of the company before the story of the next voyage begins. We may imagine Sinbad now directing a sharp glance at Sinbad the porter as he relates the details of a shipwreck or a fit of despair, now lowering his eyes modestly as he describes a cunning stratagem, now casting a broad gaze over the company of lordly friends as he recounts the story of his marriage to a beautiful and wealthy woman of noble lineage, the ruby cup, the audience with the caliph.

Now though I trusted them not, I cried down to them, "How may I come down to you? For I know not how to manage this steed, and would come among you as a friend." With that I took forth from a fold in my robe one of the jewels I had gathered from the sea bottom, and let it fall among them as earnest of my good will; whereupon the men at the looms called up to me in friendly voices, and urged me to come down to them, which I might do by turning down the corner of my carpet beside my right hand. Now when I heard those words I was loath to come down, but grasping the corner of my carpet I pulled it upward, and behold, I rose high above them. Then the old men began shouting at me in anger, but I flew all about them, making my carpet go higher and lower as I desired, till seeing another opening at the base of the cavern I directed my way thither and entered in. There I found myself in a long passageway with doors of brass and silver on both sides. One of the brazen doors being open, I directed my way within, where I discovered a stately garden with trees bearing red and yellow fruits, and a great mountain beyond the garden; and being hungry I flew low to pluck a piece of fruit, but the red fruit were rubies, and the yellow fruit topazes, whereat I rejoiced and seized as many as I could from the thick-fruited branches. On the far side of the garden I came to the base of the great mountain, where I saw a fissure in the rock, and flying into the fissure I found myself in a vast and darksome cavern, wherein was no light save a faint glimmer high above.

There is peace in Sinbad's garden. Sunlight falls on the date trees and orange trees; in sun and shade, the waters of marble fountains fall. A hidden fountain stands in a walnut grove; a pomegranate tree burns in the sun. Sinbad can distinguish the songs of blackbirds, ringdoves, and nightingales. He listens for turtledoves and mockingbirds. He has even purchased twelve parrots, which reveal themselves from time to time among the dark leaves as vivid flashes of orange and yellow. At this moment, in the warm shade of the orange tree, the voyages are bereft of enchantment. The flight through the air, the giant's eyeteeth like boar's tusks, the old man clinging to his back, the serpents the size of palm trees in the Valley of Diamonds, all are banal and boring images, of no more interest than someone else's dream or the fantasies of young children, and tainted by suspicious resemblances to the commonplace reports of all voyagers. They cannot compare with the cry of the blackbird, the sunstruck dome of a mosque, the creak of rigging in the harbor ships, the miraculous structure of a pomegranate or a camel, the shouts of the sellers of dried fruits, the beating out of copper basins in the market of the coppersmiths, the trembling blue shadow cast by falling water on a marble fountain's rim, the immense collection of precise details that compose the city of Baghdad at this moment.

▪

The story of Sinbad is set during the reign of the Caliph Haroun al Raschid, who himself is the hero of a cycle of stories in *The Arabian Nights.* In the third chapter of *Ulysses,* Stephen Dedalus walks along the beach at Sandymount and thinks:

> After he woke me up last night same dream or was it? Wait. Open hallway. Street of harlots. Remember. Haroun al Raschid.

Leopold Bloom, falling asleep beside his wife, thinks of Sinbad and the roc's egg. Earlier we learn that Bloom once attempted to write a song called *If Brian Boru could but come back and see old Dublin now,* to be "introduced into the sixth scene, the valley of diamonds, of the second edition (30 January 1893) of the grand annual Christmas pantomime *Sinbad the Sailor.*" If Bloom is Ulysses, he is also Sinbad, setting forth on a voyage through the perilous seas of Dublin. During a single day in June 1904, both Bloom and Stephen think of characters in *The Arabian Nights*; it is another of the spiritual habits that secretly unite them. Molly Bloom, toward the end of her immortal monologue, remembers her girlhood in Gibraltar: the handsome Moors with turbans, the sailors playing "All Birds Fly," the Arabs, the Moorish wall. These memories, which seem to carry her away from the husband sleeping beside her, secretly unite her with Bloom-Sinbad, the returned voyager, the sailor home from the sea.

Then I directed my carpet upward toward the gleam, but though I flew higher and higher I could not reach that height. And I could have cried out for weariness and heart-sorrow, when suddenly I drew near the light, which was an opening in the rock; and I flew out through a cave into blue sky above the salt sea. Then I rejoiced that I had escaped from the land beneath the sea, and gave thanks to Allah Almighty for my deliverance.

Yet was I sore dismayed to see the empty ocean reaching away, and to feel my precarious mount under me; whereupon I directed my carpet down to the shore of the sea, there to rest me and take counsel with myself. But so eager was I to set my feet on earth, that I took no care to secure the carpet, which rose into the air without me and returned into the opening in the cliff. So I blamed myself for my folly, yet could do naught but abide there till it should please Almighty Allah to send me relief by means of some passing ship. Thus I abode for many days and nights, feeding on wild berries that grew on bushes at the base of the cliff, till one day I caught sight of a ship; and removing my turban and placing it on the end of a branch I waved it to and fro till they espied me, and sent a boat to fetch me to them.

Beyond the warm shade of the orange tree, the late afternoon sun burns on the garden grass. The shadow of the sundial extends to the rim of the hexagon of red sand. With half-closed eyes Sinbad broods over his half-remembered voyages. If all the voyages taken together are defined as a single vast collection of sensations, is it necessary to order them chronologically? Are not other arrangements possible? Sinbad imagines the telling of other tales: a tale of shipwrecks, a tale of odors, a tale of monsters, a tale of clouds, a tale of breakfasts, a tale of murders, a tale of jewels, a tale of wives, a tale of despairs, a tale of Mondays, a tale of fauna and flora, a tale of eyes (eyes of the roc, eyes of wives, eyes of the giant, merchants' eyes).

Sinbad recites each of his voyages from start to finish in an unbroken monologue during a single day. It is not clear at what time Sinbad the porter enters his house on the first day, but starting with the second day he arrives early in the morning and sits with Sinbad the merchant until the company of friends arrives. All are served breakfast, and the entire gathering listens to the recital of a complete voyage, after which they eat dinner and depart. Sinbad's recital of the voyages therefore takes seven full days, from breakfast to dinner. But there is a second narrative movement that intersects this one. The story of Sinbad, who recites his story by day, is told by Scheherazade, who recites her story at night. There is something deeply pleasing about this scheme, which seems to permit the voyages to take place simultaneously during the day and night. But Scheherazade's recital takes much longer than Sinbad's: she begins the story at the very end of Night 536 and completes it toward the end of Night 566. It therefore takes Scheherazade thirty nights, from evening to dawn, to recite the seven voyages of Sinbad, who himself requires only seven days, from breakfast to dinner. This curious asymmetry provokes conjecture. Are we to imagine a number of unreported interruptions in Scheherazade's story—for example, bouts of lovemaking—that account for the much greater time required for her story than for Sinbad's identical one? Are we to imagine that Scheherazade speaks much more slowly than Sinbad, whose voice she adopts? Does Scheherazade perhaps begin very late at night, so that the total number of hours spent reciting the story of Sinbad is not more than the number of hours he himself requires? Are we to imagine that Scheherazade recites a much longer version of the voyages, which only the King is permitted to hear, and that we have been allowed to overhear only selected portions of those longer tales? However we account for the discrepancy, it remains true that the seven voyages narrated by Scheherazade are interrupted thirty times by the words: "And Shahrazad perceived the dawn of day and ceased saying her permitted say" (Burton). The break never comes at the end of a voyage. In the second voyage, for example, the first break comes in the middle of the opening sentence; in the third voyage, the first break comes several pages into the narrative, after the description of the frightful giant. There are thus two distinct narrative movements: that of the seven voyages, each of which forms a single narrative unit and takes a single day for Sinbad to recite, and that of Scheherazade's recital, which breaks the voyages into thirty units that never coincide with the beginning or end of a voyage. There is also a third movement to be considered. The reader may complete the entire story of Sinbad at a sitting, or he may divide his reading into smaller units, which will not necessarily coincide with the narratives of Sinbad or Scheherazade, and which will change from one reading to another.

The captain of the ship was a merchant, who heard my tale with wonder and amazement and promised me passage to the Isle of Kullah, from whence I might take ship to Baghdad-city. So we pursued our voyage from island to island and sea to sea, till one day a great serpent rose from the waves and struck at our ship, cracking the mainmast in twain and turning the sails to tatters and staving in the ship sides. We were thrown into the sea, where some drowned and others were devoured by the serpent; but by permission of the Most High I seized a plank of the ship, whereon I climbed, bestriding it as I would a horse and paddling with my feet. I clung thus two days and two nights, helped on by a wind, and on the third day shortly after sunrise the waves cast me upon dry land, where I crawled onto high ground and lay as one dead. When I woke I fed on some herbs that grew on the shore, and at once fell into a deep sleep that lasted for a day and a night; and my strength returning little by little, I soon set out to explore the place whither Destiny had directed me. I came to a wood of high trees, of which many stood without tops, or lay fallen with their roots raised high, whereat I wondered greatly, till climbing a hill I saw below me a city on the shore of the sea. But a great calamity had befallen the city, for the houses stood without roofs to cover them, great ships lay half-sunk in the harbor, and carts lay overturned in the streets; and everywhere came a sound of lamenting from the inhabitants of that town.

The trunks of the date palms in the southwest corner of the garden are enclosed from root to top in carved teakwood, encircled with gilt copper rings. Sunlight flashes on the rings of the palm trees, on the white rim of the fountain, on the hexagon's red sand. In the warm shade of the orange tree, in the northeast corner of the courtyard, it occurs to Sinbad that his voyages are nothing but illusions. He is attracted by the idea, which has come to him before. The fantastic creatures, such as the roc, the black giant, the serpents the size of palm trees, the Old Man of the Sea, are clearly the stuff of dream or legend, and dissolve into mist when set beside the sharp realities of a merchant's life in Baghdad. True, travelers have often reported strange sights, but it is well known that such accounts tend toward exaggeration and invention. As if the implausible creatures themselves were not proof enough, there is the repeated pattern of shipwreck and rescue, of hairbreadth escapes, of relentless and improbable good fortune. And then there is the suspect number of voyages: seven, that mysterious and magical number, which belongs to the planets, the metals, the colors, the precious stones, the parts of the body, the days of the week. No, the evidence points clearly to illusion, and the explanation is not far to seek: the tedium of a merchant's life, the long hours in the countinghouse, the breeding images of release. Impossible to say whether he imagined the voyages in his youth, and now remembers them as if they had actually taken place, or whether he imagined them in his old age and placed them back, far back, in a youth barely remembered. Does it matter? Sinbad is weary. On the rings of the palm trees, sunlight flashing.

There is one major difference between the A and B versions of "Sinbad the Sailor": the seventh voyage. In the seventh voyage of A, Sinbad is captured by pirates and sold to a master for whom he hunts elephants. In the seventh voyage of B, Sinbad is shipwrecked and comes to an island where he finds, under a mountain, a city whose inhabitants grow wings once a month and fly. In A, Sinbad returns alone to Baghdad; in B, he returns with a wife, and learns that he has been away for twenty-seven years. Burton, stating in a note that "All respecting Sinbad the Seaman has an especial interest," offers the reader translations of each of the seventh voyages, first B and then A. His readers have the curious privilege of reading a brief report of Sinbad's death and, immediately after it, Sinbad's account of another voyage—the voyage beyond the final voyage.

So I descended into the ruined city and asked one whom I found there what had befallen that place. Answered he, "Know, stranger, that our King hath incurred the wrath of a great Rukh, who once a year lays waste our city. Now I desire that thou tell me who thou art; for none comes hither willingly." Thereupon I acquainted him with my story, and he taking pity on me brought me food and drink from the ruins of his home; and when I was refreshed and satisfied he offered to lead me to his King, that I might acquaint him with my case; for it was a custom of that island, that strangers be brought before the King. Then I set forth with him and fared on without ceasing till we came to a great palace all in ruins, so that pillars of white marble lay scattered about the gardens, and many rooms and apartments stood without walls, and were exposed to view. We came to a garden where a great boulder lay beside a shattered fountain, and in the shadow of the boulder sat the King, who gave me a cordial welcome and bade me tell my tale. So I related to him all that I had seen and all that had befallen me from first to last, whereupon he wondered with great wonder at my adventures, and bade me sit beside him; and he called for food and drink, and I ate with him and drank with him and returned thanks to Allah Almighty, glorifying his name. Then when we had done eating I asked whether I might take ship from that port; but he sighed a sigh of deep sorrow, saying that all his ships lay sunk in the harbor; and he said no ship dared approach his isle for fear of the Rukh that was his enemy. Then the King fell into grievous silence. And I seeing the case he was in, and fearing to live out my days far from my native place, took counsel with myself, saying in my mind, "Peradventure this King will deal kindly with me, and reward me, if by permission of Allah the Glorious I rid him of his enemy the Rukh."

In the warm shade of the orange tree, Sinbad imagines another Sinbad from across the sea. He is a Sinbad who lives in a land of rocs, giants, ape-folk, immense serpents, streams strewn with pearls and rubies, valleys of diamonds. One day, intending to do business on a neighboring island, Sinbad mounts the back of a roc and sets forth through the sky. A sudden storm blows the roc off course; in the wind and rain Sinbad loses his grip and falls through the air. He splashes into a river, swims to shore, and finds himself in Baghdad. The palm trees astonish him; he has never seen a silk pillow or a camel; he is enchanted by the miraculous birds no bigger than a man's hand. He walks in wonder, entranced by a porter bent under a bundle, frightened by a ship with sails gliding magically along the river, amazed by a stone bench, a sticky date, a turban. One day he takes passage on a ship and arrives back in the land of rocs and giants. He tells his tale of wonders to a group of friends who listen in attitudes of astonishment, while beyond the open doorway rocs glide in the blue sky, serpents the size of palm trees glisten in the sun, somewhere a giant lies down and shuts his weary eyes.

Sinbad inhabits two Baghdads. The first Baghdad is a place of "ease and comfort and repose," where he lives in a great house among servants, slaves, musicians, concubines, and a rather vague "family," and where he continually entertains many friends, all of whom are lords and noblemen. It is the familiar and well-loved place, the place to which he longs to

return in the midst of his perilous voyages. The second Baghdad
is never described but is no less present. It is the hellish place of
all that is known, the place of boredom and despair, the place
that banishes surprise. In the second Baghdad he is continually
assaulted by a longing to travel, a longing so fierce, irrational,
and destructive that more than once he refers to it as an evil
desire: "the carnal man was once more seized with longing for
travel and diversion and adventure" (Burton, third voyage).
The voyages, in relation to the first Baghdad, are dangerous
temptations, succumbed to in moments of weakness; in relation
to the second Baghdad, they are release and deliverance. Or
perhaps it is more accurate to say that hellish Baghdad creates
the voyages, which in turn create heavenly Baghdad. In this
sense the two Baghdads may be seen as spiritual states between
which Sinbad continually oscillates. The restlessness of Sinbad,
as he alternately seeks rupture and repose, is so much the secret
rhythm of the story that it is difficult for us to believe in a
Sinbad who chooses one Baghdad over the other, difficult for
us to believe in a contented Sinbad who settles down peacefully
with paunch and pantofles among his friends and concubines, a
Sinbad who severs himself from the unknown, a Sinbad who
does not set forth on an eighth voyage.

Then when I had taken counsel with myself I said to the King,
"Know, O my lord, that I have a plan whereby to catch the
Rukh; which if it succeed, I ask only passage from your port."
Now when the King heard this, he said that if I spake true, he
would have me a great ship builded, and filled with pieces of
gold; but if I lied, then he would command that I be buried
alive. Then did my flesh quake, but I solaced myself, saying
within, "Better it is to be buried alive than to live out my days
in a strange land, far from my native place." Then I bethought
me of the frog folk that live under the ocean and conceal themselves in hollow dwellings when they would catch fish. And I

instructed that a great egg be fashioned of marble, fifty paces in circumference, and left hollow within, and set in the meadow-lands without the town. So the King gathered about him his engineers, his miners of marble, his sculptors and his palace architect, and devised how they should bring the stone to the field and fashion the egg therefrom. And when the work was accomplished, the people of the city gathered round it in wonder. Then I instructed that twenty great boulders be brought to the field and laid about the egg, and thick ropes fashioned by the ropemakers. Then the ropes were fastened about the boulders and the ends left in the grass. And a cunning door was in the egg, so that when the door was shut the egg was smooth. Then forty of the King's chosen soldiers entered the egg, and the door was shut behind them.

The white column of the marble sundial shimmers in the sun. It stands in the center of the garden, far beyond the leaves that shade Sinbad and allow only small spaces of light to fall on his hands and lap. The sun beats down on the white sundial and the warm shade presses against Sinbad's eyelids. In the intense light the sundial in its hexagon of red sand seems to tremble. It shimmers, it trembles, slowly it becomes a white roc's egg in the sand. The egg begins to turn slowly and unwind. It is a white turban, unwinding. Sinbad grasps an end of the turban and ties himself to the leg of a roc. He feels himself lifted high in the air and sees that he has tied himself to a serpent. He undoes the turban and falls into a dark cavern where a giant with eyeteeth like boar's tusks seizes the captain and thrusts a long spit up his backside, bringing it forth with a gush of blood at the crown of his head. Sinbad plunges the red-hot iron into the giant's eye and sees his wife lying dead at his feet. He lies down beside her and touches her cheek with his hand. Her eyes open. Tears flow from her eyes and become red and green jewels. Sinbad gathers the jewels faster and faster and runs through the cavern of corpses with jewels in his arms. He stops to drink at the side of a stream and when he lifts his head an old man asks him to carry him across on his back. Sinbad feels oppressed. The old man begins to shimmer and tremble.

In Lane, "khaleefah"; in Payne, "khalif"; in Burton, "caliph." In Lane, "Haroon Er-Rasheed"; in Payne, "Haroun er Reshid"; in Burton, "Harun al-Rashid." In Lane, "wezeer"; in Payne, "vizier"; in Burton, "wazir." In Lane, "The Story of Es-Sindibád of the Sea and Es-Sindibád of the Land"; in Payne, "Sindbad the Seaman and Sindbad the Porter"; in Burton, "Sindbad the Seaman and Sindbad the Landsman." In Lane, *The Thousand and One Nights: Commonly Called, in England, The Arabian Nights' Entertainments.* In Payne, *The Book of the Thousand Nights and One Night.* In Burton, *A Plain and Literal Translation of the Arabian Nights' Entertainments, Now Entituled The Book of the Thousand Nights and a Night.*

And behold, the sun was suddenly hid from me and the air became dark. And looking up into the sky, I saw the Rukh, which was greater and more terrible than any I had seen, and I quaked for fear of the bird. Then the Rukh espied the white egg in the meadow and alighted on the dome, brooding over it with its wings covering the egg and its legs stretching out behind on the ground. In this posture it fell asleep, whereupon I rose from out my hiding place in the side of the hill and went down to the bird, which was greater than two ships full-sailed; and my gall bladder was like to burst, for the violence of my fear. So I walked in the shadow of the Rukh, each of whose feathers was longer than a man, till I came to the door in the egg, and there I released a pin. Presently the door drew open and the King's forty soldiers came forth. And two going to one rope in the grass, and two to another, till all twenty ropes were in readiness, at a signal they rushed at the Rukh: and they placed four ropes about one leg where it lay on the grass, and four ropes about the other leg, and secured them with sliding knots; and they laid four great ropes across the tail where it rested on the grass, and they carried those ropes through the space under the tail, and secured them with sliding knots; and in like manner they carried three ropes about each wing, and secured them. Then when the work was accomplished we began to flee, but the great bird awoke. And when it made to lift its wings, lo! they were held down by great blocks of marble larger than elephants. So in its wrath the Rukh stretched down its head and seized one of the fleeing soldiers in its bill, whereat I heard his cries and saw his arms over the sides of the beak; and throwing him to the ground the Rukh thrust his bill through the man's back, so that I heard the crack of bones. Yet did I and the others escape without harm, nor could the Rukh break free of his fetters, though he thrashed and cried out in mighty cries.

Sinbad, opening his heavy-lidded eyes, sees that he is in green water at the bottom of the sea. He is able to breathe in the water, a fact that does not surprise him. He moves his hand in the water and the water becomes a green garden. Sinbad sees that he is in a garden, sitting in the shade of an orange tree. The brilliant column of the sundial glows in its hexagon of red sand. He hears the plash of fountains, the cries of blackbirds and ringdoves. It occurs to him that perhaps the garden itself is his dream, perhaps he is fast asleep on a desolate shore dreaming of the warm shade of the orange tree and the bright column of the sundial, but for the moment, at least, he chooses not to think so. Sunlight and shadow tremble on his hands: is it a breath of air stirring the leaves? He looks forward to the evening meal, flute music, the laughter of friends. He will eat chicken breasts flavored with cumin and rosewater. Sinbad is in his garden. Peace, shade, and the cry of the blackbird. Perhaps in the eve-

ning he will walk past the needlemakers' wharf to the market of
the clothmakers and look at bright-colored cloth from India,
China, Persia.

Every reading of a text is limited and contingent: no two
readings are alike. In this sense there are as many voyages as
there are readers, as many voyages as there are readings. From
an infinite number of possible readings, let us imagine one. It is
a hot summer afternoon in southern Connecticut. Under the
tall pines on the bank of the Housatonic, the shady picnic tables
look down at the brown-green water. Bright white barrels
mark the swimming area and bob up and down in low waves
made by a passing speedboat. In the shade of the far bank stand
little wharfs and white houses at the base of wooded hills. The
sky is rich blue, with a few thin, translucent sweeps of cloud.
Between two pines, Grandma sits in the orange-and-white aluminum lawn chair reading a library book with a black mask and
a knife on the cover. The boy is lying on his stomach on a
blanket next to her, not too close, reading a book. The sun is
shining on the backs of his legs but his shoulders and neck are
in shadow. He is deep in the second voyage of Sinbad and has
come to the part where Sinbad, walking in a valley surrounded
by tall mountains, discovers that the floor of the valley is strewn
with diamonds, some of which are of astonishing size. They are
probably the size of the fat pinecone lying on the blanket near
his elbow. Beyond the picnic table his father is turning the hot
dogs on the grill; drippings hiss on the charcoal. His mother is
laying out the paper plates, opening the box of red, yellow, and
blue paper cups, taking out the salt and mustard and relish and
potato salad and cucumber slices and carrot sticks. His sister is
trying to find a way to make her doll sit at the picnic table
without falling over. She is trying to lean the doll against the
thermos jug of pink lemonade. Suddenly he discovers great
serpents in the valley, serpents the size of palm trees. The small-

est of them can swallow an elephant in one gulp. Fortunately they emerge from their hiding places only at night. When dusk comes, Sinbad enters a small cave and closes the entrance with a stone. In the blackness of the cave Sinbad hears the hiss of serpents outside and for a moment the boy experiences, with intense lucidity, a double world: he is in the black cave, in the Valley of Diamonds, and at the same time he feels his arm pressing against the fuzzy blue blanket and smells the smoking hot dogs and the river. The great mountains soar, waves from the speedboat lap the sand, diamonds glisten, the sun burns down on the backs of his legs, the serpents hiss outside the cave, a pinecone the size of a valley diamond lies on the blanket beside his mother's straw beach bag and her white rubber bathing cap. He would like to prolong this moment, when the two worlds are held in harmony, he would like this moment to last forever.

And when the Rukh was thus caught, the King ordered that a great cage be built on the meadow, to keep the bird captive; for he said, it was the most wondrous bird that ever lived. Then the King ordered that the ships be raised from the harbor and made seaworthy; and when my ship was ready, he had it filled with pieces of gold. So I gave thanks to the King, and set sail with the blessing of Allah (whose name be extolled!) with some merchants of that city. We pursued our voyage and sailed from island to island and sea to sea, ceasing not to buy and sell; and whenever we stopped, I purchased goods with my gold pieces and traded with them at the next port. In this manner Allah the Most High requited me more than I erst had. In the Island of Al-Kamar I took in a great store of teakwood and an abundance of ginger and cinnamon; and there in the waves I saw fishes with wings that lay their eggs in the branches of trees that hang down in the water. In this island is a beast like a lion but covered with long black hair; this beast feedeth upon horses and hath a great tooth that it thrusts into the horses' bellies. So we fared forth from island to island and sea to sea, committing ourselves to the care of Allah, till we arrived safely at Bassorah. Here I abode a few days packing up my bales and then went on to Baghdad-city. I repaired to my quarter and entered my home, where I foregathered with my friends and relations, who rejoiced at my happy return; and I laid up my goods and valuables in my storehouses. Then I distributed alms and largesse and clothed the widow and the orphan, and fell to feasting and making merry with my companions, and soon forgot the perils and hardships I had suffered; and I applied myself to all manner of joys and pleasures and delights.

Klassik Komix #1

Cover. The cover is glossy and catches the light. Bright orange fish with big eyes and curving eyelashes swim among rubbery plants, dark red and dark green, that rise from the ocean floor. All the eyes are looking down. In the yellow sand a creature part crustacean and part man is lying on his stomach. He is wearing a long-tailed blue coat and a high white collar, and his light brown hair is lifted in the green water. Two immense orange-brown claws grow from his shoulders and sweep out before him in the sand. His face is that of a crab or lobster. From the shell of the face two long antennae rise into the green water and point in different directions. In the lower left-hand corner, not far from the claws, we see a prickly starfish, a pink rock, and a crab with bulging startled eyes. In the lower right-hand corner a tilted blue anchor, with one fluke visible, lies half buried in the sand beside a slightly open oyster that reveals two frowning eyes and a pearl.

Panel 1. A city panorama at evening. The sky is red above a row of tall black buildings with yellow windows. Stretched over the tops of the buildings, in the sky, is the supine figure of a man with a white sheet up to his chin. A dim doctor in a surgical mask bends over him, holding against his mouth a white cloth. In one hand the doctor holds a bottle marked ETHER.

Panel 2. A youngish man of indeterminate age, wearing a blue cutaway and lemon gloves and a high wing collar, stands beneath a streetlamp shaped like a lantern. Yellow light streams from the lantern into purplish darkness. His eyes are dark and melancholy and his cheeks faintly hollowed. His light brown hair is parted neatly in the middle and he rests both gloved hands on top of a polished walking stick. From his feet stretches a long shadow, which rests its hands on the shadow of a walking stick. Behind him, barely visible in the darkness, loom the wheels of a passing barouche. In the balloon beside the youngish man's head, attached by small white circles indicating thought, are the words: LET US GO THEN, YOU AND I . . .

Panel 3. He is seen from behind, walking along a narrow crooked street. The dark buildings on both sides lean toward each other. They are so close that they nearly touch at the top. Wooden signs hang before shops on both sides. One sign says TAVERN, another says HOTEL: NIGHTLY RATES. The flaps of the tavern door are open and a man with a stubble beard, a patch over one eye, and a red-and-blue-striped jersey is falling backward through the door toward the street. Above the man's head is the word CRASH!! In the tavern we see part of a table, at which men sit playing cards. A red-haired waitress bends over the table with a mug of foaming beer, exposing the top halves of large round breasts above her short lacy black costume. Across the narrow street, on the drawn shade of a yellow fourth-story window, the silhouette of a woman with thrust-out rump and upward-tilted breasts is combing her hair. In the thought balloon beside the head of the youngish man in the blue cutaway appear the words: THESE STREETS ARE PRETTY DESERTED. I'D BETTER WATCH MY STEP . . .

Panel 4. On a darker street, the close-up of a yellow window. In the window, printed in red letters, is the word E S T A U- R A N. At a dim-lit table an old man sits bent over a bowl of steaming soup. There are drifts of sawdust on the floor, and here and there in the sawdust lie oyster shells. In the left-hand corner of the panel a lemon glove resting on a polished walking stick is visible beside the edge of the window. In the thought balloon above the glove are the words: MAYBE I OUGHT TO STOP HERE. NO, NO, BETTER KEEP GOING . . . OH, DO NOT ASK WHAT IS IT . . .

Panel 5. In a well-lit square, elegantly dressed couples walk arm in arm. Wisps of yellow fog float in the air. The men wear black cutaways and black top hats with a white stripe running up the crown to indicate shine. The women wear muffs and boas and broad hats with feathers. In the background, a raven-haired woman in a long black dress is emerging from a carriage. The youngish man in the blue cutaway is shown standing among the moving couples, consulting a large gold pocket watch. In the thought balloon beside his head are the words: LET US GO AND MAKE OUR VISIT.

Panel 6. He is standing on a portico before a partly open white door. A servant in red livery looks at him with a suspicious frown.

Panel 7. He is seen from behind as he climbs a stairway. There is a small bald spot near the top of his head. Paintings of bearded men hang on both walls in heavy frames carved with fruit and leaves. On the landing above stands the white marble statue of a woman. She has white marble breasts and white marble drapery that falls in folds from white marble hips. She is taking aim with a bow and arrow.

Panel 8. A crowded lamplit room. Men in cutaways and bare-armed women in shawls and trained dresses stand holding teacups or sit languorously on couches, armchairs, and wing chairs. In the center of the room is a mahogany table on which stand a silver teapot, a silver sugar bowl, and a silver platter of buttered toast. A man with mustache and monocle leans against a white mantelpiece, reading a red book. On the cover of the book is the word POETRY. In the background a bay window gives a view of black rooftops barely visible through swatches of yellow fog. The raven-haired woman in the long black dress is standing sideways by the window, looking out. She has a very narrow waist, no wider than her wrist, and very round hips. The tightness of her corset is indicated by her thrust-out bosom, her tiny waist, and her slightly tilted appearance, as if she is straining forward at the waist. Her arms are bare and porcelain-white and her long dress, reaching to the floor, is flared and very full at the feet. Her luminous blue-black hair is pulled back tightly from her face and rests in masses of tight curls at the top of her head. Her lips are black. Over her shoulders she wears a lacy fichu, which does not conceal the round tops of her ivory breasts. Women with high-piled hair and serious expressions stand here and there, straining forward at the waist. Beside the head of a yellow-haired woman facing sideways is a speech balloon with the word: MICHELANGELO . . . Beside the head of a gray-haired woman facing forward is a speech balloon with the word: MICHELANGELO . . .

Panel 9. The youngish man in the blue cutaway stands facing a white-haired woman wearing two rows of pearls. In the speech balloon above her head are the words: I'M SO GLAD YOU COULD COME, ALFRED. Far behind them, at the bay window, we see the white arm and black hip of the raven-haired woman.

Panel 10. Alfred stands at one side of the bay window, looking furtively at the raven-haired woman who stands at the other side, looking out at the yellow fog. Her high-piled hair is pulled so tightly back that it appears to be tugging back the skin of her face and lengthening her almond eye. In the thought balloon above his head are the words: DO I DARE?

Panel 11. A close-up of the face of the raven-haired woman. Her hair is shiny black with dark-blue and purple highlights. Her eyebrows are thin and arched and purple-black. The red of her lips and the purple of her eyebrows are slightly off-center and imprint the neighboring skin with eyebrow and lip. Thin crescents of her violet irises have slid into the whites of her eyes. Her cheeks are hollow and beneath her eyes lie shadows like pale bruises. Her face is white with blue and lavender shadows.

Panel 12. A view of the building, which is black and almost entirely concealed by thick yellow patches of fog. In the street stand two men in pea jackets and wool caps. In the speech balloon above one man's head are the words: JEEZ, DIS IS SOME FOG, HUH JOE? In the speech balloon above the other man's head are the words: T'ICK EZ PEA SOUP! In a yellow bay window high above their heads two silhouettes are visible.

Panel 13. The white-haired woman stands between Alfred and the raven-haired woman at the window. The white-haired woman is looking at Alfred. In the speech balloon near her head are the words: WOULD YOU LIKE A CUP OF TEA? In the speech balloon above his head are the words: WHY YES, THAT'S VERY . . . I MEAN, IF IT ISN'T TOO MUCH TROUBLE . . .

Panel 14. Close-up of a white porcelain teacup filled with tea. Two wavy vertical lines rise in the air above the tea. A teaspoon rests in the cup and fingertips grasp the end of the spoon. On the teacup is painted a Japanese lady concealing the lower half of her face behind a red-and-black fan.

Panel 15. Alfred is shown as an infant in a diaper fastened by a big safety pin, as a toddler in shorts, as a boy of ten in a sailor suit, as a college student in cap and gown being handed a diploma, and as a fashionable young man-about-town. The infant holds a little spoon, the toddler holds a red ball in one hand and a spoon in the other hand, the boy in the sailor suit holds a sailboat in one hand and a spoon in the other hand, the college student's diploma is wrapped around a spoon, and the fashionable young man is resting his gloved hand on a walking stick shaped like an enormous spoon. In the yellow band at the top of the panel are the words: I HAVE MEASURED OUT MY LIFE WITH COFFEE SPOONS . . .

Panel 16. The raven-haired woman is half reclining on a red velvet couch, with one bare white arm extended along the couch arm. The material of her dress is stretched tightly across her rounded hip. Her lace fichu is parted slightly. The top halves of her big round breasts rise above the square décolletage of her black bodice and seem about to burst the cloth. In the lamplight her blue-black hair glitters like gunmetal. Alfred sits in a white wing chair turned partly toward the red velvet couch. He holds a teacup in one raised hand. Her blue-black melancholy eyes, fringed by long black lashes, are half closed. Beside Alfred's chair a smiling man looks down at him. In the speech balloon above the man's head are the words: LONG TIME NO SEE, OLD BOY. Behind him a stern woman in a lavender silk dress and a black lace shawl stands holding a cup of tea. In the speech balloon above her head is the word: MICHELANGELO . . .

Panel 17. Alfred is hanging on a wall. A large pin passes through the collar of his blue cutaway. The collar stretches higher than his head. The tightly bunched sleeves are pulled up to his forearms and the high wing collar comes over his ears. In one hand he holds, awkwardly, a cup of tea.

Panel 18. Alfred is sitting in his chair. The white-haired lady is standing beside him, holding the teapot. In the speech balloon above her head are the words: MORE TEA? In the speech balloon above his head are the words: WHY YES, I . . . THANK YOU, I . . . To the left of the white-haired lady we see a corner of the red velvet couch, a white upper arm, a curve of shiny blue-black hair.

Panel 19. Close-up of a plump ivory-white arm resting on the red couch arm. From the frilled edge of a green lampshade, yellow light pours. A silver bracelet with luminous white highlights loosely circles the wrist. The long, languorous hand holds a white teacup. At the ends of long fingers the sharp nails are shiny blood-red against the white porcelain. On the upsweep of the forearm lies a dusting of light-brown hairs.

Panel 20. Alfred is sitting in his chair, holding a cup of tea on his knee. The white-haired lady is standing beside him, holding a silver sugar bowl. In the speech balloon above her head are the words: I FORGET. DO YOU TAKE SUGAR? Alfred is daydreaming. In the thought balloon above his head we see a narrow street with tenements on both sides. In open windows, sad-eyed potbellied men in undershirts, smoking pipes, lean their elbows on the sills.

Panel 21. A close-up of the white-haired hostess. Lines of worry appear in her forehead. In the speech balloon beside her mouth are the words: IS ANYTHING THE MATTER?

Panel 22. Alfred in his chair, from the waist up, facing us. He has a strained smile. His speech balloon reads: I . . . I DON'T KNOW, I . . . One of his arms is resting on the chair-arm. The hand is a crab's claw. The other hand holds a teacup. The fingers remain, but the back of the hand has already turned to crabshell.

Panel 23. The crowded room. A bald man is shown half rising from a lyre-backed chair, which tips backward. He holds a tilted saucer on which a teacup is balanced on one edge. Tea from the cup hangs in the air. The man's mouth is open wide, his eyebrows are raised, one hand is pressed to his cheek. Behind him an open-mouthed woman in a blue gown stands with an arm extended and the palm up, as if to ward off a blow. Another woman cranes her neck forward, peering intently through a lorgnette. The red book has fallen from the open hand of the mustached man at the mantelpiece and has reached the level of his waist. The monocle has sprung from his eye. Everyone is staring at Alfred in his chair. Both of Alfred's hands are claws and his face is that of a gigantic crustacean. One claw holds in its pincers a teacup by the handle. On the red couch the raven-haired woman stares straight ahead, without expression.

Panel 24. On the ocean floor lies a gigantic crab. Behind it, tilted in the sand, a white wing chair stands in the green water. On the chair seat, a teacup sits on a saucer. A red fish swims above the teacup. Dark green seaweed hangs on the back of the chair and over the arms.

Panel 25. Alfred is sitting in his chair, mopping his forehead with a polka-dot handkerchief. The white-haired hostess leans toward him. Her speech balloon reads: ARE YOU SURE YOU'RE ALL RIGHT, ALFRED? His speech balloon reads: OH YES . . . YES . . . I'M ALL RIGHT!!

Panel 26. The crowded room. Faces have turned to stare at a red-jacketed butler who strides toward Alfred. The butler's right leg is swung out and the black cloth of the pant leg clings to the front of the leg and billows behind. On the cupped fingers of one hand the butler holds aloft a silver platter topped by a silver dome.

Panel 27. The butler stands bent over before Alfred. The thumb and finger of the butler's free hand grip the silver knob at the top of the dome.

Panel 28. Alfred is shown in the act of rising from the white wing chair. The teacup has fallen from his hand and is tipped sideways in the air at the side of the chair. Alfred's mouth is open, his eyes are wide, his hair stands on end. On the platter his head sits on a bed of lettuce leaves. The head looks at him with melancholy eyes. In the background the raven-haired woman watches, expressionless.

Panel 29. Beside the tea table Alfred, in graveclothes, is standing in an open coffin lined with white satin. He holds out one arm, draped in tattered cerecloth. All faces are turned to him except that of the raven-haired woman, who leans back against the red velvet couch with half-closed eyes. In the speech balloon above his head are the words: I AM LAZARUS, COME FROM THE DEAD.

Panel 30. The room, less crowded. Alfred sits in his chair sipping a cup of tea. The red couch is empty. Here and there on armchairs potbellied men sit with their eyes closed, their arms hanging over the sides, their legs extended. The raven-haired woman is standing by the bay window, looking out at the yellow fog. In a pale blue band at the top of the panel are the words: LATER THAT EVENING . . .

Panel 31. Alfred is standing at one end of the bay window, looking out at the yellow fog. The raven-haired woman is standing at the other end, looking out at the yellow fog. In the black window we see Alfred's reflection. He is facing straight ahead but his eyes are turned in the direction of the woman. In the thought balloon beside his head are the words: SHE SEEMS UNHAPPY . . .

Panel 32. The room in darkness. The dark heads of seated figures are turned toward a brightly lit screen in front of the bay window. Beside the screen stands the white-haired lady, holding a pointer. On the screen is the outline of a man, filled with an intricate network of red and blue lines. In the speech balloon above the head of the white-haired lady are the words: HERE WE HAVE ALFRED'S AUTONOMIC NERVOUS SYSTEM. PLEASE NOTE THE HIGHLY DEVELOPED INTERLIGULAR GANGLIA. ANY QUESTIONS? NEXT SLIDE, PLEASE.

Panel 33. The same as Panel 31, except that Alfred's face is turned partway toward the raven-haired woman. Three large waterdrops, representing distress, are arrayed about his head. In his speech balloon are the words: EXCUSE ME, I . . . I MEAN, I . . .

Panel 34. The same as the preceding panel. In the speech balloon beside the head of the raven-haired woman are the words: THAT IS NOT IT AT ALL.

Panel 35. Close-up of the raven-haired woman's face. Blue lines of tension crease her forehead and two black vertical lines separate her arched and blue-black eyebrows. Her pulled-back licorice hair with blue and purple highlights is a mass of tight, glinting coils at the top of her head. In her speech balloon are the words: THAT IS NOT WHAT I MEANT, AT ALL.

Panel 36. View of Alfred from behind, descending the stairway. He is dressed in doublet, ruff, and skintight hose. His calves are thin. In the thought balloon above his head are the words: NO, I AM NOT PRINCE HAMLET . . .

Panel 37. Alfred in his blue cutaway is seated at a bar before a row of empty glasses, leaning his cheek on a hand. His eyes are red and his hair is mussed. His necktie is flung over one shoulder. In the speech balloon beside his head are the words: NOR WAS MEANT TO BE!! Beside him sits a fat and double-chinned woman with forearms shaped like bowling pins. She is wearing a tight red dress with a low square neckline and a bunch of violets thrust between big round breasts. She has curly orange hair, rouged cheeks, and thick red lipstick. She is leaning toward Alfred with a gap-toothed smile. In her speech balloon are the words: CHEER UP, DEARIE.

Panel 38. Alfred is walking along a narrow crooked street. Wisps of yellow fog hang in the air. In a black shop window lit by a streetlamp he sees his reflection. The reflection is stooped, leans on a crooked blackthorn, and has a long white beard down to its baggy knees. In the thought balloon beside Alfred's head are the words: PHEW! GUESS I'M GROWING OLD . . .

Panel 39. Against a featureless black background, a gigantic orange-and-red fruit takes up nearly the entire panel. The fruit has eyes and two thick black frowning eyebrows. In the lower left-hand corner a tiny Alfred looks up at the fruit in alarm. In the thought balloon beside his head are the words: DO I DARE TO EAT A PEACH?

Panel 40. Alfred is walking near the water on a sunny beach crowded with colorful towels and striped beach umbrellas. He is wearing white flannel trousers, a white jersey with the word HARVARD on it, and a straw boater. He is passing a blanket on which lie a red radio, a bottle with the word SUN at the top and TAN at the bottom, and a girl in green sunglasses and a bright yellow bikini. She is lying on her stomach with her chin in her hands, reading a book. Her bright yellow bikini pants are stretched over a pair of very round buttocks, separated by a curving line shaped like a parenthesis. Her long legs, stretched out behind her, taper to a point. Two black eighth notes hover above her red radio. Before Alfred, in the sand, a smiling redhead in a green bikini stands sideways and holds out her arms toward a smiling brunette in a white bikini who stands facing her, bent over slightly with her knees pressed together and her calves apart. Between the girls a big blue-and-white beachball hangs in the air. The buttocks of the redhead in the green bikini resemble two grapefruit in a green silk bag and the breasts of both girls are bursting the bonds of their slender bikini tops. In the speech balloon beside the redhead is the word: CATCH!! In the speech balloon beside the brunette is the word: TEE-HEE! At the edge of the water a little boy with a red pail squats before a perfect pail-shaped mudpie. In the balloon beside Alfred's head, attached by small white circles, are the words: I SHALL WEAR WHITE FLANNEL TROUSERS, AND WALK UPON THE BEACH.

Panel 41. Alfred is walking on a deserted stretch of beach. A rock jetty extends far out in the water. On a boulder near the end of the jetty sit two mermaids combing their long blond hair. Above their heads are flagged eighth notes, joined sixteenth notes, and dotted quarter notes. In the speech balloon beside Alfred's head are the words: HOLY COW, MERMAIDS! I CAN'T BELIEVE IT! GUESS THEY'RE NOT SINGING TO ME, THOUGH . . .

Panel 42. Alfred, dressed in his blue cutaway, stands with his hands in his pockets at the bottom of the ocean. All about him, on rocks, on twists of coral, on a half-sunk treasure chest from which gold coins and a pearl necklace protrude, mermaids are seated. One mermaid, with shiny blue-black hair tumbling to her waist, sits nestled in the curved fluke of a partially sunk anchor. She leans back as she holds the shank of the anchor with one hand. The round breasts of all the mermaids peep out behind long thick hair that is blond, black, or red. All the mermaids have white and pink flowers in their hair and wear bracelets of shells. In the thought balloon beside Alfred's head are the words: WE HAVE LINGERED IN THE CHAMBERS OF THE SEA . . .

Panel 43. Alfred is lying in bed with his blanket pulled up to his chin. He is wearing a red nightcap with a white pompom.

His fingertips are visible gripping the edge of the blue blanket under his chin. One eye is open. At the foot of the bed the door is open and a gray-haired woman with eyeglasses has thrust her head in. In the speech balloon beside her head are the words: ALFRED! LAZYBONES! TIME TO GET UP! In the thought balloon above Alfred's head are the words: WAS IT ALL A DREAM?

Panel 44. Alfred in his blue cutaway is seated at a dark desk on which are an oil lamp, a bottle bearing the word INK, several quill pens, a globe on a stand, and a white bust with the word DANTE on its pedestal. Before him on the desk lies a long piece of paper curled over at the top. In his right hand he holds a quill. On the paper are the words: LET US GO THEN, YOU AND ME . . . The "ME" is crossed out and above it appears the word "I." On the wall behind the desk hangs a large oval mirror in a mahogany frame. Alfred's head, bent forward over his paper, is reflected in the mirror. Yellow lines of light radiate from the oil lamp. Brown and blue shadows lie on Alfred's hand.

R*ain*

One summer evening at about midnight a man wearing eye-glasses and a light-blue shirt made his way through the crowded lobby of a movie theater and stepped outside with a look of dismay. The marquee was hung with a crackling curtain of rain. Groups of animated women stood in the brightness of the marquee shelter, while now and then a husband or boyfriend hunched his shoulders and marched into the downpour to bring the car around. Two plump girls in tight white shorts and denim jackets stood bent together at the edge of the rain, reaching out their fingers, whispering, giggling into the backs of their hands, as if the storm were a wild and erotic joke—and all at once they pulled their jackets over their heads and ran off into the rain like two upright turtles. A sudden flash of lightning revealed black thunderclouds in a lavender sky.

Mr. Porter jingled the car keys in his pocket and looked down with a frown at his new black shoes. It was just his luck. He was wearing tan cotton pants, and the sleeves of his light-blue shirt were turned back neatly twice. With an irritable glance at his watch he walked to one end of the marquee shelter, where the dry pale sidewalk became dark hissing wet. He reached out a palm, but to his surprise he felt no rain. He placed the tips of his shoes on the line of wetness, and bending forward at the waist, stretched out his arm farther and farther until he rose on his toes. A shot rang out. Mr. Porter began to thrash the air with both arms as if he were teetering on the edge of a cliff.

As the thunder died away Mr. Porter regained his balance. He adjusted his eyeglasses, looked contemptuously at a grinning couple, and walked to a dark corner beside the ticket booth, where he stood with his back to a wall of glass-covered Coming Attractions. One showed a redheaded woman in a transparent green nightgown standing before an open door with her hands pressed to her cheeks and her mouth wide open. Mr. Porter folded his arms across his stomach. He leaned one shoulder against the ticket booth, crossed his legs so that one shoe balanced on its toe, and resolved to wait out the rain.

Soon the crowd had vanished but the rain remained. On the polished tar a traffic light threw rippling green and red reflections that mingled with the blinking lemon swirls of the marquee lights. The precise blue letters of a neon sign over a hardware store appeared in the street as an azure blur. Rain hissed on the street, drummed on car tops, made a sound like flung pebbles against a passing umbrella. It blew along the street in waves of mist. "Nice weather," said a voice. Mr. Porter started. Beside him stood a large woman who seemed to have sprung from one of the colorful Coming Attractions. Her rain-soaked orange hair was brown at the roots, her black eyebrows dripped down in wavy dark lines, the aquamarine of her eyelids flowed from the corners of her eyes. Rouge-colored drops rolled down her cheeks and dripped from her shining jaw. Mr. Porter nodded and glanced about. The marquee shelter was deserted except for a solitary figure in a tan trench coat who stood with his back to Mr. Porter and clasped in pink hands a tightly furled black umbrella with a silver point. "It's getting late," Mr. Porter said in a low voice barely above a whisper, and then he pushed against the ticket booth with his shoulder and straightened up and stepped briskly away, taking a deep

breath and lowering his head as he approached the loud, dark
cement.

As his foot swung over the line, Mr. Porter saw dark streaks
soaking into his light pant leg. By the third step he felt as if he
had stepped into a bathroom shower. Only a few pale streaks
remained in his shirt, dyed dark blue by the rain. The backs of
his hands glistened; his black watchband gleamed. His shoes
shone with a perfect finish but he feared the black polish was
being washed away by the rubbing rain. Water poured down
the back of his neck and dripped from his nose and chin. His
lenses rippled. A blurred taxi floated by, flinging at him a sheet
of water.

When he reached his Chevy hatchback, Mr. Porter stepped
from the curb into an ankle-deep steam of rushing water. He
groped along the front of the car until he came to the door on
the driver's side. At the sight of the closed window he exhaled
sharply with relief, but as he reached for his keys he was surprised to see that the lock button was raised. He opened the
door quickly and slid onto the suddenly illluminated seat, which
vanished as he shut the door. In the dark he took off his glasses
and rubbed them against his soaked shirt. When he put them on
he saw wavy blurs. Drops from his hair streamed down his
cheeks onto his lips. Fumbling in his pocket with wet, slippery
fingers, Mr. Porter drew out the zippered leather case from
which his car keys dangled. He inserted the ignition key. It did
not fit. Mr. Porter opened the door and in the amber light
examined the blurred silver shape. It appeared to be the correct
key. As he turned to insert it again, he noticed on the clean
black seat beside him a roll of butter-rum Lifesavers, and suddenly he had the odd sensation that the world was unraveling,
rushing out of control, as when, in his childhood, descending a
dark stairway, he had reached out his foot for that last, phantom
stair even as the floor, one step too soon, leaped up to meet
him. Quickly Mr. Porter looked about. On the back seat he
saw a lidless blue coffee can containing a screwdriver with a

transparent yellow handle. Beside the can lay a little naked pink plastic doll the size of a thumb.

"Stupid cars," Mr. Porter muttered, stepping out into the rain and slamming the door. A passing car swerved and honked. Under the bright blur of a solitary streetlight, four car-lengths away, stood another Chevy hatchback. Mr. Porter splashed toward it and bent down over the rear bumper. In the dripping chrome he saw his image, a colored ripple, and through his streaming lenses he read his license plate. Mr. Porter made his way to the door on the driver's side. The window was half open, though the door was locked. When he opened the door a pool of rainwater on the driver's seat reflected the amber light. On the glistening seat beside it lay a fat wet paper-back with blue page-ends. Its shiny, sticky-looking cover stuck up, revealing watery blue stains on the uppermost page. On the back seat lay a slim black umbrella.

Mr. Porter drove slowly, leaning over the wheel and squint-ing through the rain-sheeted windshield at the rainbowed tar. From time to time he rubbed the misty glass with a quick mo-tion of his left hand; his fingers left faint oily patterns on the glass. Through the dripping arches designed by the wipers he watched the stoplights and shopfronts flowing along the street in iridescent streams. Slowly, wavering silently, the bright signs and windows floated past, dripping into the street, streaming along the gutters, pouring into drains: a luminous green win-dow filled with green-tinted bicycles, a blue-glowing cardboard girl holding up a bottle of beer, a red and green pizzeria. Under a streetlamp a brilliant red stop sign glistened at the end of its stick like an enormous lollipop. Mr. Porter turned onto another street. A stone divider appeared, the stores and bars and rain-bows were replaced by large ghostly houses flanked by shad-owy trees, beyond the double arch of the wipers the black windshield was dotted with transparent crystal drops. A blink-ing stoplight flung a handful of rubies across the windshield. In the distance Mr. Porter saw the tall misty pillars of the thruway, and soon he was rising slowly into the air along a sleek entrance ramp.

He could barely see. Blurred rows of aquamarine lights stretched curving into the distance, tinting the mist. Mr. Porter felt as if he were driving at the bottom of a green swimming pool. He stayed to the right, straining through rippling lenses for the broken white line that marked the lane. A passing truck sprayed water against the windshield and for a moment Mr. Porter could see nothing but the lazy wipers, bowing left and right, left and right, like twin actors on a stage. The applause has died down, the audience is making its way to the exits, but still they bow, left and right, left and right, though the audience has left long ago and the lights are out in the deserted theater. A white streak appeared; Mr. Porter was driving in the center of two lanes. Behind him a truck was flashing its lights. Mr. Porter swerved to the right. The truck rushed past, throwing water at the side window like a fistful of sand. In the distance he saw a red glow from the shopping center. The melting exit signs announced his town.

Mr. Porter turned off at his exit and drove slowly down to an orange streetlight that spilled over its glass container into the surrounding air and dripped onto the flowing windshield. The rain was falling harder. It hammered against the car top like sharp fingernails drumming against a metal table. Who will come? No one comes, no one will ever come, though the fingernails drum drum drum against the metal table. All at once Mr. Porter remembered that he was wet, and the memory was like stepping into the rain; the drumming rain seemed to be pouring through the roof and driving his clothes against his skin. Soon he would be home. He would lie warm and dry in his bed like a freshly ironed shirt in a drawer. Looking carefully both ways, Mr. Porter turned left and passed under the dripping highway. In the near distance appeared the familiar railroad trestle. Above it the black sky glowed murky red from the shopping center across Main Street. As Mr. Porter passed under the trestle the car sank into water above its wheels, and stopped.

He waited, stepped on the gas, and waited longer; stepped on the gas, waited, stepped on the gas; waited; stepped on the gas. As he waited he noticed water seeping through the doors onto the floor. Quickly he tried again. The water was rising slowly. Mr. Porter opened the door and stepped out.

He stood up to his knees in water. And for a moment he felt like lying down in the water and closing his eyes, he imagined his body at peace, drifting away in the dark water. Mr. Porter began to pull his legs forward in the direction of the shopping center. He was more than two miles from home. A sudden downpour fell on him—he had forgotten the momentary shelter of the trestle. Through the heavy drops he passed slowly up the incline to the stoplight at Main Street. Across the street the long smear of the shopping center loomed above a deserted parking lot. The vast orange-red letters of the supermarket and the cherry-red letters of the bargain store stained the dark mist overhead and flowed in the gleaming tar. In a far corner of the parking lot stood a glass telephone booth that reminded him of an aquarium and a coffin. The light changed, and as Mr. Porter walked across the street he heard sucking and oozing sounds in his ruined shoes.

As he stepped onto the parking lot he saw his shoe disappear into a red puddle; when he lifted it he saw the polish dripping away in red-black drops. The rain was coming in sharp slanting lines, driving against his cheeks, his shirt, his shoes. Mr. Porter glanced at his watch. Through the dripping crystal he saw two wavy hands. A faint black smudge was visible on his pale wrist beside the shining black band. Mr. Porter rubbed the band with a fingertip; his finger showed a black stain. Through streaming eyeglasses he peered up at the distant telephone booth. He imagined the telephone ringing in his empty house. The parking lot was streaked with luminous bands of cherry-red and orange-red, and Mr. Porter saw red ripples in his shoes, a reddish glow in his flashing hands. His cat would prick up her ears before slowly settling her chin on her outstretched paws. Mr. Porter tried to walk quickly but he seemed to be walking through a tide. He would never arrive anywhere. His shoes were ruined, his shirt was ruined, everything was washing away. The rain was flooding him, passing through him and coming out the other side. Everything was coming undone. Black drops fell from his watchband onto his hands, blue drops fell from his shirtsleeves onto his arms. Have I wasted my life? The telephone booth was far, far away.

Mr. Porter stopped. He was standing alone under a dripping red-black sky. Behind him the railway trestle had melted away, nothing remained of the highway but a distant shimmer. His shirt was running down in blue streams onto his pants, his pants were trickling onto his shoes, his shoes were flowing away in inky streams. Everything was washing away. His cheeks were running, his eyeglasses were spilling down in bright crystal drops, flesh-colored streams fell from his shining fingertips, he was dissolving in the rain. In ripples of blue and flesh and tan and black he flowed into the shine of the tar. For a moment on an empty parking lot a bright puddle gleamed, but then the rain washed it away.

Alice, Falling

Alice, falling, sees on the top shelf of the open cupboard a jar bearing the label RASPBERRY JAM, a yew-wood tea caddy with brass fastenings and a design of handpainted plants and flowers on the lid, and a tin of lemon snaps: the dark green top shows in the center an oval containing a colored head of Prince Albert. On the bottom shelf Alice sees a porcelain dessert plate with a gilt border and a center panel showing a young man in a tilted tricorne, red jacket, and white breeches, standing beside an oak tree; a bread knife with an ivory handle carved to show a boy holding wheat in his arms; and a silver-plated cream jug with a garland of silver plated leaves and berries encircling the base. So slowly is Alice falling that she has time to take in all the details, to note the pink thistles on the lid of the tea caddy and the yellow buttons on the red jacket of the man on the dessert plate, to observe the faint reflections of her face above and below the label on the jar of raspberry jam.

*

Alice does not know how long she has been falling, but when she looks up she has the sense of a great shaft of darkness stretching interminably upward. In the alien tunnel-world she

tries to think of the bright upper world, where her sister sits on
a bank, under a tree, reading a book without pictures or conversations, but as she falls deeper and deeper it becomes harder
for her thoughts to reach so high, as if each thought is a heavy
rope that has to be hurled upward in the act of falling. And
gradually, as she falls, a change comes about: the mysterious
shaft or vertical tunnel through which she is falling begins to
seem familiar to her, with its cupboards, its shelves, its lamplit
bumps and hollows, while the upper world grows shadowy and
strange; and as she falls she has to remind herself that somewhere far above, suddenly the air is blinding blue, white-and-
yellow daisies grow in a green field, on a sloping bank her sister
sits reading in sun-checked shade.

*

The dark walls of the shaft are faintly illuminated by globed
oil lamps attached at irregular intervals to wrought-iron wall
brackets: each bracket has the shape of an elongated S-curve
turned sideways, and on the apex of the outermost curve sits a
brass mermaid holding up a cylindrical chased-brass base with
a brass adjustment knob; on the cylinder rests the globe of glass,
topped by a slender glass stem. The light from the lamps permits Alice to observe the objects that abound on the walls. In
addition to the cupboards with their shelves, she passes maps
and pictures hung on pegs, including a black-and-white engraving of Scotland showing all the counties outlined in red, and a
painting of a lion leaping onto the back of a horse: the horse's
head is twisted backward, its teeth are bared, the flared nostrils
are wide as teacups, and dark red streaks of blood course along
the shiny brown sides; a pair of oak bookshelves holding
Twenty-five Village Sermons, Bewick's Birds, Macauley's *History,
The Fair Maid of Perth, The Life and Works of Edwin Landseer,*
Pope's *Homer, Coke upon Lyttleton,* Rogers' *Pleasures of Memory,
Sir Charles Grandison, Robberies and Murders of the Most Notorious
Pirates,* Bayle's *Dictionary, Ivo and Verena, Pilgrim's Progress,* and

Gems of European Art; a barometer in a case of walnut wood
shaped like an anchor: the flukes of the anchor support the glass
disc, in which is pictured Neptune riding a sea horse within a
circle of words (RAIN, FAIR, CHANGE, STORMY); a niche containing
a marble Venus and Cupid: the winged, curly-haired boy
reaches for his bow, which his seated mother holds away: her
robe has slipped to her lap, and one breast is visible above his
reaching arm; and a Gothic-arch-topped set of small, glass-
fronted shelves on which stand a barefoot porcelain girl holding
a basket of flowers over one forearm, a pincushion set in a brass
wheelbarrow and stuck with hat pins ornamented with china
flowers, a playing-card box with a floral border and a center
panel showing a castellated mansion in Tunbridge Wells, two
small oval silhouettes framed in ivory and showing, respectively, a snub-nosed girl in a bonnet and a snub-nosed boy in a
flat-brimmed hat, a red glass rose with green glass thorns, and
a majolica snake devouring a toad.

*

Down, down, down. Would the fall *never* end? Alice has been
falling for so long that she is beginning to grow uncertain. If
the fall does end, then the vertical tunnel will be a connecting
link, a transition, a bridge between the upper world and the
unknown lower world; it will be unimportant in itself and, at
the instant of ending, it will disappear. But if the fall never ends,
then everything is changed: the fall itself becomes the adventure, and the tunnel through which she is falling becomes the
unknown world, with its magic and mystery. Alice, looking
about uncertainly, tries to decide whether she is on her way to
an adventure or whether she is in the middle of one.

*

The shaft, well, or vertical tunnel down which Alice is falling
has irregular walls of hard earth mixed with outcroppings of
rock: granite, feldspar, and basalt. The hard earth is mostly dry,

with occasional moist patches; here and there a trickle of dark water zigzags down, passing the edge of a map, slipping behind a cupboard's open door. Some of the cupboards have small dishes on top, placed back against the wall, as if to catch dripping water. The tunnel is a comfortable width for falling: Alice falls without fear of striking the walls, yet at any moment she can reach out and remove a jar from a shelf or adjust a tilted picture. Alice wonders how the shelves are reached from below. At first she imagines a very long ladder, but this presents difficulties even if the tunnel has a bottom, for how would such a long ladder get into such a narrow space? Next she imagines small openings in the walls, through which servants can enter the tunnel, but she sees no openings, no doors. Perhaps the answer is small birds who fly up from below, or from nests hidden in the darkness. It occurs to Alice that there may be another answer: the jars, the pictures, the maps, the lamps have always been here, unchanging. But how can that be? Alice, as she falls, feels a little frown creasing her forehead.

*

Falling, always falling, Alice closes her eyes and sees her sister on the bank under a tree, reading a book without pictures or conversations. The bank slopes down to a pool with reeds; the sun-shot shadow of the tree, a thick beech (*Fagus sylvatica*), trembles on the water. Circles of sun and shade move on her sister's hands. Deep in her book, Alice's sister scarcely hears the stir of leaves overhead, the distant cries of the shepherd boy, the lowing of the cattle, the rustle of Alice's dress. Gradually she becomes aware of a disturbance beside her; it is Alice, restless as always. It's difficult, thinks Alice's sister, to have a younger sister who won't ever sit still and let you read. Although Alice's sister is determined to keep her eyes fixed on the page, she feels that her attention has already been tugged away, it's as if she is being pulled out of a dream, the words are nothing but words now; irritably she places her finger at the end of a line. Raising her eyes, she is surprised to see Alice chasing a white rabbit across a field. With an impatient sigh, Alice's sister reaches into her pinafore pocket and removes a scrap of blue ribbon, which she places in her book before closing it. She rests the book carefully against a bare root. She then rises to her feet, brushing off her dress with sharp little flicks of the backs of her fingers, and begins to walk quickly after Alice through the field of daisies. When she comes to the rabbit hole under the hedge she stops and crouches down, pushing away the hedge branches, careful not to kneel on the ground. "Alice!" she calls, looking down into the dark hole. "Alice, are you there?" There is no answer. The hole is just large enough for her to enter, but it is very dirty, and very dark. For a while she looks down thoughtfully into the dark. Then she raises her head; in the distance she hears the tinkle of sheep bells; the sun burns down on the tall grass; reeds stir at the edge of the pool; under the leaning beech, sun and shade tremble on the grass, on the closed book, on a purple wildflower beside the bare root.

*

Down, down, down: she can't really see too much, down there in the dark. She can see the hem of her dress outspread by the wind of her slow falling, and the dark earthen wall of the vertical tunnel, broken here and there by eruptions of rock. The upper view is better, but it makes Alice dizzy: raising her eyes, and bending back her head, she can see the ocher bottom of a cupboard, and higher up, on the other side of the wall, the shadowy underside of a bookshelf supported by two wooden brackets shaped like elephant heads with uplifted trunks. Still higher up she sees a dim glow passing into upper darkness; the glow is from a lamp concealed by the cupboard. When Alice looks down again, she sees the top of a new object rising into view: a strip of dark wood carved with wooden leaves and wooden bunches of grapes. Beneath the strip of carved wood a glimmering mirror appears. Alice sees, at the top of the glass, her shiny black shoes with their narrow black ankle-straps and the bottoms of her blue stockings. The large mirror in its heavy frame of carved mahogany is shaped like a shield. In the dim glass Alice sees, as she falls, the outspread hem of her yellow dress, and then the bottom of her white pinafore with its blue stripe along the bottom border, and then the two pinafore pockets, each with a blue stripe along the top: one pocket holds a white handkerchief. And as if she is standing at the side of a stairway, watching someone appear at the high landing and start to descend, Alice sees in slow succession the white cotton belt, the puffed shoulder sleeves, the outspread yellow-brown hair, the dark, worried eyes under the dark eyebrows, the tense forehead; and already the shiny black shoes and blue stockings and pinafore pockets have disappeared, the bottom of the mirror is rising higher and higher, all at once the top of her head with its thick combed-back hair vanishes from view: and looking up she sees the bottom of the mirror rising higher and higher, floating away, slowly dissolving in the dark.

*

If only, Alice thinks to herself suddenly, I could let myself go! If only I could fall! For she feels, in her falling, a tension, as if she is holding herself taut against her fall. But a true fall, Alice thinks to herself, is nothing like this: it's a swoon, a release, it's like tugging at a drawer that suddenly comes unstuck. Alice, as she falls, is tense with alertness: she holds herself in readiness, though for what she isn't certain, she looks around eagerly, she takes in everything with sharpened awareness. Her fall is the opposite of a sleep: she has never been so awake. But if I were truly falling, Alice thinks to herself, then I would let myself go, myself go, myself go.

*

It occurs to Alice that she is of course dreaming. She has simply fallen asleep on the bank with her head in her sister's lap. Soon she will wake up, and the tunnel, the cupboards, the maps, the mirror, the jar of raspberry jam, all will vanish away, leaving only the bank of sun-patched shade, the sunny field, the distant farmyard. But suppose, Alice thinks to herself, the bank too is a dream? If the bank is a dream, then she will wake up somewhere else. But where will that be? Alice tries to think where she might wake up, if she doesn't wake up with her head in her sister's lap. Maybe she will wake up in Lapland, or China. But if she wakes up in Lapland, or China, will she still be Alice, or will she be someone else? Alice tries to imagine another Alice, dreaming: the other Alice has short brown hair, likes rice pudding, and has a cat called Arabella. But mightn't this Alice also be a dream? Who then is the dreamer? Alice imagines a series of Alices, each dreaming the other, stretching back and back, farther and farther, back and back and back and back and back.

*

On the afternoon of July 4, 1862, a boating party of five was to be seen on the Isis, heading upriver from Oxford to God-stow. It was a cloudless blue day. Heat-haze shimmered over the meadows on both sides of the water. Charles Lutwidge Dodgson, mathematical tutor at Christ Church, Oxford, and deacon of the Church of England, having changed from the black clergyman's clothes he always wore in Oxford to white flannel trousers, black boots, and a white straw boater, sat facing the back of his friend Robinson Duckworth, who rowed stroke to Dodgson's bow. In the stern, facing Duckworth, sat the three Liddell sisters, daughters of the Dean of Christ Church: Edith, age 8; Alice, age 10; and Lorina, age 13. The girls, seated on cushions, wore white cotton frocks, white socks, black shoes, and hats with brims. In the boat stood a kettle and a large basket full of cakes; on river expeditions Dodgson liked to stop and take tea in the shadow of a haycock. "The story was actually composed and spoken *over my shoulder*," Duckworth recalled some years later, "for the benefit of Alice Liddell, who was acting as 'cox' of our gig. I remember turning round and saying, 'Dodgson, is this an extempore romance of yours?' And he replied: 'Yes, I'm inventing as we go along.' " Twenty-five years later Dodgson recalled: "I distinctly remember now, as I write, how, in a desperate attempt to strike out some new line of fairy-lore, I had sent my heroine straight down a rabbit-hole, to begin with, without the least idea what was to happen afterwards." He remembered the stillness of that afternoon: the cloudless blue sky, the watery mirror of the river, the tinkle of drops falling from the oars. Mrs. Hargreaves—as Dodgson always referred to Alice, after her marriage—also recalled the day sharply: the blazing summer afternoon, the heat-haze shimmering over the meadows, the shadow cast by the haycocks near Godstow.

*

Alice is growing thirsty, and as she falls slowly past a cupboard she opens the doors. She sees a bottle labeled GINGER BEER and grasps it as she falls, but the bottom of the bottle catches on the edge of the shelf and the bottle slips from her fingers. Alice covers her ears, widens her eyes, and opens her mouth to scream. But she sees the bottle of ginger beer falling lazily in front of her and not plunging down like a stone in a well. The bottle is tilted like the hand of a clock pointing to ten; at once Alice reaches out and seizes the bottle firmly. When she brings it close to her face she sees with disappointment that there is scarcely a swallow of ginger beer left. She wonders how long the bottle has been sitting on the shelf, for it simply won't do to drink from an old bottle, or one that has been used by someone else. She will have to speak to the housekeeper, if she ever finds one. How neat and clean the shelves are! The housekeeper must have a fine feather duster. But it must be a very long feather duster, to reach so high. Alice feels that her thoughts are growing confused, and without another moment's hesitation she raises the bottle to her lips and swallows the ginger beer. "Why," Alice says to herself in surprise, "this isn't ginger beer at all! It is nothing but soda water! I shall certainly have to speak to someone about this. Fancy if all labels meant something else, so that you never knew what you were going to eat. Please, Miss, would you care for more buttered toast? And out comes roast duck and dumplings. But that isn't what I mean, exactly." Alice is no longer certain what she means, exactly; when she looks up she can see the cupboard vanishing in the dark. As she falls past another cupboard, she manages to place the bottle inside. At the last moment she realizes that the label is still not right, since the bottle is now empty. But, Alice thinks to herself as the cupboard rises into the dark, it isn't as wrong as it was before.

*

It occurs to Alice that the shaft is a prison: she cannot climb out, she cannot escape. It may be that she can stop falling, by reaching out and grasping the top of a cupboard, the edge of a niche, or a protruding piece of stone; but even if the cupboard does not tear out of the wall, even if the edge of the niche does not crumble, and the stone not break, what possible use will it be to hang there like a coat on a peg, while her fingers and arms grow tireder and tireder? There are no doors or windows in the walls of her prison, no stairs or ladders: it seems more sensible to keep falling, and to hope for an end of falling, than to stop and think about regaining the upper world. Perhaps if she had stopped very early in her fall, it might not have been too late. Alice tries to imagine herself sitting on top of a cupboard as she looks up and cries for help: her legs dangle against the cupboard doors, she grasps the rim of the cupboard top, she raises her face and shouts for her sister. It occurs to Alice that she has never once cried out, in all her falling; until this moment, when it is too late, the idea has never come to her.

*

Down, down, down: something must be wrong, Alice thinks to herself, for the fall should surely be over by now. And a doubt steals over her, like a cloud shadow over a pool on a summer's day. Did she do the right thing, when she jumped into the rabbit hole? Wasn't she guilty of a certain rashness? Shouldn't she have considered more carefully, before taking such a step? But the leap into the rabbit hole was the same as the leap to her feet beside her sister: it was the final motion of a single impulse, as if she had leaped from the bank directly into the rabbit hole. The mistake was to have jumped up in the first place. Alice tries to recall her feeling of restlessness on the bank, under the tree, beside her sister, but she recalls only the warm, drowsy shade, the sunny field of daisies, the blue, blue sky. Of course, it was the White Rabbit that made her jump up in excitement. But is a rabbit with a waistcoat and watch really so remarkable, when you stop to think about it? Was it really necessary for her to jump up without a moment's hesitation and run off so rashly, without considering anyone's feelings but her own? Her sister will be worried; when she looks up from her book, Alice will be gone; her day will be ruined. And is it possible, Alice thinks to herself, that the rabbit was only the usual sort of rabbit, after all? Is it possible that she had been daydreaming again, there on the bank beside her sister? Alice, doubting, feels a little burst of bitterness in her heart.

*

In the darkness, lit here and there by the dim glow of oil lamps, Alice feels a sudden revulsion: the tunnel walls oppress her, the cupboards bore her to death, she can't stand it for another second—and still she continues falling, past the always rising maps, the pictures, the cupboards, the bookshelves. She can hardly breathe in the dank, close air. It is like a long railway journey, without conversation and without any hope of taking tea. Above, the darkness pushes down on her like a column of stone; below, the darkness sweeps slowly upward, sticking to the dark above, increasing its height and weight. There is absolutely nothing to do. Do cats eat bats? Do bats eat cats? Do rats eat mats? Do blats eat clats? This can't go on much longer, Alice thinks to herself, and opens her mouth to scream, but does not scream.

*

There is no illustration of Alice falling, and so we must imagine the Tenniel drawing: Alice in black and white, falling against a dark background of minute cross-hatchings, upon which we can make out the bottom corner of a cupboard. Alice is wearing black shoes, white stockings with black shading, a white dress and white pinafore. Her long hair is lifted away from her face on both sides; her wide dress billows. Her elbows are held away from her sides and her forearms are held stiffly before her, at different heights; the fingers of the lower hand are spread tensely, the fingers of the upper hand are curved as if she is playing an invisible piano. Under her black eyebrows her black eyes are wide and brooding. The creases of her pinafore are indicated by several series of short parallel lines; the shadow of an arm across her pinafore shows as cross-hatching. In the lower right-hand corner is Tenniel's monogram: a large *T* crossed with a small *J*. The illustration is without a frame, and is fitted into the text in such a way that the words continue down the right-hand side of the drawing for most of the page before stretching across the entire width of the page for the last six lines. Alice is therefore falling alongside the text that describes her fall, and at the same time is enclosed by the text; if she falls any farther, she will bump into words. Pictured in the act of falling, Alice remains motionless: she is fixed forever in her fall.

*

There are four dreams of falling. The first is dreamed by Alice, asleep on the bank with her head in her sister's lap: she dreams of falling down a long vertical tunnel or well. The second is the dream that Alice tells her sister, when falling leaves wake her on the bank: her tale includes the story of the long fall through the dark well. The third is the dream of Alice's sister, alone on the bank, in the setting sun: she dreams of Alice telling her dream, which includes the story of the fall through the dark tunnel. The fourth is Alice's sister's dream of Alice as a grown woman: she dreams of grown-up Alice telling the dream of Wonderland to little children gathered about her. Alice is therefore caught in a circle of dream-falls: no sooner does she wake than she begins to fall again down the dark tunnel, as she recounts her dream to her sister, and no sooner does she run off to tea than she begins to fall again, in her sister's dream; and even as a grown woman she is still falling through the dark, as the bright-eyed children look up at her with eager faces. It appears, then, that Alice can never escape from her dream: once she plunges into the rabbit hole, once she leaves the safe, predictable world of her sister, she can never return; once she starts to fall, she can never stop falling.

*

Down, down, down: Alice tries not to be unhappy, for what would be the use of *that*, but as she falls she bursts into sudden tears. "Come," Alice says to herself rather sharply, "there's no use in crying like that!" And no sooner has she spoken than she stops crying, for Alice always tries to listen to her own advice. She wipes her cheeks with the backs of her hands; a few tears drip from her chin, and Alice ignores them as she falls past a closed cupboard with six tiles over the doors. The tiles show rustic figures in sepia, blue, and black: a shepherd resting under a tree, a boy in a stream, a girl feeding tame rabbits, a woman and child resting from collecting sticks, a seated girl with goat and kid, and a young woman carrying a pail across a stream. The cupboard vanishes into the upper dark, and Alice, glancing down, sees a curious sight: in the air directly under her chin there are three tears, falling as she falls. For a while she watches the tears, pressing her chin against her neck and frowning down to see them; then she lifts out the handkerchief in her pinafore pocket and carefully wipes away the tears, as if she is erasing them.

*

If only, Alice thinks to herself, I weren't so tired! If only I could rest! For it's tiring to be always falling, falling down the rabbit hole. Alice wonders if it is possible to rest awhile. She doesn't want to catch hold of a cupboard or bookshelf, for fear of bringing it down; and in any case, to hang against a wall with your legs resting on air is hardly Alice's idea of a proper way to rest. Indeed, the act of falling requires no effort; Alice is puzzled why she should be tired of doing something that requires no effort. Is it possible that the fall itself is a rest? Alice tries to imagine what it would be like to sit on a chair as she falls. It would be very pleasant, she thinks, to curl up in a corner of a great armchair and close her eyes. But would there be room for an armchair in the narrow tunnel? Wouldn't it knock against the cupboard doors? And if she should fall asleep, and tumble out of the armchair, what then? But if she tumbled out of the armchair, wouldn't she simply fall through the air, as she is doing now? Again Alice feels that she is growing confused, and she decides to rest by raising her hands, interlocking her fingers, and leaning her cheek on her clasped hands. For a while she falls this way, with her eyes closed and her head resting lightly on her hands.

*

As in a dream, Alice remembers: she was sitting on the bank beside her sister. It was hot, even in the shade. Her legs hurt from sitting on the ground, her stockings itched, a gnat kept bumping against her hair. Her sister sat motionless over her book and refused to look up—even her fingers gripping the edges of the book were motionless, like table legs with claws gripping a ball, and her neck was bent in a tense, unnatural way, which meant that she didn't want to be disturbed in her reading. The grass was tickly and sharp. Alice's skin itched, but she also felt an inner itching, as if all her bones needed to be scratched. Of course she loved her sister dearly, but just at that moment she would have liked to pick up a stone and crush her sister in the eyes. She was a wicked girl, to have thoughts like that. Her brain felt hot. Her ankles itched. Her blood itched. She felt that at any moment she was going to split open, like a seed pod. That was when, she remembers, she heard the noise in the grass.

*

Alice, raising her head abruptly, suddenly thinks of the White Rabbit: she had seen it pop down the rabbit hole and had gone down after it. He must therefore be under her, falling as she is falling. Of course, Alice reflects, it's possible that she alone has fallen down this endless well, while the White Rabbit has remained high above, in the tunnel-like part of the rabbit hole before the sudden drop. It's also possible that the White Rabbit has fallen much more swiftly than she, and has long ago come to the bottom, if there *is* a bottom. But Alice doesn't recall any other opening in the tunnel-like part of the rabbit hole; and the maps, the cupboards, the bookshelves all suggest a familiar, much-frequented portion of the White Rabbit's home. And then, there is actually no reason to think that the White Rabbit should fall more quickly than she. It is therefore very likely that the White Rabbit is just below her, falling in the dark; and so certain does her reasoning strike her that, looking down into the dark, she seems to see a faint motion there, in the blackness through which she is already passing.

*

Why, of course, Alice thinks to herself: the White Rabbit lives here. I am falling through the White Rabbit's home. Why hadn't she thought of it just that way before? But what a curious sort of home it was—more like a chimney, really. Alice has never heard of a chimney with maps and cupboards on the walls; it would never do to start a fire here. Is it perhaps an entrance hall? But what sort of entrance hall can it be, with no place to leave your visiting card and no stand to put your umbrella in? Is it a stairway, then? Alice wonders whether a stairway must have stairs in it, in order to be a stairway. And as she continues falling she looks with sudden interest, as if searching for a clue, at the crowded walls, where she sees a glass-covered engraving of two dogs fighting over the nest of a heron; a wall bracket shaped like a swan with lifted wings, supporting a marble stat-uette of Whittington Listening to the Bells of London: he is seated on a block carved with the word WHITTINGTON, his right hand is raised, his forefinger is pointing up, his head is cocked to one side; and a marble shelf holding a clock: the round dial is set in a dark blue porcelain vase surmounted by two white porcelain angels, and the vase rests on a pediment decorated with pink porcelain flowers. On the pediment, on each side of the vase, sits a naked child with flowers in his lap; one child holds up a butterfly, the other clutches an arrow. The hands are pointing to 2:05, and Alice wonders, as she falls past, whether the time is the same as the time on the bank, under the tree, where her sister sits reading, or whether it is some other time.

*

Falling through darkness, Alice imagines herself rising: past the clock, past the bottle of ginger beer, past the shield-shaped mirror, where she sees her hair pressed to the sides of her head, past the cupboard with the jar of raspberry jam, past so many shelves and maps and pictures that they begin to slide into each other like the dissolving views in the Polytechnic, higher and higher, until she reaches the place where the horizontal tunnel begins—and pulling herself onto the path, she makes her way through the dark toward a distant lightness, which reveals itself suddenly as the opening of the rabbit hole. Alice climbs out of the hole under the hedge into the brilliant day. Sunlight burns down on the field. The sky is the troubling blue of stained-glass windows or magic lantern slides. Across a field of knee-high grass she sees her sister reading a book on a sloping bank in the shade of a beech tree. The beech, the bank, the sister are very still, as if they are made of porcelain. Alice runs across the field with her hair streaming out behind her and comes to the shady bank. All is still. Her sister does not move, does not raise her eyes from the book. Over the far fields the bright blue sky burns down. All is still.

*

On her sister's lap, Alice lies dreaming. Leafshadows move on her face and arms. She is far from the long grass bending in the wind, from the pool rippling to the waving of the reeds, from the sheep bells tinkling, the cries of the shepherd boy, the lowing of the cows in the distance. Alice's sister doesn't want to disturb her sleep and sits very still in the warm shade of the bank. It is a hot, drowsy day. When Alice fell asleep, Alice's sister continued reading for a while, but now she has laid the book aside on the grass, for she is feeling a little sleepy herself, and it's difficult to read for very long without changing the position of your arm and hands, which she doesn't wish to do for fear of waking Alice. She watches Alice breathing gently in and out. Strands of hair lie rippling over Alice's cheek and shoulder; a single hair, escaping from the rest, curves across her cheek and lies at the corner of her mouth. Her forehead is smooth, but a slight tension shows between the eyebrows, which are darker than her hair: Alice is closed deeply in sleep. In the warm shade her sister feels drowsy, but she knows she must not sleep: she must watch over Alice, here on the shady bank. Sleep is strange, Alice's sister thinks to herself: you are there and not there. Alice seems far away, like a princess in a tower. Alice's sister would like to pick up her book again, but her hand remains motionless; she would like to shift her position, for her left leg is beginning to tingle, but she does not move. It is very quiet. Are we mistaken to see in the brightness and stillness of this afternoon an echo of the afternoon on the Isis? In the brightness a darkness forms: the tunnel is a shadow cast by the sunny day. May we perhaps think of a story as an internal shadow, a leap into the dark? In a distant field, cows are lowing. Under a shady tree, Alice's sister keeps watch. Deeply Alice lies sleeping.

*

A long, low hall lit by a row of oil lamps hanging from the ceiling. A row of many doors, evenly spaced, all around the hall. In the middle of the hall a small three-legged table made of glass: a tiny gold key lies on top. On the right-hand wall, a dark red curtain hanging to the floor. Behind the curtain, but not yet visible, a small door about fifteen inches high. Behind the small door, a garden of bright flowers and cool fountains. In the left-hand wall, rear, an opening: the entrance to a dark corridor or passage. The long passage leads to an unseen heap of sticks and dry leaves. Above the heap, a shaft, well, or vertical tunnel, stretching up into blackness.

*

Alice, falling, imagines that the tunnel comes to an end in a heap of sticks and dry leaves. In the instant that her foot touches the first stick, she realizes two things: that the tunnel does not exist, and that she is about to wake up with her head in her sister's lap. And indeed, already through the black wall she can see a shimmer of sun, the cupboards and maps are growing translucent, she can hear the tinkle of sheep bells in the fields. With a sharp, sudden motion of her mind she banishes the heap of sticks and dry leaves. And as when, in a darkened room, a heavy church or stone bridge becomes airy and impalpable, staining your hand with color as you pass your arm through the magic lantern's beam of dust-swirling light, so Alice's foot passes soundlessly through the heap of sticks and dry leaves, and she continues falling. Is it possible, Alice wonders, to resist the tug of the upper world, which even now, as she falls in darkness, entices her to wake? For should she wake, she would find herself on the bank, with itching bones, beside her sister, who will still be reading her book without pictures or conversations. Alice wonders whether it is possible to fall out of the bottom of a dream, into some deeper place. She would like to fall far, very far, so far that she will separate herself forever from the dreamer above, by whose waking she doesn't wish to be disturbed. Have they anything in common, really? Sooner or later the girl in her sister's lap will wake and rub her eyes. And in that moment she will sweep away the tunnel walls, the cupboards, the maps, the dark, replacing them with the tree, the book, the sun-dappled shade. But for dream-Alice the tree, the book, the sun-dappled shade are only a trembling and shimmering, a vanishing—for here there are only the hard walls of the tunnel, the solid shelves, the glistening glass jars, the lifted hair, the wind of her slow falling. And who's to say, Alice thinks to herself, that one's more a dream than the other? And is it possible, Alice wonders, that she will stop falling only when she releases herself utterly from the upper world, with its flickers of sunlight, its murmur of sheep bells, its green-blue shimmer of field and sky? Then in her toes she will feel the tingle of the end of falling. And with a sense of urgency, as if only now has she begun to fall, Alice bends her mind downward toward the upstreaming dark, looking expectantly at a map showing the Division of English Land by the Peace of 886 A.D. between King Alfred and the Danes, at a shelf on which sits a glass-domed arrangement of artificial leaves and flowers composed of knitting wool stitched over wire frames, at a painting in a carved gilt frame: in a parlor window-nook a woman with her hair parted in the middle is sitting in a maroon armchair with buttoned upholstery and an exposed frame of polished mahogany; in her lap she holds knitting needles and the beginning of a

gray shawl, but her hands are idle, she is looking out the window; one gray strand leads to a ball of yarn on the floor, where
a black kitten with green eyes and tilted head lifts one paw as if
to strike the yarn-ball; the room is dark brown, but sunlight
pours through the open window; in the yard stand blossoming
apple trees; through the trees we see glimpses of a sun-flooded
field; a brown stream, glinting with sunlight, winds like a path
into the shimmering distance, vanishes into a dark wood.

The Invention of Robert Herendeen

I

I trace the origin of my perilous gift to an idle morning in the fourth grade. I was seated at my desk before an open geography book with double columns of small print. A gray photograph in one corner showed a banana tree with a sharply focused trunk and high, blurred fruit. In front of me sat Diana Cerino. For a while I studied her complicated black hair and her two raspberry-red barrettes, one of which was tilted at a disturbing angle. I considered how I might go about fixing it without attracting her attention, but already I was losing interest in Diana Cerino's barrette and in fact her entire existence and was wishing I'd bought one of the pink rubber balls I had seen that morning at Rappoport's candy store in a shallow box next to the cash register. The box held a tightly packed layer of fifteen identical pink rubber balls arranged in three rows of five. A second layer of eight pink rubber balls rested neatly on the depressions formed by each group of four adjacent balls in the first layer. On the very top, where there was room for three more balls, sat a single pink rubber ball, king of the mountain. The balls cost fifteen cents apiece and I had exactly fifteen cents in my pocket but I had needed time to make up my mind. Now my desire for the unbought ball made me tense and irritable. The minute hand of the big round clock prepared for its jump but did not jump. I sometimes wondered about those clocks. Did time just stop during those suspended moments and then pass in a rush? Was an hour a kind of corpse that sat up with a grin once a minute, only to collapse again with its arms folded on its chest? Was my entire life going to consist of blank stretches of deadness punctuated by feverish rushes? The pink rubber ball would have sat very nicely on the pencil trough between my yellow pencil and the inkwell. Desperately I desired that ball. I saw its precise shade of dark pink, the hair-breadth raised line that encircled the ball and divided it exactly in two, the black, stamped star. I could smell a faint pink rubbery aroma, I felt a bursting sensation in my brain, and there, seated in my pencil trough between my yellow pencil and the inkwell . . . Ghostly and translucent, it seemed to be trembling slightly. I could see the dim glow of the overhead lights at the top of its smooth pink roundness, shading to darker pink toward the bottom. A peachlike pink bloom dusted the surface. Already my palm tingled in anticipation—but the minute hand jumped, Diana Cerino creaked in her seat, the phantom ball rolled from the desk, dropped to the floor, bounced silently away . . .

My name is Robert Herendeen. But really, should I continue? And here let me say that I begin this report against the grain of my own better nature, for I've never cared for the confessional tone so dear to our contemporary romantics. If in the course of this rigorous record I happen to bring forth my own feelings, it is I hope never for their own sake but solely for the sake of those other phenomena which I propose to examine in the clear light of—the clear light of!—and which, even now, when I look back on them—but this sentence is already quite long enough.

I was a precocious dreamer. At the age of one I lay in my crib and saw forest paths winding among fat trees full of cupboards and stairways. At five I imagined detailed houses with many-paned windows and precise fireplaces, all of which mocked the conventional squares with rectangle roofs that alone my childish fingers could manage. Yes, even then I was aware of the painful rift between the vivid images my mind created and the mediocre drawings, clay figures, and stories that I brought to birth in the material world—always to the hysterical praise of some aunt or schoolteacher, who would raise her clasped hands to her throat in an ecstasy of admiration. In the second grade I imagined a story that would fill many volumes and take up an entire shelf in the library, but somehow I never progressed beyond the first chapter. I invented wonderful toys that I never knew how to embody in actual wood or metal. One day in the fourth grade I saw on my desk a pink rubber ball but did not yet understand its meaning. I was very good at making detailed maps of South America and Australia, though I was reproached for my tendency to insert an eccentric twist of coastline here, a little green island just over there. I was well liked by my classmates and received A in everything, but my sense of secret failure was so sharp that I felt stunned with sorrow.

With the onset of adolescence my powers of imagination, so lively and varied during childhood, took a conventional turn. My sexual fantasies were precise, obsessive, and inaccurate. I was particularly fond of imagining the slow, the very slow, the dreamily slow raising of a dark wool skirt or light summer dress to reveal pastel underpants molding themselves to disturbing bulges. I imagined that girls were quite smooth under there, like rubber dolls, until one day a schoolmate with a beet-colored birthmark on his jaw carefully unfolded a wrinkled photograph. After that I imagined prodigious growths, exuberant and impossible burgeonings. In high school I amused myself by mentally removing the skirts and slips of girls who stood writing on the blackboard. I waited for them to turn, to look at the entire class seated in suspenseful silence, to begin to realize . . . but they never did, those brazen girls, they just brushed the chalk from their fingers and ambled back to their seats with that little

tick-tock motion of hips as if nothing had happened. One evening in the winter of senior year I placed my right hand on the
bare upper thigh beneath the charcoal-gray skirt of Carol Ed-
mondston. She looked thoughtful, as if she were trying to remember an address. That spring I took up oil painting without
success and planned with a friend a long summer trip that never
materialized.

I went to a good but remote Eastern college and there, amid
the hills and snows of northern New England, I became a serious student. I declared myself an idealist, despised all intellectual
endeavor tainted by the practical, and double-majored in English and Philosophy, both of which I chose because they bore
no relation whatever to actual life. I spent fourteen hours a day
in the library and soon earned the respect of my professors, a
fact that only heightened my sense of secret failure. About this
time my first headaches began. One night in the spring of junior
year I undressed Celia Ann Hodges on her oval braided rug
during a romantic thunderstorm and was forced to make certain
adjustments in the imaginary women who haunted my mind.
In the summer between junior and senior year I wrote in ten
weeks the draft of a six-hundred-page novel (ten pages a day,
six days a week) but for some reason stopped at the end of the
penultimate chapter and never completed it. In November, December, and January of senior year I began a comedy, a tragedy,
and a tragicomedy, respectively, all three of which I destroyed
one night during spring break. Shortly afterward I received
Highest Honors for my senior thesis, "The Role of Metaphor
in the Philosophy of Locke." On the night before graduation I
stayed up till dawn explaining to a girl I had met at midnight
that great work can be accomplished only in solitude, and the
next day, an hour after returning my cap and gown, I traveled
by train to my family home in southern Connecticut.

My father, pleased by my good grades but troubled by the
vagueness of my plans, had agreed to let me live at home for a
year before I went to law school or business school or took

some job or other or did something, anything. I moved into the spare room in the attic and threw myself into several ambitious literary projects, which soon came to nothing. I began to invent a series of artists' lives that I planned to assemble in a book of fictional biographies, but one night I noticed that all of them were failed artists and I abruptly abandoned the plan. By mid-August I was going to bed at five in the morning and waking at one in the afternoon. I began reading long books, which fired my ambition without leading to anything in particular: *The Anatomy of Melancholy*, *The Decline and Fall of the Roman Empire*, the complete letters of Byron in twelve volumes. By October I was sullen and irritable. I refused to apply to graduate school, stating to my father that I would rather hang myself than enter a finishing school for mediocrity. My father said that I couldn't hang myself without a rope and that a rope cost money. My father's ironic attitude caused a coolness between us but he did not press matters after that. I began borrowing books on architecture from the library and invented in vivid detail gorgeous villas, gardens, palaces, country estates, amusement parks. On December 31 I wrote a thirty-four-page suicide note that I destroyed on January 1. In the spring I left home to work in a bookstore in a small town near my college and returned a month later with the plan for an American epic in fifty cantos, one for each state. My father agreed to support me for one more year if I promised to apply to business school in the fall. I returned to my attic life. The book came to nothing and I took up the study of Latin and Italian. At this period I began to have dull, gentle, persistent headaches, nothing bad, not really, but definitely noticeable. One warm spring night an exhilarating idea came to me.

In the week before my idea I had been puzzling over a problem. It seemed to me that a distinction should be made between two types of artistic sterility. In one type, the imagination remains a horrible blank, its mechanism simply refuses to create images, or else produces hopelessly banal or dead ones, greenish little corpses with waxen features. Would-be artists suffering from this form of sterility can do nothing but admit defeat, turning their attention to less exacting pursuits or perhaps shooting themselves between the eyes, as the case may be. In the second type, the imagination remains strong, perhaps too strong, and the sufferer's torment consists in his inability to embody his meticulous imaginings in a medium. This type, though superficially resembling the first, since both issue in nothingness, is nevertheless far more hopeful, for its cure depends on the discovery and mastery of a medium. My own case was clearly of the second type, since my image-making faculty, far from being impaired, was almost disturbingly strong and resulted in vivid, detailed, elaborate eidola, which longed for release.

My parents' house stood about a mile from a small public beach where I sometimes strolled at night. On the warm spring night when my idea came to me I was walking on the hard sand below the ragged line of mussel shells, cracked crabshells, and seaweed. The brilliant moon, much too round, gleamed in the wet flat sand by the water's edge. I thought of my uncertain future, my failed past, my oddly becalmed present—cast up as I was in the attic of my father's house—my restlessness, my wistfulness, my inner riot mixed with outer calm, my headaches, my eyeaches, my sense of not yet having entered into my proper adulthood combined with my sense of being eighty-seven years old, my rancor, my languor, my soul-soreness, my sighs. I was beginning to enjoy this list and wondered whether I could extend it indefinitely when all at once I felt tired, immensely tired, as if I had not slept in a long time. It occurred to me that I hadn't really slept well for a long time, even as a child I was a terrible sleeper, the slightest noise startled me awake. By this time I had come to an abandoned lifeguard chair and in obedience to an obscure impulse I began climbing up the side in order to sit looking out over the moonlit water with a melancholy expression. It was as I was climbing up the side that my idea came to me and I reached the top in a state of high excitement. I decided to invent a human being by means of the full and rigorous application of my powers of imagination. Instead of resorting to words, which merely obscured and distorted the crystalline clarity of my inner vision, I would employ the stuff of imagination itself. That is to say, I would mentally mold a being whose existence would be sustained by the detail and energy of my relentless dreaming. My ambition was to create not an actual human being or a mere work of art but rather a being who existed in a realm parallel to the other two—a third realm, obedient to the laws of physical bodies but utterly discarnate.

I hadn't expected my task to be an easy one, in fact I distrusted all forms of work accomplished without difficulty, but within a week I was snappish with failure. In my effort to be rigorous I had proceeded step by step, from the inside out, in the manner of a painter who imagines the musculature beneath the skin, but what I achieved was only a heap of dead parts—a rib cage, a pile of twisting bluish-red arteries, a carefully molded heel shading into vagueness. What I needed was something else, something else entirely. One night I thought of the name Olivia. At once an image formed. Silently she hovered before my imagination's eye. There were vague places here and there, her hair was uncertain, I knew nothing about her knees, her nose, her history, but these were matters that I could attend to at leisure.

Leisure! Well, I suppose so. But from that moment I knew no peace, only the obscure ecstasy of creation. I made elementary errors, revised my mistakes, pushed on. Despite my vivid sexual imaginings in adolescence and beyond, despite Celia Ann Hodges, I had never made the attempt to visualize a girl or woman or any human being in exhaustive detail. I spent two nights and two days imagining her hands, summoning them out of vagueness into the precision of being. On the third night I realized that I had still failed to envision the exact pattern of veins on the back of each hand, the movements of the skin between the fingers, the intricate configuration of creases on each reddish knuckle. It seemed to me that only by an act of fanatical precision could I knit her into existence, rescue her from the continual tug of vagueness that is only one step removed from nothingness. I lavished a ferocity of attention on her eyelids, the folds and shadows of her ears, the muscles of her neck. Her clothes proved unexpectedly difficult to see precisely: the puckers of skirt at the waist, the arrangement of threads in the front and back of a button, the system of creases in the sleeve of a moving arm. Although she had appeared to me in a rather demure costume—dark blue denim skirt reaching to her knees, plain white cotton blouse with small transparent buttons—I rejected the temptations of modesty and applied to her breasts, her thighs, the folds of her vulva, the coloring and structure of her buttocks, the same rigor of attention that I applied to her eyebrows and toes.

Sometimes, in weariness, I removed my attention from her to contemplate some peaceful inner landscape. Then I returned in alarm to find odd gaps and distortions in her, as if without my sustained attention she tended toward dissolution. One night she walked from my desk to my reading chair and sat down; I realized that I had failed to imagine the precise system of motions that constitute a human walk, and threw myself into new feats of arduous imagining. Errors repeatedly erupted. One night when she walked from my attic room down two flights of stairs to the living room, I realized that I had been careless in managing her stair-by-stair descent, permitting her to fade away and reappear in the manner of a trite ghost.

It was these fadings, these absences of attention, that I found most difficult to overcome, in the laborious weeks that followed; and as the nights grew warmer, and through my attic window I smelled the dark green scents of summer and heard the shouts of children, the clang of a bell, the rush of roller skates on driveways, the soft *thunk thunk* of a dribbled basketball, I had the sense of being borne up by all the rich blue summer night and carried toward a far, desired shore.

On the night of July 16 my work was done. In the center of my dark room the unlit standing lamp with the bent brass neck stood looking down at the leather pad of my crowded desk. The cracked leather desk-chair where I had been sitting was partly turned to one side. I was lying on the bed by the double window, beneath the drawn blinds that reached to the bottom of the slightly raised windowframe. Bits of moonlight entered through the edges of the blinds and polished a leg of the mahogany desk, a few brass buttons in the back of the leather chair, a coffee cup resting on a book. She stood at the side of the desk, resting one carefully veined hand on a corner. She was gazing toward a window. Suddenly she lifted her other hand and swept a piece of hair back over an ear. It was a gesture we had practiced many times. Beneath the white cotton sleeve of her lifted arm I knew that a long vein in her forearm pressed through the skin and curved toward the inner bend of her elbow. Her nostrils tensed at the sound of a distant car; a faint breathing was audible. Perhaps it was a memory of the last feverish and draining months, perhaps it was the clarity of her presence there, perhaps it was the sense of a long task carried to fulfillment, anyway I felt in my chest a deep upwelling, my nose burned, my eyes prickled, and turning my face away I paid Olivia the dark homage of my tears.

II

I ask myself: was there a flaw, a little fatal flaw? Was there at the very outset an error in conception or construction that by the operation of unalterable laws was bound to bring my work to a disastrous end? Without arrogance I think I may answer: No. Oh, there may have been some very minor lapse here or there, some lack of precise imagining that spoke of Olivia's kinship with all that is unshaped and unborn, but the vividness, the clarity, of her being was beyond all doubt. Indeed I would

argue that insofar as our existence is confirmed or strengthened
by our presence in a mind outside our own, her existence was
far richer than that of the beings we call human. For we are
imagined carelessly and in patches, you and I, we're ghosts and
phantoms all, fading away and reappearing at the whim of amateur imaginers, whereas Olivia—well, Olivia was imagined
with an artist's passionate exactitude. And just as the enticing
vividness of a painting or statue derives in part from the intensity of our attention, so the creature I had pressed forth night
after night from the malleable stuff of my imagination flourished by virtue of the accumulated acts of attention that I had
lavished upon her. Then why, at the very moment of my
triumph, did I feel a twist of anxiety?

For I was anxious, I won't deny it. Slowly, night after night,
I had brought my creature into being, and in the consuming
passion of my task I hadn't given much thought to exactly what
was to become of her. The artist sells his painting, or leans the
unsold canvas solidly against the unyielding wall. The writer
multiplies his creatures in editions of many thousands, or perhaps places his heavy typescript, bound in black, in the bottom
drawer of his desk where in its slowly spun cocoon of dust it
grows secret rainbow wings as it prepares to burst forth into
the light of posterity's dazzling day. But what of those who
summon into existence a being of the third realm? Aye, what of
us? Do you think it's easy for us, we solitary ones, we attic
dwellers and noontime dreamers, with the mark of midnight on
our brow? In the nights that followed it seemed to me that
Olivia looked at me with a questioning gaze. Of course she
didn't just stand there always. I liked to send her off on little
journeys into the midnight streets of my town, where she could
walk unnoticed and undisturbed. But it was precisely these early
wanderings that impressed on me a certain aimlessness in her
way of life, and led me to construct for her a wondrous dwelling.

I chose the stretch of woodland at the north end of town

beyond the park and the new shopping center. There, drawing
on my architectural studies of a year ago, I built a many-roomed
mansion in the full mad flower of late-nineteenth-century eclec-
ticism, complete with towers and cross gables, Gothic windows
with heavy drip-moldings, Italianate scrolled brackets under the
projecting eaves. I laid the grounds with an overgrown English
garden containing meandering paths, dim pools, and moldering
statues. The images came with surprising swiftness, as if I had
already created them and were now simply permitting them to
realize their nature. The extravagance of it all struck me as
peculiarly suitable for Olivia. For wasn't it expressive of a secret
extravagance in her nature that I had suspected from the beginning, despite her air of detachment? In any case Olivia now had
a home to go to when she wasn't with me or wandering alone
through the streets of the town. She lived there with her handsome but solitary father who designed intricate electronic equip-
ment and had a passion for chess problems, classic military
battles, and cryptic crossword puzzles, and her rather dim
mother who played the piano and was rumored to rise at noon.
There was also a sickly grandmother with uncombed white hair
who visited for months at a time and rarely left her room. They
had a housekeeper, a Mrs. Nelson, who came every Thursday.
In addition to her bedroom on the second floor, Olivia had a
tower room all to herself, where she liked to read. No one paid
much attention to Olivia, who came and went as she pleased,
took occasional part-time jobs that she always quit within two
weeks, read long Russian novels while drinking tea with honey,
and appeared to be waiting for something.

At this period I was leading an extremely solitary life. I stayed
up all night, went to bed at six or seven in the morning, and
slept until three in the afternoon. I avoided my parents as much
as possible and began eating dinner alone in the kitchen long
after they were through. These strategies, developed at first to
enable me to proceed undisturbed with my various projects,
now permitted me to spend a great deal of time with Olivia.

She was particularly vivid to me after eleven o'clock, when my parents went to bed and the whole summer night lay open before us. I would imagine her opening the front screen door and the front wooden door, making her way through the moonlit living room past the mahogany bookcase, past the round mahogany table with the old chain-pull lamp . . . Or I would creep down the attic stairs and down the carpeted stairs and through the moonlit living room into the warm dark-blue summer night. Olivia would be waiting for me. I would see her sitting in the front yard against a fencepost that divided her face into moonlight and shadow, or perhaps waiting around a corner under a sugar maple. And we would set off on a long, detailed, scrupulously imagined walk.

All streets pleased us: the ranch house neighborhood with its rows of identical basketball posts that cast long precise shadows ending in parallelograms, the rural lanes shaded by tall syca-mores and Norway maples, the small center of town with its red and yellow window displays: a basket of cheeses wrapped in bright green cellophane, a luminous arrangement of volley-balls and gleaming tennis rackets and exercise bikes, a watch rising and falling in a glass of water, a mannequin with tight black curls, yellow bikini, and silver sunglasses. Olivia studied these displays avidly. She liked to seek out some incongruous detail, like the white plastic spoon resting on the shiny black seat of an exercise bike. She always waited till the last moment before ducking into doorways at the approach of car lights, a habit that made me uneasy; my uneasiness made her impatient. I was calmer on dark rural roads in the north part of town, where crickets shrilled in the long spaces of dark between the light-pools of solitary streetlights. It was understood between us that I was in love with Olivia and that she did not love anyone.

One hot evening as I lay on my bed in the dark and awaited the adventures of the night, I heard a faintly creaking footstep on the attic stairs. I sat up instantly. It was much too early for

Olivia, who at that very moment was brushing her hair on the other side of town with a tortoiseshell hairbrush that had recently sprung into existence. The hairbrush bothered me. I didn't like things springing into existence, but there it was and I couldn't get rid of it. Another footstep sounded. It was unheard of for my mother or father to intrude on my privacy. After a pause there was another footstep higher up, and in this intermittent and ghostly manner the footsteps ascended, sometimes creaking and sometimes failing to creak, as if the climber were fading in and out of existence. As I imagined the foot rising to the topmost stair in preparation for entering the cold part of the attic, there was a startling knock on the door. "Come in!" I half shouted. The door stuck in the jamb, hesitated, and flew open.

Framed by attic light, my shadowy father loomed in the doorway. He was smoking his curved pipe and wearing his robe and slippers. The room was dark except for the light coming from the open door, and as my father hesitated I said, "I wasn't asleep, just resting. You can turn on the—"

"I wouldn't dream of it," he said dryly, shuffling forward in the half-dark and stepping over books standing in knee-high piles on the ragged rug. A pile of books toppled softly but my father kept coming.

"I see you're working," he remarked. "No, don't get up, I'll be only a minute. There?" He pointed with his pipe at the shadowy armchair wedged into a corner near the head of the bed. He sat down heavily, removed his pipe, and looked down at the bowl. I could hear him breathing heavily from his climb. "I'm afraid what I have to say is drearily predictable." He thrust the pipe into his mouth and sucked rapidly, covering and uncovering the bowl with two fingers. "Terrible draw. You wouldn't happen to have a pipe cleaner. Never mind." He removed the pipe from his mouth, brought it close to his eye, and lowered it to his knee. "Trite scene, the elderly father admonishing his wayward son. However. I want you to come to a

definite decision about your future. I have no objection to supporting your"—here he made a fluttering motion with one
hand—"curious way of life, but I cannot do so indefinitely. I
understand of course that there are more things in heaven and
earth than are dreamt of in my philosophy. I certainly hope so.
But it isn't so much my philosophy I'm thinking of as my
bankbook. You don't happen to have a match. Deuce take it.
Never mind. Your mother and I are in agreement, a remarkable
fact in itself and one worth pondering. Sooner or later you're
going to have to make your own way in the world and I suggest
you give the matter some serious thought. Fortunately for you,
my pipe has gone out. Bear in mind that this interview is as
disagreeable to me as it is to you. It is, however, over. Oof,
these old bones. No no, please. Sit still. I prefer to be thought
of as a ghost. Well then, Rob. Have a profitable evening, or
should I say morning. Life is—well, yes: life. Night."

Slowly he shuffled from the room, stepping with exaggerated
care over bookpiles and strewn underwear. In the light of the
doorway he looked massive and wild. A thick ruff of iron-gray
hair circled his skull. I listened to his footsteps creaking intermittently down the attic stairs.

Now this was a triply unwelcome intrusion. In the first place,
I had been looking forward eagerly to my night of roaming
with Olivia, and my attention was now scattered. In the second
place, I had carefully put aside the tedious consideration of my
ludicrous future. And in the third place, I hadn't been paying
much attention to my aging father, whose sudden appearance
struck me with all the force of a haunting. He had been more or
less reasonable with me, in his ironic way—a brilliant maneuver, for it had undermined my capacity to feel indignation.

That night Olivia was waiting for me in one of the Scotch
pines in the side yard. She climbed down, shaking the branches,
and brushed the needles from her blouse and skirt. Olivia was
like that: despite her quietness, her air of remoteness, she had
bursts of mischievous gaiety. "This is for you, Robert," she

said, and handed me a pinecone. I was unused to her voice, which struck me as a little ghostly. "And this is for me." She thrust a pinecone in her hair. "Tonight I'd like to go to—oh, Paris. Why don't we go to Paris? That way." She pointed down the road. Her playful mood unnerved me, and fevered me too, for she had more dash and daring than I; that night we wandered farther than ever before, beyond the parkway at the north end of town, and returned only when the streetlamps grew pale against the graying of the sky.

Am I understood? Am I? To be with Olivia was for me a serene exhilaration, a fierce peacefulness. Our intimacy was that which only a creator and creature can know. Unable to imagine my life without her, I began to wait for her each night with a harsh, a hectic impatience that only her appearance could soothe away.

Sometimes an uneasiness came over me. Lying on my bed with one arm bent behind my neck, I would stare at my dark piles of books, my desolate desk, my disastrous life. Then when I pushed aside the blinds, the lustrous moon in the dark blue summer night would turn to cigarette ash, the velvety night sky would be the color of bruises and decay, my trafficking in forbidden creations would be a knifeblade twisting in my temple: and as if nourished by hopelessness, invigorated by despair, all the more fervently Olivia and I would hurl ourselves into the pathways of the unchanging summer night. Have I discussed my headaches?

By headache I do not mean the sharp pain at the side or back of the head, or perhaps behind an eye, the banal consequence of conventional stress. No, I have in mind the headache that is a band of metal tightening around the bones of the skull. I have in mind the inner blossom of fire, leaving behind charred and smoking places. And let us not forget the ratlike nibbling headache that gnaws its way slowly through the soft white sweet matter of the brain until it presses its furred back against the inside of the cranium, nor the fabulous winged headache with brilliant red and green feathers and gold-black claws that clutch and squeeze while the heavy wings beat faster and faster, nor the many-branched headache, the thornbush headache that swells and swells to fill the entire skull, pushing its glistening thorns against the soft backs of the eyes until the branches burst through the bloody eye sockets—such are the headaches that must be distinguished from those others, for these are creation's dark sisters, shadows of the brilliant dream. Shall we continue?

One night Olivia was lingering in town before a display of soup cans in a variety-store window that glowed now red, now green, now red, now green, to the rhythm of a desperately bored stoplight. My headache glowed now red, now green, and as I urged her to come away, please come away, away from all this, I was startled to see a figure emerge from a nearby door-way and approach us. This had never happened before and I felt a constriction in my chest as if some vital organ were being squeezed by a malign hand. Olivia turned without surprise. She introduced us. I disliked him immediately, but really, dislike is too gentle a term for that inner quivering, that intimate raw red tickle of revulsion as if all one's nerve endings were trembling in the stream of an unwholesome effluence. This Orville—Orville!—came smiling up to us. I saw at once that it was a mock-ing smile. The very set of his slouched shoulders was insolent. "What a pleasant surprise," he said, with deliberate falseness. He was tall and thin and paper-pale, and would have been gaunt were it not for a disturbing fleshiness about him: plumpish soft hands, a softness about his chin, even a little potbelly that pressed through his shirt. He wore faded bluejeans and old run-ning shoes and a soiled white dress-shirt. He reminded me of a soft white tuber growing secretly in moist soil. "Olivia has told me so much about you," he continued. "Actually she's never mentioned you. What did you say your name was? Harold?"

"We were just going," I remarked.

"Then I'll join you," he said and walked alongside Olivia, standing too close to her. "Ah, the night! What would we do without it? It's a wonderful invention. Youth, clair de lune, dreamlike distortion, spiritual transfiguration—even death. They start you off with 'Twinkle Twinkle, Little Star' and before you know it you're crooning '*O sink hernieder, Nacht der Liebe!*' Match?" He reached into his shirt pocket and drew out half a cigarette.

He was, Olivia informed me when he had left (abruptly, with mocking bow), the son of a friend of a friend of her mother's. He had driven his mother and her friend to Olivia's mother's house one night, in order to have use of the family car, and on his return he had seen Olivia on the stairs. "Nice painting," he had remarked, jerking his thumb at her. "Is it an original?" Since then he had shown up a few times, asking for Olivia; she had spoken to him once, indifferently. This brief, unsatisfactory history, the episode of our meeting, his disagreeable name, in fact everything about him filled me with irritable unease. My instinctive, brutal revulsion wasn't simply a response to his physical person, his mockery, his air of knowing some unsavory secret he was itching to reveal, his whole spiritual bag of tricks, but to something else that I found difficult to define but that revealed itself more clearly on later occasions.

Later occasions, did I say? Yes, later occasions—there were plenty of those. Night after night he would pop out at us from behind some maple trunk or lamppost and join us in our wanderings. Under the pressure of his presence the nights changed shape, became sadly deformed. Orville was by nature an intruder, a violator, and it showed in his slightest gestures: he leaped up to rip down handfuls of maple leaves, leaned over moonlit fences to break off flowers that he sniffed and tossed away. One night he pointed to the open door of an attached garage and began slinking along the driveway, beckoning. I was outraged but saw that Olivia wanted to follow. We crept into the dark garage and made our way along a narrow path between a station wagon on one side and on the other a pair of garbage cans, a basket of lawn tools, two bicycles, a hot-water heater wrapped in insulation. The black inner door opened to a moon-lit porch. Orville sat on a chaise longue and smoked a cigarette, leaving the smoking butt in a bouquet of ceramic flowers. I saw that he was bent on goading me and in response I assumed an expression of intense boredom. Leaping suddenly to his feet he opened the porch door and beckoned us into the moonlit back yard. He led us under a taut badminton net, past a wicker arm-chair on which a badminton birdie lay on its side, and through a tall hedge into another back yard, where a yellow toy dump-truck sat beside a gardening glove, and then along a driveway bordered with zinnias until we came out on a leafy street.

"Night's dreamlike freedom," Orville said, sweeping out an arm. "Existence as dream. Eh, Robert? Dare me to climb that roof over there and sit smoking on the chimney. Dare me to enter that window and bring back a bunch of grapes from the icebox. No? And yet, on such a night, when the moon resem-bles a beautiful head of cauliflower, one feels, ho hum, that anything might happen. Here, watch this. See that pole?" He lowered his head and began running hard toward a nearby tele-phone pole. "Stop!" Olivia cried, but he kept plunging for-ward. At the last moment I snapped my head away. When I turned I saw the moonlit telephone pole. Its long shadow stretched across a neatly trimmed lawn, stood up against the bright white side of a house, bent across the pale roof. Orville, with mocking smile, stepped out from behind the pole. He placed a hand on his stomach and bowed. I glanced at Olivia, who was looking down at her hands.

Minor intrusions, you say, trivial violations; and yet they oppressed me. Those melodramatic entrances, those mocking innuendos, those little monologues on the dreamlike nature of existence—and once, removing half a cigarette from his pocket, he placed it on his thumbnail and said, "Here's an interesting trick." He flipped the cigarette into the blue darkness, shaded his eyes, and cupped an ear, listening intently. At last he turned up his palms with a look of exaggerated bewilderment. "Vanished," he said. "Kaput. An illusion—like life itself, one is tempted to add." Bitterly I resented his influence over Olivia. True, she treated him with indifference, even contempt, yet I noticed that she accepted his presence as if it were as natural as the night itself. He for his part had a subtly disturbing effect on her, for in his presence she seemed to me less vital, less richly particular, as if her full nature were being constricted by his mockery into a faded, wooden version of itself.

As for me, I could not understand his poisonous presence each night. Whatever route I took, however hard I tried, sooner or later he would step out to greet us with a look of false surprise; and a nervousness came over me as I tried to account for him, tried to interpret his obscure hints.

"Consider what a dreamlike existence I lead," he said one night, stepping out suddenly from behind a hollyhock and joining us as we walked. "Today I rose at noon, breakfasted at one, at two considered how I might earn a living without the necessity of leaving my room, opened a novel at three, a moment later raised my eyes to discover that romantic night had fallen —and here I am, a shadow among shadows, gliding beneath the ridiculously round moon, which reminds me of a Necco wafer. The other day my mother asked me what I was going to do with my wife. She said wife, not life, but didn't notice the slip because she was thinking about something else at the time and because I'm practically a figment of her imagination anyway. Those houses look like candy. And look at this! Someone seems to have been extremely careless." Bending over abruptly, he began to roll up a leg of his narrow jeans. At the top of his running shoe began a white sock and at the top of the sock I saw or seemed to see nothing—emptiness—nothing at all. "Stop that!" I said angrily. Orville, grinning up at me, rolled down his pant leg. "A trick of all-transforming night," he said, looking at me upside down. Olivia stood with averted eyes. I remember the blackness of her lashes against her brilliant white skin.

In the nights that followed I began to sense a remoteness in Olivia. She seemed a little tired, a little listless; it was as if she had fewer gestures at her command. She avoided my eyes. Was she, even then, preparing her departure? Scrupulously I planned intricate night-wanderings in little-known parts of town, but always I had the feeling that her inner attention was elsewhere; and from behind every house corner, from behind every fir tree and hydrangea bush, I waited for that fiend Orville to appear. One night Olivia held both elbows and gave a little shiver. "Summer's almost over," she said. Her words pierced me like a farewell; I noticed it was cool. "Curtain," Orville said, and gave a sneering bow.

But the nights grew hot again. As if to oblige me, Orville caught a cold and took to his bed. We resumed our carefree wandering, Olivia and I, through the summer-lovely streets, past the sprinklers on the lawns of ranch houses, under the thruway overpass, along rural lanes lined by sycamores and low stone walls; and all was happy, all was well; only sometimes I would raise my head and look about in confusion, as if I had lost track of something; and a pain, a little pain, began in the back of one eye, beating with the rhythm of my heartbeat.

"Oh Robert," my father said one evening as I ate alone in the kitchen. The swinging door shut behind him; the breeze of its closing touched my face. "About our little talk." He stood with his hands clasped behind his back. "Have you made up your mind? Interesting expression: to make up your mind. As if the mind were an unmade bed."

"I'm not feeling well," I said, scraping back my chair.

Late one night when I was feeling tired, terribly tired, I waited longer than usual before setting forth on my night journey. It was after midnight. Outside I waited impatiently for Olivia. She had not been looking well lately. I searched the yard, walked around the block, set off hesitantly and returned. It was a windy night, nervous gray-blue clouds rushed across the sky, covering and uncovering the moon. I climbed the two staircases to my attic room, descended suddenly and waited outside, returned to my room. There I sat down at my desk for no particular reason and immediately stood up and joined myself on the bed. Through the slightly raised window I heard a soft riot of crickets and a faint rustle or susurration that puzzled me before I suddenly solved it: the dim rush of trucks on the distant thruway. I imagined the austere, heavy-shouldered tribe of truckdrivers crossing and crisscrossing the night, stopping at islands of yellow light in the darkness to sit on gleaming red stools and loop their fingers in the handles of heavy, thick-edged cups. The stools creaked under the truckdrivers and mingled with the chirr of crickets and the distant rustle of trucks. On the attic steps I heard a faint creaking. Slowly her footsteps ascended. I saw the series of comic mishaps—I returning to my room, she looking for me in vain before going off, I descending to look for her in vain—and as I waited for the door to open I remembered the night when I had finished my work and Olivia stood resting one hand on my desk and staring at the window. What had she been thinking? I felt a burst of tenderness and unease, my head was beating like a drum, suddenly the door opened with a cracking sound.

Slouched and slack, with a look of exaggerated innocence, flourishing an unlit cigarette, he slinked his way forward over the black bookpiles, the strewn underwear, the stray shoes and slippers lying on their sides. "Match?" he said, throwing himself into my reading chair and hooking a leg over the arm.

"Where is she?" I demanded.

"Where she's always been." He gave a soft snort of laughter and looked about. "Nice setup you've got here. Not my style exactly, but then, what is. Match?"

"Look, I'm not feeling well. What do you want?"

"But I've just told you. Oh: here's one. A pause as the villain of the piece strikes a match. In the sudden spurt of the hellish match-flame his pale satanic features—which reminds me, Robert, that line of yours was awful. 'Look, I'm not feeling well.

What do you want?' Very third-rate stuff. Have you noticed that whenever people feel deeply they speak in cliches? I love you. Do you love me? Don't leave me. Don't. The real justification for cynicism is that it improves one's style. She asked me to bring you this."

He reached into his shirt pocket and removed a folded envelope. I snatched it from him and removed a folded piece of paper. I shook it open and saw at the top of the page the words *Dear Robert*. The page itself was blank.

"Is this some sort of joke?" I said angrily.

"Now now, don't lose your temper, Robert. Artists should never lose control. I hope you're not losing control, Robert. Not losing control, are you? You know, you don't understand the first thing about her, you don't even believe in her, no one is called Olivia, and besides, what's the point of it all? It's hopeless, pal. Might as well throw in the towel. Time to hang up your tights, buster. You're all washed up. It's all over, bub. This is it."

He reached into his pants pocket and removed a small black gun. He pointed it at me and his face knotted in rage. I threw up an arm. A stream of water shot past my cheek at the window curtain. He gave a gulp of unpleasant laughter.

I looked at him with contempt.

"But then, Robert, how does that line go? I forget." He laid a long finger along his cheek and frowned in thought. "Oh, I have it. We are such stuff and nonsense as dreams are made of. And what about me? Poor li'l ol' me? Sprung up out of god knows where, ill conceived, hastily patched together, a few threadbare gestures—difficult to be civilized, all things considered, under the circumstances. You really might have given it more thought."

"I don't know what you—"

"Not that I hold it against you, Herendeen old world-shaker. It suits my, my what, well say my sense of ironic detachment, not to mention my um charming cynicism and my attraction to extremes. And so I live out my life at the edge of the plausible. An example to us all. God bless us one and all, and Tiny Tim. Here. Pick a card."

He produced from a pocket a fistful of cards and held them fanlike before him. On the glossy backs were pictured a young nun kneeling in prayer, her palms pressed together at her throat, her eyes raised yearningly.

"I don't have to listen to you."

"Of course not! And yet you do, don't you. Here. This one?" He held out daintily a card chosen from one end. I snatched it from him with disdain. On the other side was a slightly blurred black-and-white photograph of the same nun standing with her back to the viewer and looking over her shoulder with a smile. Her wimple was down and her long blond hair lay fanned across her back. She was holding up her habit, revealing black high heels, black fishnet stockings, tense black garters, and the round white bottom of one firm buttock.

I swept my hand through his outspread cards. "You're nothing but a pack of cards!" I said. Falling slowly, as if they were dry leaves, the cards floated down to the bed, to the floor, to the arms of the chair, and lay still.

"Very nice, Robert. Very nicely done. A nice effect." Suddenly he sat upright. "It's unbearably hot in here. Mind if I take off my head?" Placing his hands on his jaw he began pushing, pushing, his eyes were twisted in anguish—"Stop!" I commanded. He dropped his hands and looked at me with a sly smile.

"Why certainly, Robert. Anything you say." His expression changed to intense concern. "May I speak frankly? You're not a well man, Robert. Maybe you ought to—you know, go away for a while." He sighed. "And now I'm tired. Why is that? Good God!" He glanced at his wrist, which was without a watch. "So late already? By jingo, I hope to heaven she. By Jove, I hope it isn't too late to."

"I'm not listening to any more of this crazy—"

"Have it your way, Bob. Hey, what are you—"

I squeezed past the chair, stumbled over a bookpile, scraped against a bookshelf. At the door I looked back at him. "Nighty-night," he said, wiggling his fingertips, but I was already half-way down the attic stairs, already the screen door was closing behind me.

III

It was late, a brisk wind blew; now and then in the dark streets the obsidian windows gave off a shine of streetlights. Once I passed a faint yellow glow behind a curtain, where per-haps in a flowered armchair under a brass standing lamp an insomniac in summer pajamas sat reading a thick novel set in Berlin or Morocco. In my anxiety I followed an erratic route: scarcely had I passed the first corner-post of a black front porch when I found myself rounding the final post of a porch two blocks away, no sooner had I passed that porch than I found myself before a luminous window containing tennis rackets and exercise bikes, the edge of the window shaded into a winding lane bordered by tall thistles and tiger lilies, and turning a corner I came to the edge of a dark wood. Olivia's house was invisible from the road. I made my way along a path of pinecones and oak leaves, stumbling in the dark. Around a bend the house loomed on a rise, all its windows ablaze, its black towers and gables sharply outlined against the stormy sky. A faint sound of music and voices drifted down to me. I passed several cars parked on the side of the unlit path and soon found myself in an overgrown garden. A weathered statue with decayed, pocked breasts and a single arm stood tilted at a dangerous angle; the arm was held out gracefully, and someone had hung a watering can from the thumbless hand. I passed a crumbling fountain, a child's wagon containing a three-pronged gardening tool and half a tennis ball, an immense bush with heavy black blossoms. A topiary hedge had been cut to resemble a swan, but the swan was badly in need of trimming: it had a ruffled, shaggy look, and here and there long stems poked up, as if the swan were bursting at the seams. There was something hasty and slapdash about this garden, as if it had not been thought out very carefully, small paths branched off in all directions, and following one path I came to a cul de sac that turned out to be the side of the high front porch. Through the balusters that began at the height of my head I saw glowing yellow windows beyond which shadows moved. Holding to the posts I made my way through bushes and flowers to the front of the porch and climbed the stone steps to the front door, which opened suddenly to release a big tawny cat who hesitated before rushing past me into the wilderness of the garden. "Poor kitty," murmured a woman with eyeglasses who stood holding the inner doorknob and peering into the dark. Without changing the direction of her glance she said, "Please come in, I'm so glad you could come," and as I stepped past her into the hall she turned to me with a puzzled expression.

"Robert Herendeen," I said, "and you must be Olivia's mother." "Oh no, heavens," she said, raising a spread hand to the top of her chest, "whatever gave you, oh no, I'm just answering the—you know, the door. May I take your coat, Roger? You don't seem to have a coat, do you. Are you a friend of—"

"Yes, she's expecting me." Through a doorway I saw a crowd of revelers in eye-masks, and brushing past a leaning coat tree and an umbrella stand containing an orange yardstick I entered the room. At a glossy black piano sat a woman in a brilliant green dress and a pink eye-mask, playing barbershop quartet tunes while she leaned forward to peer at a sheet of music held open by a bright yellow Schirmer album of Beethoven sonatas. Three masked and bearded men stood singing with their arms around each other's shoulders. Masked men and women talked in loud groups, a glass fell on its side and a ruby liquid rushed across a tabletop, a silver-masked woman in bluejeans and a gray sweatshirt threw back her head to laugh and plunged her frizzy long blond hair into a passing tray of drinks. A hand with long mint-green nails appeared in front of me, holding a black mask by its rubber string. I slipped the mask over my eyes and pushed my way through the crowded room toward another doorway, which admitted me to a den or sitting room where revelers sat on couches and armchairs. An elderly woman in white pants handed me a narrow glass on a stem, containing a green liquid. I took a sip and felt a burn in my throat; someone applauded. A tall fellow with a red mask waggled his fingers at me. Was he here, then, too? I found another door and passed into the dim-lit kitchen. On the counter beside an empty dishrack sat a masked woman in a knee-length skirt, her hands tucked under her thighs, one leg swinging slowly back and forth as she talked to someone who sat on the floor in the dark. At the end of the kitchen I opened a door and found myself in a hall. It appeared not to be the front hall, for in one direction I saw a high, closed door and in the other I saw rows of doors leading into darkness. I walked toward the dark, past paneled doors with fluted glass knobs, until the corridor ended at a transverse hall. I turned left. As I proceeded along the almost dark corridor, past closed doors, the black gleam of a mirror, a high-backed narrow chair on which sat a black telephone, I realized that I had only a vague sense of this part of the house, which seemed to extend back and back. Here other hallways began to branch left and right, the doors were of different sizes, through an open arch I saw a room with armchairs and glass-doored bookcases; and as I continued I felt that I was penetrating deeper and deeper into a region where rooms and corridors sprouted in the lush, extravagant dark.

One of the halls ended in a carpeted stairway and I began to climb. On the dark landing I bumped a small table; something rattled glassily and slowly became still. Four more stairs led to an upper hallway, dark except for a weak night-light in the baseboard. At the end of the hall I turned into another hall, where all was black except for a strip of yellow light running along the bottom and up the side of a barely open black door that rested against the jamb. I made my way to the door and stood listening but heard no sound. "Olivia," I whispered, "are you there?" Slowly I pushed open the paneled door, which revealed a big empty bed with the reading light on. The covers of the bed were turned down and a panda lay under the blanket, holding out stiffly both plump paws. There was a tall mahogany bureau, a desk with a fat typewriter squatting on it, an armchair with its back to me. A standing lamp shone down over the armchair's left shoulder. Olivia's black hair at the top of the chair was glossy as licorice. I tiptoed up to her and bent over.

The black wig sat on the head of a big floppy doll propped up on four books. In the doll's lap was an open copy of *Anna Karenina*. "Very funny," I said, looking about sharply. Under the bed-light the panda avoided my stare.

I returned to the hall and made my way into the dark, running my fingertips along the papered walls, the doorjambs, the paneled doors, until I came to a sudden opening in the wall. A short corridor led to a many-paned window. Through the panes I saw buttery yellow light from a lower window spilling onto ragged bushes. Beyond the bushes a dark wooden swing dangled above the ground, its fallen rope twisted in the grass. Black tree-branches crossed my window and through them I saw a dark blue sky with rushing blue-gray clouds. Short flights of stairs began at my left and right. I chose a flight and made my way along a hall that was intersected by another hall, and it seemed to me that I was going to spend the rest of my life wandering the prolific hallways of that always branching house, when I came to a door that opened onto a flight of wooden steps.

I turned on a switch that illuminated a faint amber night-light and began to climb. The walls were studs separated by vertical, rippling strips of insulation from which pink twists of fibers escaped at the sides. On a nail hung a leather glove with burst fingertips. At the top of the stairs I came to a crude wooden door fastened by a hook. I unlatched the hook and stepped over the steep doorsill into a pile of wood shavings at the bottom of a narrow stairway. Four steps led to a landing, four more steps to another, four steps to a third landing, and in this manner the stairway turned at landing after landing until it abandoned all pretense and became a rickety circular stairway with a creaking rail. My thighs ached, my breath came sharp, far away I heard the dim sound of a piano, and all at once I came to a low door no higher than my neck. I turned the knob and the door opened easily.

"So there you are," I said and bowed my way beneath the low lintel into the tower room.

Six of the eight walls were lined with bookshelves from top to bottom. The seventh wall contained a casement window, beneath which sat a reading chair; against the eighth wall stood a dressing table with a large oval mirror. Olivia sat at the dressing table with her back to me and her mirrored face looking directly at me. A green mask covered her eyes. She wore a black dress, black stockings, a pearl necklace, and a pink-and-green party hat. She was leaning forward and appeared to be studying her face in the mirror, which reflected part of the open door, my hand on the knob, and part of my shirt and pants. Still holding the door I bent over to see myself in the mirror, startled at the black mask over my eyes, which I had forgotten.

"You're just in time," Olivia said, reaching behind her neck to unclasp the pearl necklace. On the dressing table stood an open jewelbox, a row of faceted glass vials, and a bald wig stand that disturbed me for some reason.

"Are you going to the party?"

"I've already been." She placed the necklace in the blue velvet tray of the jewelbox and leaned forward again. The black window reflected a wall of books. I closed the door behind me and stood uneasily in the large octagonal room. Olivia reached through an eye-slit of her mask, removed something small and dark, and placed it carefully on the dressing table. As she reached into the other eye-slit I took a step forward and saw her remove a pair of false eyelashes, which she placed beside the first pair. A feeling of anxiety came over me and I said, "Olivia, let's leave this place, let's go for a walk, it's hard to breathe in here, Olivia." And indeed I felt that something wrong was happening, that things were beginning to get out of hand. "Don't be absurd," Olivia said, slipping off her long blood-red fingernails one by one and placing all ten of them side by side on the dressing table, where they resembled the visible tips of invisible hands. Slowly she removed a glittering earring hidden by her hair. She placed the second earring beside the first in the velvety jewelbox. Then she reached behind her neck to unclasp a glossy black cluster of hanging hair. She held it up for a moment, examining it with her head tipped to one side before laying it on the table. It looked like a black squirrel. Then she swung halfway around in her chair, drew her silky black dress up to her thighs, and unclasped her garters one by one. Swiftly she rolled down each black stocking in turn, and gave them a little kick. "There," she said, wriggling her toes, "that's a relief!" In the lamplight her bare legs looked glossy and smooth. She reached an arm behind her neck. With a sharp ripping sound she pulled a black zipper partway down. She reached her other arm behind her back and pulled the zipper down to her waist. "Olivia," I said. She gave a little yawn, stretched out her arms, and looked vaguely about. She slipped off her pink and-green party hat and placed it next to the wig stand. She slipped off a chain bracelet and dropped it on the table with a sharp little rattle. She slipped off her watch, slipped off a glittering ring, and raising her hands to the sides of her head she slipped off her hair and mask, placing them carefully over the wig stand.

The top of her head was smooth and blank. In the mirror I saw her faded eyes, her flat, painted eyebrows. Her nose was little and hard. With a sigh she stood up. Wearily she drew the black dress over her head, revealing a black half-slip and a black bra. "Olivia," I said, "that's enough now, enough, enough now," and somewhere I heard a footstep creaking on a stair. "Olivia," I said, but already she was removing her half-slip, already she was stepping out of her underpants, unhooking her black bra. Her breasts were smooth and flattish and without nipples. Wearily she slipped out of her cluster of pubic curls, leaving herself smooth and hard. "*Tn*," she said, and stood stiffly there. "What," I said, "what did you say." Her limbs shimmered in the lamplight. One arm was held out as if to be offered to someone crossing the street. The masked wig stand looked at me.

"Olivia?" I said, reaching out a hand but not moving. I felt that if only I could return to the meandering hallways then perhaps I might begin all over again, but behind me I heard a clattering, the door began to shake, all at once it sprang open.

Huffing and puffing, taking deep exaggerated breaths, holding one hand over his chest, Orville entered. "So there"—pause for gasping—"you"—pause for gasping—"are!" His running shoes were covered with wood shavings. He strode over to Olivia, picked her up by the elbows, and laid her against the reading chair like an old lamp. And indeed she had begun to resemble an old standing lamp, with a dull brass base and three light sockets with burned-out bulbs. "That's all, then," he said. "We won't be needing this anymore." He went over to the desk and removed the oval mirror, leaning it against a wall of books. He went to the casement window and slipped off one of the hinged frames. A brisk wind blew into the room, fluttering the hair of the wig stand, knocking over a glass vial. Orville laid the hinged frame against the mirror. He looked about, strode up to a wall, and began pushing against the shelves. The walls began to move back and forth, I could feel the tower trembling. "Stop that!" I said. In rage he turned to me and stamped his foot, which plunged through the floor. Splinters flew; puffs of dust rose up. "I hope you're satisfied!" he cried. He looked at me with hatred as I turned to the door. It seemed to have grown smaller—I could barely squeeze my way through.

I hurried down the turning wooden stairs, which seemed to be swaying under my footsteps. Above me I heard sounds as of ripping and muffled thumping. I came to a landing, I flung myself down the steps to another landing—and as I descended, the landings seemed to rise faster and faster to meet me. I stepped into a pile of shavings, climbed over a threshold that came up to my knees, clattered down a flimsy flight of splintery steps, emerged in a hall. As I hurried along I could hear bits of plaster falling with the delicate sound of spilled sugar. Other hallways branched from the hall, and I must have made a wrong turn somehow, for I could not find the carpeted stairway going down. Ahead of me in the darkness I saw a line of light under a door. I felt a sudden need to say farewell to her room, and when I came up to it I pushed lightly against the door. It swung briskly inward and clattered against the wall. In a big bed an old woman with streaming white hair stared at me over the tops of her reading glasses. Her mouth was large and brightly lipsticked. Her hand gripped the top of her nightdress and her mouth was opening wider and wider as I shut the door and rushed on. The floor was trembling slightly, bits of plaster struck my arms, and I noticed that the corridor was lined with pieces of furniture: a small table, a wing chair, a grandfather clock. The furniture began to collect more thickly and jut into the hall, so that it was necessary for me to squeeze between sharp edges and climb over the arms of old stuffed chairs, as in certain dreams, terrible dreams, where you— Somewhere I heard a sound of shattering glass. I was wondering whether to turn back when the hall ended in a small door no higher than my knees. I knelt down and tried to peer through the tiny keyhole, then pushed the door open and scraped my way through.

I found myself in what appeared to be a low storage space. My hand pressed into something soft and rubbery that gave a wheezing squeak. I snatched my hand away and brushed against a shape that began to fall over, giving a soft "*Waaa.*" Something poked up before me and I felt the cold top of a ladder, rising through a trap door. I swung my leg through the opening and began to climb down. Cloth rose up on all sides of me, it was as though I were sinking helplessly into a morass of thick, yielding folds—and half drowning in that mass of musty perfumed dresses I made my way down to the floor of a closet. There I thrust my way through clutching sleeves and buckles to a door that opened onto a hall.

In the branching corridors I turned left and right while plaster fell from the trembling walls. Behind me a picture struck the floor sharply, like the blade of a guillotine. I came to a door, pulled it open, and entered the dark kitchen. In the black dish-rack a pointed black party hat sat upside down in the silverware box. I hurried through a door and found myself in the lamplit room of couches and armchairs, deserted except for a tired-looking woman with gray hair pulled back tight who was picking up teacups and glasses. Without looking up at me, she handed me a small wooden bowl containing a few peanut halves lying among glistening brown skins. I carried the bowl into the next room. Everyone had left, the room was nearly dark. Black furniture loomed against the night-blue windows. On the dark-gleaming piano bench I placed the bowl beside an abandoned mask. I tore off my mask and knocked my leg against a sharp corner as I hurried through the room and out into the front hall. Heavy pieces of plaster were falling, I could feel a fine dust sifting down. Somewhere above I heard a loud snap or crack. Before me the coat tree began to fall slowly, dreamily, landing with a muffled thud among its coats. I stepped over it, fumbled at the front door, and ran out onto the porch. One of the thick corner-posts appeared to be buckling. I ran down the stone steps onto a flagstone path, where I leaped over something that might have been a cat, and as I escaped from the collapsing house into the ruined garden, which was already wavering and dissolving under a rushing sky, it seemed to me that if only I could remain calm remain calm remain calm then I might be able to imagine what would happen to me next.

Eisenheim the Illusionist

In the last years of the nineteenth century, when the Empire of the Hapsburgs was nearing the end of its long dissolution, the art of magic flourished as never before. In obscure villages of Moravia and Galicia, from the Istrian peninsula to the mists of Bukovina, bearded and black-caped magicians in market squares astonished townspeople by drawing streams of dazzling silk handkerchiefs from empty paper cones, removing billiard balls from children's ears, and throwing into the air decks of cards that assumed the shapes of fountains, snakes, and angels before returning to the hand. In cities and larger towns, from Zagreb to Lvov, from Budapest to Vienna, on the stages of opera houses, town halls, and magic theaters, traveling conjurers equipped with the latest apparatus enchanted sophisticated audiences with elaborate stage illusions. It was the age of levitations and decapitations, of ghostly apparitions and sudden vanishings, as if the tottering Empire were revealing through the medium of its magicians its secret desire for annihilation. Among the remarkable conjurers of that time, none achieved the heights of illusion attained by Eisenheim, whose enigmatic final performance was viewed by some as a triumph of the magician's art, by others as a fateful sign.

Eisenheim, né Eduard Abramowitz, was born in Bratislava in 1859 or 1860. Little is known of his early years, or indeed of his entire life outside the realm of illusion. For the scant facts we are obliged to rely on the dubious memoirs of magicians, on comments in contemporary newspaper stories and trade periodicals, on promotional material and brochures for magic acts; here and there the diary entry of a countess or ambassador records attendance at a performance in Paris, Cracow, Vienna. Eisenheim's father was a highly respected cabinetmaker, whose ornamental gilt cupboards and skilfully carved lowboys with lion-paw feet and brass handles shaped like snarling lions graced the halls of the gentry of Bratislava. The boy was the eldest of four children; like many Bratislavan Jews, the family spoke German and called their city Pressburg, although they understood as much Slovak and Magyar as was necessary for the proper conduct of business. Eduard went to work early in his father's shop. For the rest of his life he would retain a fondness for smooth pieces of wood joined seamlessly by mortise and tenon. By the age of seventeen he was himself a skilled cabinetmaker, a fact noted more than once by fellow magicians who admired Eisenheim's skill in constructing trick cabinets of breathtaking ingenuity. The young craftsman was already a passionate amateur magician, who is said to have entertained family and friends with card sleights and a disappearing-ring trick that required a small beechwood box of his own construction. He would place a borrowed ring inside, fasten the box tightly with twine, and quietly remove the ring as he handed the box to a spectator. The beechwood box, with its secret panel, was able to withstand the most minute examination.

A chance encounter with a traveling magician is said to have been the cause of Eisenheim's lifelong passion for magic. The story goes that one day, returning from school, the boy saw a man in black sitting under a plane tree. The man called him over and lazily, indifferently, removed from the boy's ear first one coin and then another, and then a third, coin after coin, a whole handful of coins, which suddenly turned into a bunch of red roses. From the roses the man in black drew out a white billiard ball, which turned into a wooden flute that suddenly vanished. One version of the story adds that the man himself then vanished, along with the plane tree. Stories, like conjuring tricks, are invented because history is inadequate to our dreams, but in this case it is reasonable to suppose that the future master had been profoundly affected by some early experience of conjuring. Eduard had once seen a magic shop, without much interest; he now returned with passion. On dark winter mornings on the way to school he would remove his gloves to practice manipulating balls and coins with chilled fingers in the pockets of his coat. He enchanted his three sisters with intricate shadowgraphs representing Rumpelstiltskin and Rapunzel, American buffalos and Indians, the golem of Prague. Later a local conjurer called Ignazc Molnar taught him juggling for the sake of coordinating movements of the eye and hand. Once, on a dare, the thirteen-year-old boy carried an egg on a soda straw all the way to Bratislava Castle and back. Much later, when all this was far behind him, the Master would be sitting gloomily in the corner of a Viennese apartment where a party was being held in his honor, and reaching up wearily he would startle his hostess by producing from the air five billiard balls that he proceeded to juggle flawlessly.

But who can unravel the mystery of the passion that infects an entire life, bending it away from its former course in one irrevocable swerve? Abramowitz seems to have accepted his fate slowly. It was as if he kept trying to evade the disturbing knowledge of his difference. At the age of twenty-four he was still an expert cabinetmaker who did occasional parlor tricks.

As if suddenly, Eisenheim appeared at a theater in Vienna and began his exhilarating and fatal career. The brilliant newcomer was twenty-eight years old. In fact, contemporary records show that the cabinetmaker from Bratislava had appeared in private performances for at least a year before moving to the Austrian

capital. Although the years preceding the first private performances remain mysterious, it is clear that Abramowitz gradually shifted his attention more and more fully to magic, by way
of the trick chests and cabinets that he had begun to supply to
local magicians. Eisenheim's nature was like that: he proceeded
slowly and cautiously, step by step, and then, as if he had earned
the right to be daring, he would take a sudden leap.

The first public performances were noted less for their daring
than for their subtle mastery of the stage illusions of the day,
although even then there were artful twists and variations. One
of Eisenheim's early successes was The Mysterious Orange
Tree, a feat made famous by Robert-Houdin. A borrowed
handkerchief was placed in a small box and handed to a member
of the audience. An assistant strode onto the stage, bearing in
his arms a small green orange tree in a box. He placed the box
on the magician's table and stepped away. At a word from
Eisenheim, accompanied by a pass of his wand, blossoms began
to appear on the tree. A moment later, oranges began to
emerge; Eisenheim plucked several and handed them to members of the audience. Suddenly two butterflies rose from the
leaves, carrying a handkerchief. The spectator, opening his box,
discovered that his handkerchief had disappeared; somehow the
butterflies had found it in the tree. The illusion depended on
two separate deceptions: the mechanical tree itself, which produced real flowers, real fruit, and mechanical butterflies by
means of concealed mechanisms; and the removal of the handkerchief from the trick box as it was handed to the spectator.
Eisenheim quickly developed a variation that proved popular:
the tree grew larger each time he covered it with a red silk cloth,
the branches produced oranges, apples, pears, and plums, at the
end a whole flock of colorful, real butterflies rose up and fluttered over the audience, where children screamed with delight
as they reached up to snatch the delicate silken shapes, and at
last, under a black velvet cloth that was suddenly lifted, the tree
was transformed into a bird-cage containing the missing handkerchief.

At this period, Eisenheim wore the traditional silk hat, frock coat, and cape and performed with an ebony wand tipped with ivory. The one distinctive note was his pair of black gloves. He began each performance by stepping swiftly through the closed curtains onto the stage apron, removing the gloves, and tossing them into the air, where they turned into a pair of sleek ravens.

Early critics were quick to note the young magician's interest in uncanny effects, as in his popular Phantom Portrait. On a darkened stage, a large blank canvas was illuminated by lime-light. As Eisenheim made passes with his right hand, the white canvas gradually and mysteriously gave birth to a brighter and brighter painting. Now, it is well known among magicians and mediums that a canvas of unbleached muslin may be painted with chemical solutions that appear invisible when dry; if sulphate of iron is used for blue, nitrate of bismuth for yellow, and copper sulphate for brown, the picture will appear if sprayed with a weak solution of prussiate of potash. An atomizer, concealed in the conjurer's sleeve, gradually brings out the invisible portrait. Eisenheim increased the mysterious effect by producing full-length portraits that began to exhibit lifelike movements of the eyes and lips. The fiendish portrait of an archduke, or a devil, or Eisenheim himself would then read the contents of sealed envelopes, before vanishing at a pass of the magician's wand.

However skilful, a conjurer cannot earn and sustain a major reputation without producing original feats of his own devising. It was clear that the restless young magician would not be content with producing clever variations of familiar tricks, and by 1890 his performances regularly concluded with an illusion of striking originality. A large mirror in a carved frame stood on the stage, facing the audience. A spectator was invited onto the stage, where he was asked to walk around the mirror and examine it to his satisfaction. Eisenheim then asked the spectator to don a hooded red robe and positioned him some ten feet from the mirror, where the vivid red reflection was clearly visible to the audience; the theater was darkened, except for a brightening light that came from within the mirror itself. As the spectator waved his robed arms about, and bowed to his bowing reflection, and leaned from side to side, his reflection began to show signs of disobedience—it crossed its arms over its chest instead of waving them about, it refused to bow. Suddenly the reflection grimaced, removed a knife, and stabbed itself in the chest. The reflection collapsed onto the reflected floor. Now a ghostlike white form rose from the dead reflection and hovered in the mirror; all at once the ghost emerged from the glass, floated toward the startled and sometimes terrified spectator, and at the bidding of Eisenheim rose into the dark and vanished. This masterful illusion mystified even professional magicians, who agreed only that the mirror was a trick cabinet with black-lined doors at the rear and a hidden assistant. The lights were probably concealed in the frame between the glass and the lightly silvered back; as the lights grew brighter the mirror became transparent and a red-robed assistant showed himself in the glass. The ghost was more difficult to explain, despite a long tradition of stage ghosts; it was said that concealed magic lanterns produced the phantom, but no other magician was able to imitate the effect. Even in these early years, before Eisenheim achieved disturbing effects unheard of in the history of stage magic, there was a touch of the uncanny about his illusions; and some said even then that Eisenheim was not a showman at all, but a wizard who had sold his soul to the devil in return for unholy powers.

Eisenheim was a man of medium height, with broad shoulders and large, long-fingered hands. His most striking feature was his powerful head: the black intense eyes in the austerely pale face, the broad black beard, the thrusting forehead with its receding hairline, all lent an appearance of unusual mental force. The newspaper accounts mention a minor trait that must have been highly effective: when he leaned his head forward, in intense concentration, there appeared over his right eyebrow a large vein shaped like an inverted *Y*.

As the last decade of the old century wore on, Eisenheim gradually came to be acknowledged as the foremost magician of his day. These were the years of the great European tours, which brought him to Egyptian Hall in London and the Théâtre Robert-Houdin in Paris, to royal courts and ducal palaces, to halls in Berlin and Milan, Zurich and Salamanca. Although his repertoire continued to include perfected variations of popular illusions like The Vanishing Lady, The Blue Room, The Flying Watch, The Spirit Cabinet (or Specters of the Inner Sanctum), The Enchanted House, The Magic Kettle, and The Arabian Sack Mystery, he appeared to grow increasingly impatient with known effects and began rapidly replacing them with striking inventions of his own. Among the most notable illusions of those years were The Tower of Babel, in which a small black cone mysteriously grew until it filled the entire stage; The Satanic Crystal Ball, in which a ghostly form summoned from hell smashed through the glass globe and rushed out onto the stage with unearthly cries; and The Book of Demons, in which black smoke rose from an ancient book, which suddenly burst into flames that released hideous dwarfs in hairy jerkins who ran howling across the stage. In 1898 he opened his own theater in Vienna, called simply Eisenheimhaus, or The House of Eisenheim, as if that were his real home and all other dwellings illusory. It was here that he presented The Pied Piper of Hamelin. Holding his wand like a flute, Eisenheim led children from the audience into a misty hill with a cavelike opening and then, with a pass of his wand, caused the entire hill to vanish into thin air. Moments later a black chest materialized, from which the children emerged and looked around in bewilderment before running back to their parents. The children told their parents they had been in a wondrous mountain, with golden tables and chairs and white angels flying in the air; they had no idea how they had gotten into the box, or what had happened to them. A few complaints were made; and when, in another performance, a frightened child told his mother that he had been in hell and seen the devil, who was green and breathed fire, the chief of the Viennese police, one Walther Uhl, paid Eisenheim a visit. The Pied Piper of Hamelin never appeared again, but two results had emerged: a certain disturbing quality in Eisenheim's art was now officially acknowledged, and it was rumored that the stern master was being closely watched by Franz Josef's secret police. This last was unlikely, for the Emperor, unlike his notorious grandfather, took little interest in police espionage; but the rumor surrounded Eisenheim like a mist, blurring his sharp outline, darkening his features, and enhancing his formidable reputation.

Eisenheim was not without rivals, whose challenges he invariably met with a decisiveness, some would say ferocity, that left no doubt of his self-esteem. Two incidents of the last years of the century left a deep impression among contemporaries. In Vienna in 1898 a magician called Benedetti had appeared. Benedetti, whose real name was Paul Henri Cortot, of Lyon, was a master illusionist of extraordinary smoothness and skill; his mistake was to challenge Eisenheim by presenting imitations of original Eisenheim illusions, with clever variations, much as Eisenheim had once alluded to his predecessors in order to outdo them. Eisenheim learned of his rival's presumption and let it be known through the speaking portrait of a devil that ruin awaits the proud. The very next night, on Benedetti's stage, a speaking portrait of Eisenheim intoned in comic accents that ruin awaits the proud. Eisenheim, a proud and brooding man, did not allude to the insult during his Sunday night performance. On Monday night, Benedetti's act went awry: the wand leaped from his fingers and rolled across the stage; two fishbowls with watertight lids came crashing to the floor from beneath Benedetti's cloak; the speaking portrait remained mute; the levitating lady was seen to be resting on black wires. The excitable Benedetti, vowing revenge, accused Eisenheim of criminal tampering; two nights later, before a packed house, Benedetti stepped into a black cabinet, drew a curtain, and was

never seen again. The investigation by Herr Uhl failed to produce a trace of foul play. Some said the unfortunate Benedetti
had simply chosen the most convenient way of escaping to
another city, under a new name, far from the scene of his notorious debacle; others were convinced that Eisenheim had somehow spirited him off, perhaps to hell. Viennese society was
enchanted by the scandal, which made the round of the cafés;
and Herr Uhl was seen more than once in a stall of the theater,
nodding his head appreciatively at some particularly striking
effect.

If Benedetti proved too easy a rival, a far more formidable
challenge was posed by the mysterious Passauer. Ernst Passauer
was said to be Bavarian; his first Viennese performance was
watched closely by the Austrians, who were forced to admit
that the German was a master of striking originality. Passauer
took the city by storm; and for the first time there was talk that
Eisenheim had met his match, perhaps even—was it possible?
—his master. Unlike the impetuous and foolhardy Benedetti,
Passauer made no allusion to the Viennese wizard; some saw in
this less a sign of professional decorum than an assertion of
arrogant indifference, as if the German refused to acknowledge
the possibility of a rival. But the pattern of their performances,
that autumn, was the very rhythm of rivalry: Eisenheim played
on Sunday, Wednesday, and Friday nights, and Passauer on
Tuesday, Thursday, and Saturday nights. It was noted that as
his rival presented illusions of bold originality, Eisenheim's own
illusions became more daring and dangerous; it was as if the
two of them had outsoared the confines of the magician's art
and existed in some new realm of dextrous wonder, of sinister
beauty. In this high but by no means innocent realm, the two
masters vied for supremacy before audiences that were increasingly the same. Some said that Eisenheim appeared to be struggling or straining against the relentless pressure of his brilliant
rival; others argued that Eisenheim had never displayed such
mastery; and as the heavy century lumbered to its close, all

awaited the decisive event that would release them from the tension of an unresolved battle.

And it came: one night in mid-December, after a particularly daring illusion, in which Passauer caused first his right arm to vanish, then his left arm, then his feet, until nothing was left of him but his disembodied head floating before a black velvet curtain, the head permitted itself to wonder whether Herr "Eisenzeit," or Iron Age, had ever seen a trick of that kind. The mocking allusion caused the audience to gasp. The limelight went out; when it came on, the stage contained nothing but a heap of black cloth, which began to flutter and billow until it gradually assumed the shape of Passauer, who bowed coolly to tumultuous applause; but the ring of a quiet challenge was not lost in the general uproar. The following night Eisenheim played to a packed, expectant house. He ignored the challenge while performing a series of new illusions that in no way resembled Passauer's act. As he took his final bow, he remarked casually that Passauer's hour had passed. The fate of the unfortunate Benedetti had not been forgotten, and it was said that if the demand for Passauer's next performance had been met, the entire city of Vienna would have become a magic theater.

Passauer's final performance was one of frightening brilliance; it was well attended by professional magicians, who agreed later that as a single performance it outshone the greatest of Eisenheim's evenings. Passauer began by flinging into the air a handful of coins that assumed the shape of a bird and flew out over the heads of the audience, flapping its jingling wings of coins; from a silver thimble held in the flat of his hand he removed a tablecloth, a small mahogany table, and a silver salver on which sat a steaming roast duck. At the climax of the evening, he caused the properties of the stage to vanish one by one: the magician's table, the beautiful assistant, the far wall, the curtain. Standing alone in a vanished world, he looked at the audience with an expression that grew more and more fierce. Suddenly he burst into a demonic laugh, and reaching up to his face he tore off a rubber mask and revealed himself to be Eisenheim. The collective gasp sounded like a great furnace igniting; some-one burst into hysterical sobs. The audience, understanding at last, rose to its feet and cheered the great master of illusion, who himself had been his own greatest rival and had at the end unmasked himself. In his box, Herr Uhl rose to his feet and joined in the applause. He had enjoyed the performance im-mensely.

Perhaps it was the strain of that sustained deception, perhaps it was the sense of being alone, utterly alone, in any case Eisen-heim did not give another performance in the last weeks of the fading century. As the new century came in with a fireworks display in the Prater and a hundred-gun salute from the grounds of the Imperial Palace, Eisenheim remained in his Vienna apart-ment, with its distant view of the same river that flowed through his childhood city. The unexplained period of rest con-tinued, developing into a temporary withdrawal from perfor-mance, some said a retirement; Eisenheim himself said nothing. In late January he returned to Bratislava to attend to details of his father's business; a week later he was in Linz; within a month he had purchased a three-story villa in the famous wooded hills on the outskirts of Vienna. He was forty or forty-one, an age when a man takes a hard look at his life. He had never married, although romantic rumors occasionally united him with one or another of his assistants; he was handsome in a stern way, wealthy, and said to be so strong that he could do thirty knee-bends on a single leg. Not long after his move to the Wiener-wald he began to court Sophie Ritter, the twenty-six-year-old daughter of a local landowner who disapproved of Eisenheim's profession and was a staunch supporter of Lueger's anti-Semitic Christian Social party; the girl appears to have been in love with Eisenheim, but at the last moment something went wrong, she withdrew abruptly, and a month later married a grain merchant from Graz. For a year Eisenheim lived like a reclusive country squire. He took riding lessons in the mornings, in the afternoons practiced with pistols at his private shooting range, planted a spring garden, stocked his ponds, designed a new orchard. In a meadow at the back of his house he supervised the building of a long low shedlike structure that became known as the Teufelsfabrik, or Devil's Factory, for it housed his collection of trick cabinets, deceptive mirrors, haunted portraits, and magic caskets. The walls were lined with cupboards that had sliding glass doors and held Eisenheim's formidable collection of magical apparatus: vanishing bird-cages, inexhaustible punch bowls, devil's targets, Schiller's bells, watch-spring flowers, trick bouquets, and an array of secret devices used in sleight-of-hand feats: ball shells, coin droppers, elastic handkerchief-pulls for making handkerchiefs vanish, dummy cigars, color-changing tubes for handkerchief tricks, hollow thumb-tips, miniature spirit lamps for the magical lighting of candles, false fingers, black silk ball-tubes. In the basement of the factory was a large room in which he conducted chemical and electrical experiments, and a curtained darkroom; Eisenheim was a close student of photography and the new art of cinematography. Often he was seen working late at night, and some said that ghostly forms appeared in the dim-lit windows.

On the first of January, 1901, Eisenheim suddenly returned to his city apartment with its view of the Danube and the Vienna hills. Three days later he reappeared on stage. A local wit remarked that the master of illusion had simply omitted the year 1900, which with its two zeros no doubt struck him as illusory. The yearlong absence of the Master had sharpened expectations, and the standing-room-only crowd was tensely quiet as the curtains parted on a stage strikingly bare except for a plain wooden chair before a small glass table. For some in that audience, the table already signaled a revolution; others were puzzled or disappointed. From the right wing Eisenheim strode onto the stage. A flurry of whispers was quickly hushed. The Master wore a plain dark suit and had shaved off his beard.

Without a word he sat down on the wooden chair behind the table and faced the audience. He placed his hands lightly on the tabletop, where they remained during the entire performance. He stared directly before him, leaning forward slightly and appearing to concentrate with terrific force.

In the middle of the eighteenth century the magician's table was a large table draped to the floor; beneath the cloth an assistant reached through a hole in the tabletop to remove objects concealed by a large cone. The modern table of Eisenheim's day had a short cloth that exposed the table legs, but the disappearance of the hidden assistant and the general simplification of design in no sense changed the nature of the table, which remained an ingenious machine equipped with innumerable contrivances to aid the magician in the art of deception: hidden receptacles or *servantes* into which disappearing objects secretly dropped, invisible wells and traps, concealed pistons, built-in spring-pulls for effecting the disappearance of silk handkerchiefs. Eisenheim's transparent glass table announced the end of the magician's table as it had been known throughout the history of stage magic. This radical simplification was not only esthetic: it meant the refusal of certain kinds of mechanical aid, the elimination of certain effects.

And the audience grew restless: nothing much appeared to be happening. A balding man in a business suit sat at a table, frowning. After fifteen minutes a slight disturbance or darkening in the air was noticeable near the surface of the table. Eisenheim concentrated fiercely; over his right eyebrow the famous vein, shaped like an inverted Y, pressed through the skin of his forehead. The air seemed to tremble and thicken—and before him, on the glass table, a dark shape slowly formed. It appeared to be a small box, about the size of a jewelbox. For a while its edges quivered slightly, as if it were made of black smoke. Suddenly Eisenheim raised his eyes, which one witness described as black mirrors that reflected nothing; he looked drained and weary. A moment later he pushed back his chair, stood up, and bowed. The applause was uncertain; people did not know what they had seen.

Eisenheim next invited spectators to come onto the stage and examine the box on the table. One woman, reaching for the box and feeling nothing, nothing at all, stepped back and raised a hand to her throat. A girl of sixteen, sweeping her hand through the black box, cried out as if in pain.

The rest of the performance consisted of two more "materializations": a sphere and a wand. After members of the audience had satisfied themselves of the immaterial nature of the objects, Eisenheim picked up the wand and waved it over the box. He next lifted the lid of the box, placed the sphere inside, and closed the lid. When he invited spectators onto the stage, their hands passed through empty air. Eisenheim opened the box, removed the sphere, and laid it on the table between the box and the wand. He bowed, and the curtain closed.

Despite a hesitant, perplexed, and somewhat disappointed response from that first audience, the reviews were enthusiastic; one critic called it a major event in the history of stage illusions. He connected Eisenheim's phantom objects with the larger tradition of stage ghosts, which he traced back to Robertson's Phantasmagoria at the end of the eighteenth century. From concealed magic lanterns Robertson had projected images onto smoke rising from braziers to create eerie effects. By the middle of the nineteenth century magicians were terrifying spectators with a far more striking technique: a hidden assistant, dressed like a ghost and standing in a pit between the stage and the auditorium, was reflected onto the stage through a tilted sheet of glass invisible to the audience. Modern ghosts were based on the technique of the black velvet backdrop: overhead lights were directed toward the front of the stage, and black-covered white objects appeared to materialize when the covers were pulled away by invisible black-hooded assistants dressed in black. But Eisenheim's phantoms, those immaterial materializations, made use of no machinery at all—they appeared to emerge from the mind of the magician. The effect was startling, the unknown device ingenious. The writer considered and rejected the possibility of hidden magic lanterns and mirrors; discussed the properties of the cinematograph recently developed by the Lumière brothers and used by contemporary magicians to produce unusual effects of a different kind; and speculated on possible scientific techniques whereby Eisenheim might have caused the air literally to thicken and darken. Was it possible that one of the Lumière machines, directed onto slightly misted air above the table, might have produced the phantom objects? But no one had detected any mist, no one had seen the necessary beam of light. However Eisenheim had accomplished the illusion, the effect was incomparable; it appeared that he was summoning objects into existence by the sheer effort of his mind. In this the master illusionist was rejecting the modern conjurer's increasing reliance on machinery and returning the spectator to the troubled heart of magic, which yearned beyond the constricting world of ingenuity and artifice toward the dark realm of transgression.

The long review, heavy with *fin de siècle* portentousness and shot through with a secret restlessness or longing, was the first of several that placed Eisenheim beyond the world of conjuring and saw in him an expression of spiritual striving, as if his art could no longer be talked about in the old way.

During the next performance Eisenheim sat for thirty-five minutes at his glass table in front of a respectful but increasingly restless audience before the darkening was observed. When he sat back, evidently spent from his exertions, there stood on the table the head and shoulders of a young woman. The details of witnesses differ, but all reports agree that the head was of a young woman of perhaps eighteen or twenty with short dark hair and heavy-lidded eyes. She faced the audience calmly, a little dreamily, as if she had just wakened from sleep, and spoke her name: Greta. Fräulein Greta answered questions from the audience. She said she came from Brünn; she was seventeen years old; her father was a lens grinder; she did not know how she had come here. Behind her, Eisenheim sat slumped in his seat, his broad face pale as marble, his eyes staring as if sightlessly. After a while Fräulein Greta appeared to grow tired. Eisenheim gathered himself up and fixed her with his stare; gradually she wavered and grew dim, and slowly vanished.

With Fräulein Greta, Eisenheim triumphed over the doubters. As word of the new illusion spread, and audiences waited with a kind of fearful patience for the darkening of the air above the glass table, it became clear that Eisenheim had touched a nerve. Greta-fever was in the air. It was said that Fräulein Greta was really Marie Vetsera, who had died with Crown Prince Rudolf in the bedroom of his hunting lodge at Mayerling; it was said that Fräulein Greta, with her dark, sad eyes, was the girlhood spirit of the Empress Elizabeth, who at the age of sixty had been stabbed to death in Geneva by an Italian anarchist. It was said that Fräulein Greta knew things, all sorts of things, and could tell secrets about the other world. For a while Eisenheim was taken up by the spiritualists, who claimed him for one of their own: here at last was absolute proof of the materialization of spirit forms. A society of disaffected Blavatskyites called the Daughters of Dawn elected Eisenheim to an honorary membership, and three bearded members of a Salzburg Institute for Psychic Research began attending performances with black notebooks in hand. Magicians heaped scorn on the mediumistic confraternity but could not explain or duplicate the illusion; a shrewd group of mediums, realizing they could not reproduce the Eisenheim phenomena, accused him of fraud while defending themselves against the magicians' charges. Eisenheim's rigorous silence was taken by all sides as a sign of approval. The "manifestations," as they began to be called, soon included the head of a dark-haired man of about thirty, who called himself Frankel and demonstrated conventional tricks of mind reading and telepathy before fading away. What puzzled the professionals was not the mind reading but the production of Frankel himself. The possibility of exerting a physical influence on air was repeatedly argued; it was suggested in some quarters that Eisenheim had prepared the air in advance with a thickening agent and treated it with invisible chemical solutions, but this allusion to the timeworn trick of the muslin canvas convinced no one.

In late March Eisenheim left Vienna on an Imperial tour that included bookings in Ljubljana, Prague, Teplitz, Budapest, Kolozsvar, Czernowitz, Tarnopol, Uzghorod. In Vienna, the return of the Master was awaited with an impatience bordering on frenzy. A much-publicized case was that of Anna Scherer, the dark-eyed sixteen-year-old daughter of a Vienna banker, who declared that she felt a deep spiritual bond with Greta and could not bear life without her. The troubled girl ran away from home and was discovered by the police two days later wandering disheveled in the wooded hills northeast of the city; when she returned home she shut herself in her room and wept violently and uncontrollably for six hours a day. An eighteen-year-old youth was arrested at night on the grounds of Eisenheim's villa and later confessed that he had planned to break into the Devil's Factory and learn the secret of raising the dead. Devotees of Greta and Frankel met in small groups to discuss the Master, and it was rumored that in a remote village in Carinthia he had demonstrated magical powers of a still more thrilling and disturbing kind.

And the Master returned, and the curtains opened, and fingers tightened on the blue velvet chair-arms. On a bare stage stood nothing but a simple chair. Eisenheim, looking pale and tired, with shadowy hollows in his temples, walked to the chair and sat down with his large, long hands resting on his knees. He fixed his stare at the air and sat rigidly for forty minutes, while rivulets of sweat trickled along his high-boned cheeks and a thick vein pressed through the skin of his forehead. Gradually a darkening of the air was discernible and a shape slowly emerged. At first it seemed a wavering and indistinct form, like shimmers above a radiator on a wintry day, but soon there was a thickening, and before the slumped form of Eisenheim stood a beautiful boy. His large brown eyes, fringed with dark lashes, looked out trustingly, if a little dreamily; he had a profusion of thick hay-colored curls and wore a school uniform with dark green shorts and high gray socks. He seemed surprised and shy, uncomfortable before the audience, but as he began to walk about he became more animated and told his name: Elis. Many commented on the striking contrast between the angelic boy and the dark, brooding magician. The sweetness of the creature cast a spell over the audience, broken only when a woman was invited onto the stage. As she bent over to run her fingers through Elis's hair, her hand passed through empty air. She gave a cry that sounded like a moan and hurried from the stage in confusion. Later she said that the air had felt cold, very cold.

Greta and Frankel were forgotten in an outbreak of Elis-fever. The immaterial boy was said to be the most enchanting illusion ever created by a magician; the spiritualist camp maintained that Elis was the spirit of a boy who had died in Helgoland in 1787. Elis-fever grew to such a pitch that often sobs and screams would erupt from tense, constricted throats as the air before Eisenheim slowly began to darken and the beautiful boy took shape. Elis did not engage in the conventions of magic, but simply walked about on the stage, answering questions put to him by the audience or asking questions of his own. He said that his parents were dead; he seemed uncertain of many things, and grew confused when asked how he had come to be there. Sometimes he left the stage and walked slowly along the aisle, while hands reached out and grasped empty air. After half an hour Eisenheim would cause him to waver and grow dim, and Elis would vanish away. Screams often accompanied the disappearance of the beautiful boy; and after a particularly troubling episode, in which a young woman leaped onto the stage and began clawing the vanishing form, Herr Uhl was once again seen in attendance at the theater, watching with an expression of keen interest.

He was in attendance when Eisenheim stunned the house by producing a companion for Elis, a girl who called herself Rosa. She had long dark hair and black, dreamy eyes and Slavic cheekbones; she spoke slowly and seriously, often pausing to think of the exact word. Elis seemed shy of her and at first refused to speak in her presence. Rosa said she was twelve years old; she said she knew the secrets of the past and future, and offered to predict the death of anyone present. A young man with thin cheeks, evidently a student, raised his hand. Rosa stepped to the edge of the stage and stared at him for a long while with her earnest eyes; when she turned away she said that he would cough up blood in November and would die of tuberculosis before the end of the following summer. Pale, visibly shaken, the young man began to protest angrily, then sat down suddenly and covered his face with his hands.

Rosa and Elis were soon fast friends. It was touching to observe Elis's gradual overcoming of shyness and the growth of his intense attachment to her. Immediately after his appearance he would begin to look around sweetly, with his large, anxious eyes, as if searching for his Rosa. As Eisenheim stared with rigid intensity, Elis would play by himself but steal secret glances at the air in front of the magician. The boy would grow more and more agitated as the air began to darken; and a look of almost painful rapture would glow on his face as Rosa appeared with her high cheekbones and her black, dreamy eyes. Often the children would play by themselves onstage, as if oblivious of an audience. They would hold hands and walk along imaginary paths, swinging their arms back and forth, or they would water invisible flowers with an invisible watering can; and the exquisite charm of their gestures was noted by more than one witness. During these games Rosa would sing songs of haunting, melancholy beauty in an unfamiliar Low German dialect.

It remains unclear precisely when the rumor arose that Eisenheim would be arrested and his theater closed. Some said that Uhl had intended it from the beginning and had simply been waiting for the opportune moment; others pointed to particular incidents. One such incident occurred in late summer, when a disturbance took place in the audience not long after the appearance of Elis and Rosa. At first there were sharp whispers, and angry shushes, and suddenly a woman began to rise and then leaned violently away as a child rose from the aisle-seat beside her. The child, a boy of about six, walked down the aisle and climbed the stairs to the stage, where he stood smiling at the audience, who immediately recognized that he was of the race of Elis and Rosa. Although the mysterious child never appeared again, spectators now began to look nervously at their neighbors; and it was in this charged atmosphere that the rumor of impending arrest sprang up and would not go away. The mere sight of Herr Uhl in his box each night caused tense whispers. It began to seem as if the policeman and the magician were engaged in a secret battle: it was said that Herr Uhl was planning a dramatic arrest, and Eisenheim a brilliant escape. Eisenheim for his part ignored the whispers and did nothing to modify the disturbing effects that Elis and Rosa had on his audience; and as if to defy the forces gathering against him, one evening he brought forth another figure, an ugly old woman in a black dress who frightened Elis and Rosa and caused fearful cries from the audience before she melted away.

The official reason given for the arrest of the Master, and the seizure of his theater, was the disturbance of public order; the police reports, in preparation for more than a year, listed more than one hundred incidents. But Herr Uhl's private papers reveal a deeper cause. The chief of police was an intelligent and well-read man who was himself an amateur conjurer, and he was not unduly troubled by the occasional extreme public responses to Eisenheim's illusions, although he recorded each instance scrupulously and asked himself whether such effects were consonant with public safety and decorum. No, what disturbed Herr Uhl was something else, something for which he had difficulty finding a name. The phrase "crossing of boundaries" occurs pejoratively more than once in his notebooks; by it he appears to mean that certain distinctions must be strictly maintained. Art and life constituted one such distinction; illusion and reality, another. Eisenheim deliberately crossed boundaries and therefore disturbed the essence of things. In effect, Herr Uhl was accusing Eisenheim of shaking the foundations of the universe, of undermining reality, and in consequence of doing something far worse: subverting the Empire. For where would the Empire be, once the idea of boundaries became blurred and uncertain?

On the night of February 14, 1902—a cold, clear night, when horseshoes rang sharply on the avenues, and fashionable women in chin-high black boas plunged their forearms into heavy, furry muffs—twelve uniformed policemen took their seats in the audience of Eisenheimhaus. The decision to arrest the Master during a performance was later disputed; the public arrest was apparently intended to send a warning to devotees of Eisenheim, and perhaps to other magicians as well. Immediately after the appearance of Rosa, Herr Uhl left his box. Moments later he strode through a side door onto the stage and announced the arrest of Eisenheim in the name of His Imperial Majesty and the City of Vienna. Twelve officers stepped into the aisles and stood at attention. Eisenheim turned his head wearily toward the intruding figure and did not move. Elis and Rosa, who had been standing at the edge of the stage, began to look about fearfully: the lovely boy shook his head and murmured "No" in his angelic voice, while Rosa hugged herself tightly and began to hum a low melody that sounded like a drawn-out moan or keen. Herr Uhl, who had paused some ten feet from Eisenheim in order to permit the grave Master to rise unaided, saw at once that things were getting out of hand—someone in the audience began murmuring "No," the chant was taken up. Swiftly Uhl strode to the seated magician and placed a hand on his shoulder. That was when it happened: his hand fell through Eisenheim's shoulder, he appeared to stumble, and in a fury he began striking at the magician, who re-

mained seated calmly through the paroxysm of meaningless
blows. At last the officer drew his sword and sliced through
Eisenheim, who at this point rose with great dignity and turned
to Elis and Rosa. They looked at him imploringly as they wavered and grew dim. The Master then turned to the audience;
and slowly, gravely, he bowed. The applause began in scattered
sections and grew louder and wilder until the curtains were seen
to tremble. Six officers leaped onto the stage and attempted to
seize Eisenheim, who looked at them with an expression of such
melancholy that one policeman felt a shadow pass over his
heart. And now a nervousness rippled through the crowd as the
Master seemed to gather himself for some final effort: his face
became rigid with concentration, the famous vein pressed
through his forehead, the unseeing eyes were dark autumn
nights when the wind picks up and branches creak. A shudder
was seen to pass along his arms. It spread to his legs, and from
the crowd rose the sound of a great inrush of breath as Eisenheim began his unthinkable final act: bending the black flame of
his gaze inward, locked in savage concentration, he began to
unknit the threads of his being. Wavering, slowly fading, he
stood dark and unmoving there. In the Master's face some
claimed to see, as he dissolved before their eyes, a look of fearful
exaltation. Others said that at the end he raised his face and
uttered a cry of icy desolation. When it was over the audience
rose to its feet. Herr Uhl promptly arrested a young man in the
front row, and a precarious order was maintained. On a drab
stage, empty except for a single wooden chair, policemen in
uniform looked tensely about.

Later that night the police ransacked the apartment with a
distant view of the Danube, but Eisenheim was not there. The
failed arrest was in one respect highly successful: the Master was
never seen again. In the Devil's Factory trick mirrors were
found, exquisite cabinets with secret panels, ingenious chests
and boxes representing high instances of the art of deception,
but not a clue about the famous illusions, not one, nothing.

Some said that Eisenheim had created an illusory Eisenheim from the first day of the new century; others said that the Master had gradually grown illusory from trafficking with illusions. Someone suggested that Herr Uhl was himself an illusion, a carefully staged part of the final performance. Arguments arose over whether it was all done with lenses and mirrors, or whether the Jew from Bratislava had sold his soul to the devil for the dark gift of magic. All agreed that it was a sign of the times; and as precise memories faded, and the everyday world of coffee cups, doctors' visits, and war rumors returned, a secret relief penetrated the souls of the faithful, who knew that the Master had passed safely out of the crumbling order of history into the indestructible realm of mystery and dream.

"The Barnum Museum," "The Eighth Voyage of Sinbad,"
and "Klassik Komix #1" appeared previously
in Grand Street.
"Rain" appeared previously in The Paris Review.
"Alice, Falling" appeared previously in Antaeus.
"Eisenheim the Illusionist" appeared previously as
"The Illusionist" in Esquire.